The Spinning House Affair

House Affair

By

Jane Taylor

TP

ThunderPoint Publishing Ltd.

First Published in Great Britain in 2021 by
ThunderPoint Publishing Limited
Summit House
4-5 Mitchell Street
Edinburgh
Scotland EH6 7BD

This book is a work of fiction. Names, places, characters and
locations are used fictitiously and any resemblance to actual
persons, living or dead, is purely coincidental and a product of the
author's creativity.

Cover Image © vera prokopchuk / shutterstock.com
Cover Design © Huw Francis

ISBN: 978-1-910946-78-7 (Paperback)
ISBN: 978-1-910946-79-4 (eBook)

www.thunderpoint.scot

Dedication

For George, Charlotte, Nancy, Marnie and Henry, with love.

1 – LENT TERM

'Yer 'orse, sir,' proclaimed the stable lad in a loud and willing voice, dragging a mounting block across the cobbles. It was just after eight o'clock on a bitterly cold morning in February, barely light. Dr Lucien Prideaux of Downing College, Cambridge, offered him but a perfunctory nod as he took up the reins.

'Shouldn't be out too long this morning, sir, if I was you,' ventured the boy.

The don sniffed. Light was sullen at that hour with a submerged greenness about it. A serrated edge to the air grazed his chin. Snow seemed likely.

The boy gave a shrug towards the learned man's back in a *suit-yourself-then* manner. Next day, he would announce to anyone who would listen to him: 'I told him. I *did* tell him.' But he could hardly take credit for hindsight because it was not the weather that was to be the undoing of Lucien Prideaux that morning.

Since being out early for this purpose was a daily ritual of some twenty years' standing, Prideaux lost no time in setting out. Regular people were already out on the streets that morning, many of whom would have been familiar with the sight of the man on his horse proceeding towards the southern boundary of the town. At that stage, there was no reason for any of them to pay much attention to the university fellow who held himself stiffly and whose demeanour was generally stern, but whose features, on closer inspection, still bore traces of a certain urbane attractiveness.

His course – it never varied, he had no time for leisurely innovation – was up towards the Gog Magog hills, a pair of chalky elevations overlooking the southern aspect of the town with a small dip between them through which ran the road leading towards Cambridge from the south. To the foot of the Gogs, then, would he make his way this morning, as always, and no further – no, never further. How these particular hills came to be so named was entirely lost by then, he reminded himself as he watched them rise up in the distance. But of course, Gog and Magog were two malevolent Biblical giants who were destined to be overcome by the power of good on the Day of Judgement – a notion which always gave him a passing sense of satisfaction.

Leaving the town behind him, he urged his horse into a temporary canter along the grassy aftermath of a ploughed field. It was not a pretty animal but it was serviceable and all too grudgingly familiar with this trajectory. All he sought on these daily expeditions was a brief escape from the four walls of his study in Downing where the demands and evasions of his students, the heavy stench of the river Cam seeping in odious pulses under cracks in his windowsill, the irritating flecks of black soot from his fire settling on his papers, and books (mounds of them, all very well ordered) all seemed set to promote in him an anxiety of one sort or another. Was it really surprising, then, that the effect achieved by these enemies of his equilibrium was to draw him towards a more spacious and tranquil atmosphere in which he might allow his thoughts to meander for a short while, unchallenged?

This particular outing took place in the mid-1890s, when townsfolk high and low in Cambridge were beginning to brace themselves for the uncertainties that lay ahead. There was an almost palpable tick-tocking of old, nearly spent time rolling towards the 20th century, virtually lying in wait upon the horizon at that point. Such a curious point in time made people twitchy and unpredictable, as Prideaux well knew. For himself, he would keep all unreasoned apprehension at a sensible arm's length – had long regarded most of the proposed celebrations in the town as excessive, if not foolish, in fact. On a more worrying note, though, he had begun to sense that a period of trouble might again be brewing between the fenland town and the ancient university grafted onto it as, regrettably, it had a habit of doing. It was probably to be expected, he told himself: after all, we are strange bedfellows. Why, it was barely twenty years ago that the Mayor of Cambridge, the unfortunately named John Death, was burned in effigy by mobs of undergraduates angered at the arrest of seven of their fellows for causing a disturbance at a concert attended by civic dignitaries in the Corn Exchange. The very notion of something as stable as a unified entity identifying itself as "Cambridge" struck him this day, as it often did, as a hopeless illusion, given the thoroughly unfixed quality of the place. Consider the fluidity of the river itself on its slouching, malodorous drift through the artfully reclaimed pockets of land at the edge of the East Anglian fens upon which Cambridge now stood … Consider, also, he once informed a visitor from afar in what his god-daughter Aurelia – a rather flighty miss, to his way of thinking, though disarmingly sweet – called, with the tongue-in-cheek manner she always managed to pull off, his "off-hand-superior" tone… Yes, consider, for a moment, the cosmopolitan flux of university people, the manifestation of whose genius and singular individuality might be alarming or provocative to some. Harken, too, to the almost vanished footprints of ancient Carmelites, Friars of the Sack, White Canons, Augustinians, Grey Friars, Dominicans and Benedictines who had settled here, favouring its remoteness, giving way later to primitive Methodists, Friends, Wesleyans, Congregationalists, Presbyterians, Baptists, Calvinists and all sorts – each jostling for a place alongside the distinctly Anglican nature of the College chapels. Not to mention the presence of one newly completed, very large, Gothic-styled Roman Catholic Church. Well, indeed, the place was steeped in the sheer variety of medieval religion and its moral sensibilities – of that he was proud to attest. And so on and so forth.

Thus daydreaming, and every so often tweaking the thick college scarf he wore tied in a neat fold under his chin in such a way that it would warm his nose whilst moistening his chapped chin, the don continued his ride at a steady, syncopated trot before allowing the horse to settle into the halting walk it preferred.

In due course he arrived at the marker for his return: a wooden stump on which was carved: "Cambridge: two miles" accompanied by an arrow pointing back towards his starting point. As he steered the horse round for his return, he noted the pallor of a mist settling on the spread of buildings down there in the distance, further reducing the town and causing it to be defined less by the uplifting architecture of its ancient colleges than by all the vague indications of a fairly nondescript settlement, an essentially provincial place, a backwater, even, where extraordinary invention somehow managed to rub shoulders with deadening dullness, great beauty with ugliness, and the exalted with – oh, make no mistake about it – with *evil*. For all that, it also occurred to him that those glorious pinnacles he knew so well – now blunted by distance and almost indistinguishable from the huddled maze of lower buildings belittling them – *might*, in more favourable circumstances, lead the way towards an enlightened experiment in sympathetic co-existence between two distinct cultures as opposed to the place being, in his experience, a cauldron of rivalry and petty disputes, making all seem small-minded and niggardly at such a remove.

But no more of this. For at a modest height he was apt to feel, on the whole, thankfully removed from the austere fiefdom of his College and able to raise his spirits somewhat. Perhaps this was his version of happiness. Perhaps it accounted in some part for his commitment to his morning ride, whatever the weather.

It was just then that an intriguing distraction diverted his attention, drawing him back inside the realm of the present. He suddenly spotted, not twenty yards in front of him, something white and flimsy fluttering in a forlorn but striking way against the rough brown hues of the rutted dirt road leading back to the town. He could make out only that it was an insubstantial thing, its whispering fronds light as an ostrich feather. Drawing closer until he could peer more accurately at it, he recognised that it was indeed just that – a sinuous white feather.

A little further ahead of him, also apparently descending towards the town, he then noticed a lady. Her back view suggested that she was in as self-absorbed a reverie as he was. She was wearing a wide-brimmed velvet hat, scarlet in colour, set at a slant on her head where it bobbed to the rhythm of her horse through the stillness of the dull air – lacking only what was surely this splendid but endangered feather. He should therefore lose no time in reclaiming the disconnected embellishment and returning it to its owner. Accordingly, he nimbly dismounted and brushed the item back and forth against his breeches to remove a few spots of debris before urging his horse – who snorted twice, with a theatrical toss of its head – into a short, fitful run.

He drew level with the lady rider and lost no time in enquiring whether she might have lost something. Opening her mouth in alarm, she probed her head with a gloved hand, registering recognition of that fact, and proceeded to thank him profusely for rescuing the adornment. For, as she proceeded to explain, it was a hat which would lose its *pith* altogether if deprived of such a flourish, wouldn't he agree? She followed this with a telling giggle, as if to draw him into a friendly pact with her. Any innuendo intended by the woman was naturally lost on the scholarly Lucien Prideaux, therefore any ambiguity about this unusual encounter simply hovered, unappreciated, in the general coldness surrounding them.

Now there seemed to be no reason at all why they should not proceed side by side: after all, they were going the same way. Although he would have preferred to re-enter his own private thoughts uninterrupted, perhaps it was not too unpleasant to play the escort for a while. In any case, short of making a rude dash for it, he could really see no alternative.

In due course the town assumed its normal perspective once more as those familiar steeples began to re-assert themselves. The sky, meanwhile, deepened its gloom, and there was an increasing heaviness about the air. Yes, it will snow, he thought to himself. Just as well, then, to be heading back to his college without delay.

Just then a hunting horn sounded some way off. A canny fox, skulking nearby, raised its head with a blank stare as the riding pair passed the hedge inside which it crouched, stone-eyed, its flanks pounding. Noticing the animal in the periphery of his vision, Lucian Prideaux ventured to point it out, adding: 'The fox likes this weather because it makes the hounds wild and nervous, you know.' He had been a hunting man in his youth and prided himself on a degree of rural knowledge as well as the more arcane stuff of his subject, which was ancient history.

'Oh, indeed,' replied his companion, nodding sagely.

As houses on the outskirts of the town hove into view, given certain shifts in the external mood of the morning due to the ominous weather, Lucian Prideaux considered that it might be an opportune moment to take leave of the woman. But no, she would have none of it, begging him to accompany her at least to a point past the railway station, where she might feel safely enclosed by the busy streets. By now the shops and street markets were open and boys with brooms were dodging passing carts in their daily effort to keep the gutters clear. For the present, therefore, he acquiesced and rode on with her, his eyes thoughtfully lowered and his head tilted slightly to one side as if to prohibit any further interaction between them, resigning himself to her unwanted company out of a sense of ingrained courtesy.

The urgent, puffing trail of the steam train just then arriving from London muted the hollow clatter of horses' hooves on the rise of the railway bridge as the two riders crossed it. Lucien Prideaux felt a little cheered by the thought that in a mile or less along this main road leading into town his college would soon present itself conveniently to the left.

It was at this point that the first group of undergraduates milling about on the pavement broke out of their huddled conversation to stop and stare. As a shy man who never courted the attention of others, Prideaux saw at once that fingers were being pointed towards him, followed by rude and worrying sniggers. What was this impertinence? He felt his garments to test whether anything was awry.

Not long after this he began to curse his own lazy thinking. A spark in his mind ignited the following timely questions in quick succession: how come the woman by his side had appeared in front of him like that *if she had not been following him in the first place*, only to turn back just as he did so that he would find himself positioned behind her on the return journey? Was it a deliberate act on her part? What manner of ruse could this be? What purpose had she in mind?

In rising discomfort, he now set his gaze with resolute grimness straight ahead and urged his horse to move faster. Surely, he surmised, little in the way of obligation remained to him in relation to this person now they had left the railway bridge behind them. But no. The woman was spurring her own horse forward in an audacious mirror movement of his own so that, neck and neck, they must furiously trot on, as if bound together. Worse, when he reigned in his horse in an attempt to deflect her – so did she hers; and when he made a futile attempt at a dash for home – so did she.

A peel of hideous laughter escaped the lady who was plainly exulting in the increasing attention they were attracting from both sides of the street. It was in this indecorous manner that the unlikely pair cantered erratically past the new Catholic Church, frowning and gaunt in its Gothic splendour, after which they were hemmed in by high buildings on both sides of the road.

By now, to his horror, it was evident to Lucien Prideaux that a fresh audience was forming up ahead as if alerted by the periodic cries of various groups they had lately passed. He saw a thickening of the crowd stopping to stare and laugh, formed mostly of undergraduates but also of tradesmen and a smattering of professional people and academics heading for their offices, laboratories, lecture halls and libraries. For some reason, this hooting, gesturing mass of impudent mockers seemed bent on turning him into a public spectacle, a laughing stock, a common jest.

At the same time, he could scarcely fail to mark another development in the behaviour of the spectators. It took the form of a spontaneous round of rude applause aimed towards the lady when she finally chose to slow down, making exaggerated waves towards all and sundry with evident delight in her mischievousness before suddenly abandoning Prideaux of her own will, spurring her horse in the direction of Magdalene Bridge where she veered off into a side road on the hill with a most dreadful shriek of triumph.

Belatedly, forensic thoughts slipped into his mind. Maybe she had been rouged. Maybe her hair was a vivid, unnatural red under that absurd hat of hers. And about that hat: it was as they parted company that she reached up, grasped it, and tossed the gaudy thing in one last extravagant gesture towards her impromptu audience.

Mindless of either the eccentricity he had been driven to or the outrage of his horse which was accustomed to a sedate stroll home requiring only modest energy on its own part, Prideaux entered Downing College at last by its handsome gate, urging the animal down the graceful, tree-lined avenue at almost a gallop, whereupon he dismounted with a nimble leap, as though he were a young man again. He flung the sweat-stained reins towards the stable boy before vanishing inside, at speed.

Overcome by a feeling of dread, the awful truth finally dawned on him: could it be that she was that notorious local courtesan they called Mrs Blanche Marchmont? He was wrought with dismay at this unsettling notion. The woman's antics would surely ruin him, and he lost no time in racing up the familiar staircase leading to the sanctuary of his rooms. Because by then there was no doubt in his mind that one way and another he had been *had*, fully and squarely.

Folly, folly, folly, he repeated to himself aloud, breathing heavily in a futile attempt to escape the awfulness of the moment which made him feel as though he had been disassembled and left in shards.

If his surmise proved to be true, how would he ever live it down? For who in Cambridge had *not* heard of that lady?

*

Back on the street at the height of the fracas, it happened that more hand-waving of a significant kind was being both proffered and received at the precise moment that Lucian Prideaux and his

7

erstwhile companion shot past. Harry Hobbs, a second year Downing undergraduate, happened to be strolling towards his morning lecture. He couldn't repress a grin and a small cheer of his own when he felt the heat of Lucien Prideaux's horse rushing past, recognising instantly the dark outline of his tutor. Glancing around him for an opportunity to share his own mirth with others, Harry raised a hand to another onlooker standing on the opposite side of the road. This was his friend and fellow student Arthur Moody – whose own short-sightedness failed to register the greeting. Instead, it was taken up by Rose Whipple, a servant at Arthur's lodging house, who happened to be walking not far behind him.

*

Also watching this debacle unfold with some bemusement was William Travers, proprietor of the town's daily newspaper, *The Mercury*, whose office was on the same side of the road where Arthur Moody stood. He, too, was stopped in his tracks by such an uncommon sight. From where he stood, he also recognized Harry Hobbs, an undergraduate he was acquainted with, having been up at Downing College himself with Harry's father in days gone by. And he noticed how Harry gave a fulsome wave aimed at someone standing on his own side of the road. And how a town girl standing nearby also raised her hand, as if in response. This was odd. Was there something binding them?

As the disturbance began to die down William Travers turned his eyes towards the upper level of buildings on the opposite side of the road, seeking a slice of open sky to inform him of the state of the worsening weather. He traced the awkward shape of a weak trapezium of light cast by a platinum sky which cut through shadow lines cast by a number of terraced attics. Hmmm … snow, surely, and soon. When he drew his eyes down to street level again, it was to weigh up, with a wry smile to himself, the quintet of buildings he held in his sights. These were: The Fountain Inn, Downing College, The Police Station, The Spinning House, and The Baptist Church – all cheek by jowl, with not an alleyway between them. And there you have it, he thought to himself: liberation and progress; restraint and redemption: the fallen and the risen. All in a single terrace.

Instead of continuing on to *The Mercury*, as he had intended, he abruptly changed his mind, re-tracing his steps to his home in nearby Park Terrace where, suppressing a sigh, he felt he ought to await the arrival of his dear friend Lucien Prideaux, who would, without a doubt, be seeking him out before long in the light of these strange events.

*

Oh dear oh dear oh dear: why did she have to wave back at that young man? Why that reflex raising of her own arm to respond to his? Surely, her gesture spoke only of willingness – the willingness of a servant towards a gentleman who regularly called on his friends at the lodging house where certain young Downing men lived and where she worked as a housemaid. This establishment was in Warkworth Terrace, just across the twenty-five acres of open parkland in the middle of Cambridge called Parker's Piece. Yet try as she might, Rose Whipple could not fathom why he chose to wave his arm at her at that moment of confusion when there was a bit of an uproar going on in the street. For her own part, the raising of her right arm in response was wholly automatic, a reflex reaction, and she did it in good faith simply because she recognized him. For from time to time, in the natural course of things, Rose Whipple and Harry Hobbs had passed by each other with a nod on the stairs of the house in Warkworth Terrace. He had never once acknowledged her before in the street, nor she him – of course he hadn't – yet undoubtedly he had waved at her, and so she waved back at him. Might this action be construed as forward of her?

All of a sudden a gaunt, heavily set man in a black gown materialised on the pavement beside Rose, displacing such thoughts. Before she could formulate any sort of reaction to his close proximity, he grabbed her roughly by the arm. 'Come with me, young woman,' he ordered, and she felt an obligation to do so, being in no doubt of his superior strength and status. She recognized him immediately as one of the University's proctors responsible for enforcing student discipline in the town. He had to be the new one, surely – the one with a reputation for severity. She was aware that a proctor had extraordinary powers to gate a young man if he failed to observe the nightly curfew, or if he failed to be in college for the requisite number of days each term, along with all manner of other misdemeanours he might be prone to. They could even send him down for good if his offence was deemed grave enough to be brought before the university: for cheating, maybe, or defrauding a local vendor, or gambling at the race course at nearby Newmarket. Or attempting to hang himself. All, certainly, shameful practices in Rose's own estimation. But the Proctor was entitled also to arrest young women of the town, perfectly legally. That she knew as well.

This Proctor standing before Rose was an academic man of rank within the University. More importantly, he was a man of excessive enthusiasm when it came to interpreting his powers – which were indeed considerable. Especially, as it was well known, when he was in pursuit of local women. For it was the case that young women were deemed by a great many University people to present a grave danger to the young men studying there. Therefore such women who were caught associating in any way with an undergraduate could be summarily arrested by the Proctor on the assumption that they were guilty of soliciting. These unfortunates would be promptly shut away in the Spinning House nearby and "tried" the next morning at a rudimentary Vice-Chancellor's court held there for the purpose of rubber-stamping their misdemeanours. They could be given a sentence of up to three weeks incarceration in that place of correction for their alleged wickedness. It was said that on one day alone towards the beginning of this particular academic year the Proctor had committed no less than fifteen girls to the Spinning House. As he drew her towards this fearful destination, Rose now had cause to wonder whether the sheer volume of arrests was the Proctor's way of performing a kind of exorcism, laid on in public especially for the witness of the respectable people of the town, some of whom now paused to gawp at this diversion.

The Spinning House was a flat-fronted building with a bulky front door fortified with slatted planks held within a Norman arch. A large lantern was suspended on a brass fitment above the arch to illuminate this door after dark, although no passer-by would be tempted to view the pale rays it gave out as a welcoming sign. Stoutly built, with no embellishment to suggest that it was anything other than what it was, Rose noticed that the house was beginning to show its age in terms of its architectural style – perhaps amplified by the steady seepage of generations of despair its incumbents had left behind in the stains of its crumbling brickwork. As Proctor and housemaid stood attached to each other, it announced itself to her as a place where shame could be contained in such a way that it would not taint worthy folk living freely beyond its confines.

Perhaps that was its purpose. It made a kind of sense to her. Its sturdiness spoke to her, perversely, of grim pride, as though in a dull, stubborn sort of way it could stand its own ground beside the glories of the churches and Colleges surrounding it.

Had she been arrested? For what, then? Did the Proctor need no reason at all to pluck a vulnerable girl out and about on the business of her employer? Perspiring with embarrassment despite the chilliness, she focussed her eyes on the pavement in the hope that she would not become just another public diversion hot on the heels of the last, a follow-up act to the drama which had just unfolded on what had once promised to be such an ordinary morning. 'Oh sir, please, no,' she managed to blurt out as they waited to be admitted, shrinking against the door whilst the Proctor attacked a knocker encrusted with a sickly green patina, with all the gusto of the self-righteous, ignoring his captive.

'Name?' he demanded whilst they waited for a response, and she wondered how colourful would be the bruise on her right arm where his fist still gripped her.

'Rose Whipple, sir,' she replied. 'But, sir, there has been a mistake. I am wanted at my house. I have employment.'

'Wanted you may be,' he told her, eyeing her with disdain. 'But you will cease talking forthwith if you do not wish to earn yourself more trouble than you have accrued already.'

The door opened a crack and a wizened face showed itself – only to turn away and call out: 'Matron, oh, Matron, it's the Proctor with another girl.' But that lady was already hot on her heels and motioned the pair inside whilst the other scurried off.

*

It happened that just then two town constables were standing on the road not far from the Spinning House, who silently observed the progress of the courtesan's rude teasing of the university man followed by Rose Whipple's arrest from start to finish, without making any attempt to intervene in either event.

'I reckon we might have a situation here,' mentioned one to the other.

'No doubt about it,' the other agreed. 'And there is nothing whatsoever we can do about it.'

*

'Gracious, Dr Demetrius, you hev been busy today,' opined the matron of the Spinning House. 'This is the second one today, and it's not yet nine o'clock. What hev we got here, then?' she added, turning her attention to his prey. Rose became aware of a steady groaning sound coming from further inside. At the same time several shrill cries seemed to indicate a female altercation taking place somewhere off the dark main corridor.

'I am Rose Whipple, ma'am,' pre-empted Rose in as level a voice as she could manage, and with the reckless bravery of the innocent. 'I work at a respectable lodging house in Warkworth Terrace. You can check, if you please, and the landlady, Mrs Mawkins, will surely vouch for me. I have done no wrong. I should never have been brought here.'

'Well, now. Is that right? Pooh. It's what they all say.'

'I beg you. I am telling the truth.'

'Don't be impertinent, girl,' said Matron. 'No one is listening to you. We've heard it all before, haven't we, sir?' They both surveyed the girl, still attached to the Proctor. 'Now then,' she continued, turning with abrupt purpose to face Rose close up. 'Know you this, girl: the Proctor is going to charge you. That's how it works. So come along with me now, and it will be all the better for you if you do it quietly.'

In a moment of madness prompted by shock, Rose Whipple considered trying to box her way past the substantial figures of both the Proctor and the Matron in a bid to escape. Her whole future suddenly seemed to hang on her ability to get out of that place. But she was in no doubt that such an action would be futile. That was when her fright began to curdle into a low sense of confusion. She hung her head and allowed herself to be drawn forward.

*

Meanwhile, back on the streets of Cambridge, people were drawing up their collars against the bitter cold. Like a slow wave creeping up a beach before tumbling in on itself by gravity, all had been swiftly restored to normality in the wake of the route recently taken by the courtesan and the don. The hams hanging in their five vertical tiers outside Selby's Tea Coffee and Dining Rooms had not even shuddered at her passing. Merry, the Undertaker, continued with his cart towards the hospital, entirely unaware of what had just taken place due to the mental arithmetic going on in his mind as he calculated an estimate for the removal of another body (it was

12

a prosperous time of year for him – treacherous winter, harbouring all sorts of horrible pulmonary complaints). The butter seller in Cambridge Yard resumed his weighing out of each pound of butter with the merest shake of his head at what had just passed, rolling his rich yellow wares dexterously between two flat boards. The iron rims of cartwheels screeched on uneven surfaces of stone and cobbles, and an asphalt trolley steamed in fiery denial of the worsening weather as another stretch of new road was laid down, its heady smell competing with the stink of the fish curing going on in Bridge Street. The clink of empty iron milk urns on floats returning to country farms empty after their morning deliveries, and the sound of the muffin man ringing his bell to attract attention of passers-by acted as an uneven percussion for a man in a jaunty suit of many colours playing a barrel organ in order to solicit funds. At least two college servants collecting dirty crockery from nearby student lodging houses with their big baskets on wheels seemed mystified by the diversion, shaking their heads in accord. Predictably, on the hour, a scramble of bicycles sped by signalling the end of a morning lecture, ridden by young men in the flowing black gowns they were obliged to wear at all times.

A little while later, a hush descended, muffling any residue of gossip about the recent happenings. It was as though townspeople and university folk alike were suddenly rendered deaf to the sounds of the street. This was because it had begun to snow for the first time that winter.

But one woman, swaying from side to side as she pedalled her tricycle, was smiling to herself. *The north wind doth blow, and we shall have snow …* Brittle cold it may be, but snow, just at that first instance of its appearance, felt welcome. It promised to grant a disguise for all rough edges, and must surely offer a brief respite to personal worries, dissolving them in its whiteness just as it promised the illusion of comfort and an untainted tomorrow.

*

Shortly after lunch Bernadette, the diminutive Irish housemaid, opened the front door of William Travers's handsome town house in Park Terrace and pointed a clearly harassed Lucien Prideaux towards his friend's study. This was a place he'd visited countless times before for the comfortable purpose of engaging in a reasonable conversation with a man who he had known since their youth, when they had both attended the local grammar school followed by admittance as scholarship boys to Downing College. This time, he darted past the maid without so much as his customary 'Good afternoon, Bernadette', forgetting to remove his top coat as he kicked off a few meaty snowflakes sticking to his boots.

'Oh, Travers,' he groaned – deeply, deeply grateful to be in the comfortable presence of the newspaperman. 'I am humiliated.' All that William Travers offered in return was a questioning smile, determined not to compound his old friend's indignity by admitting that he himself had been a witness to it all.

'The sheer scandal of it, Travers,' continued the victim, quite unable to settle. 'You know, something has got to be done about these dreadful women.' Prideaux was relieved to note, thanks to one or two subtle indications from his friend, that he would be spared from explaining the whole ghastly event in detail. But he knew exactly what it was he wanted to get off his chest and began to speak as though Travers himself possessed superior powers of intervention and judgement, so that, at the end of the day, he would be able to *make things right*.

As a publisher of daily news, William Travers was all too familiar with the expectations of those who approached him with their grievances from time to time and, as was his way, he tended to use his bearing rather than words to express his commiseration, not willing to commit himself by responding directly to their concerns.

'Come now, you know very well these creatures are vermin, Travers,' Prideaux persisted. 'And you are aware that their sinful deeds are multiplying, I am sure.' This had been rehearsed during the short walk from Downing College to the Travers house on Park Terrace, as he attempted to reassemble himself. 'You see,' he said, still smarting, 'I, my friend, have been the target of *grossly wanton behaviour*. Through no fault of my own whatsoever. When are people going to do something about the dreadful problem with prostitution that we have in this town?'

'Is there a charge that might be brought against the woman, do you think?' Travers enquired.

'I don't know about that,' Prideaux was forced to reply. What he took to be Travers's initial passivity meant that the shock of being used as a clown in front of the young men in his charge must now necessitate the turning of his rage inward. But he was not done yet.

'Well, then … ?' said Travers.

'But you see, she *wins*, Travers,' he added, unwilling just yet to let it go (winning, after all, was in his own gift, something a man in his position rather took for granted). 'So what do you say? I must go to ground on this, swallow my pride? Even though you can be sure that undergraduates of my own college will take the liberty of sniggering at me from henceforth and I will have no choice but to pretend not to notice? Bah! The woman has made sport of me. *How dare the creature*!' he exclaimed. 'She has interfered with my standing. She has turned me into a figure of ridicule. Such people should not be allowed to think they can get away with it. Surely you agree?'

If only it were that simple, thought William Travers, saddened to witness his friend's wounded outrage. The Marchmont woman's notoriety was long established by then – to the extent that she had become what most would describe as a Cambridge "character" in her own way. There were plenty of well-known "characters" at the University as well, of course, although their peccadilloes were admired, on the whole, rather than excoriated. No doubt she had earned for herself some sway with men of influence in the town by now, having accumulated enough revealing matter about some of them to guarantee her safe passage. With luck, though, she was past her prime and would one day soon purchase a house in the countryside with her illicit gains and cease to trouble upright men like Prideaux, mused Travers. But it wasn't the first time that a number of individuals of good standing from both the town and the university felt entitled to suggest privately to the newspaper proprietor that he take an editorial stance on the issue that people were beginning to call a menace. He was aware, too, in more detail than Prideaux could guess, that this one woman was only the tip of the iceberg and that a situation with ramifications for both the town and the university was almost certainly on the cards.

'Come, draw closer to the fire,' he offered, keen to supply the opportunity for an impasse. 'Let me give it a poke and we will warm ourselves up. Goodness gracious, it looks cold outside.'

This was true: a pall had descended over the grassy expanse of Parker's Piece stretching out in front of the Travers household which it overlooked directly, giving the house its fine prospect. The two men surveyed the scene outside for a moment from behind parted curtains, drawn to feathers of snow falling heavily. How it emphasised the cosy contrast of the room in which they were sitting. This comfortable room served as William Travers's home office, where he conducted what he called his "other business" – those matters of property and retail investments. He was an Alderman on the Town Council, and the house on Park Terrace, a fine three storey building with wrought iron balconies on each of its floors, was one of the grandest of all Cambridge town houses.

'It looks as though it is settling,' said Prideaux after a thoughtful pause, attempting to discipline his disappointment, but only as a mark of respect for their friendship. It was at this point that Travers's wife Alice, prefiguring her appearance with a gentle knock, as she always did, was followed closely into the room by Bernadette, bearing a large tray in her outstretched arms. 'Set it down there, please, Bernadette,' Alice instructed, and Bernadette placed the tray on the neat surface of the newspaperman's ample desk before swiftly departing the room with a quick bob. Prideaux felt himself about to make a comment, opening his mouth then deciding otherwise and closing it. It would run something like … See? There's a pleasant, uncorrupted girl, despite being Irish and no doubt poor. Why can't there be more of her kind about and less of the sinful type who prey upon university men? … But he held his peace because this was surely a feeble notion coming from a man who considered himself superior to whining, especially in front of a woman such as Alice Travers, for whom he had nothing but admiration. As though in telepathic compensation for his bruised feelings, she beckoned him towards the source of the warm waft of freshly baked fruit scones that caught in his nostrils, combined with a wonderful scent of coffee just brewed and laced thoughtfully with a drop of brandy. Was there another as fragrant and considerate as Alice Travers in the whole of Cambridge? He doubted it. She must have got wind of his sudden arrival and intuited his discomfort. Travers was a lucky man indeed.

*

So this, then, was how it would be: she would be "tried" in the Vice Chancellor's "court" convened in the Spinning House the next day on a "charge" of "offering temptation" to a young undergraduate. This much was conveyed to Rose. She was warned that her sentence could lead to further remand in The Spinning House, although Matron hinted that if she was lucky and kept her peace it might not amount to such a horror, this being her first offence. 'Take my word, girl, and keep your eyes down and your mouth shut while they hear your case,' advised Matron.

'But surely I must tell them I have been wrongfully taken?'

Matron let out a single snort. 'They don't ask for evidence, you silly girl.' Another piece of advice followed: that if she had any sense at all she would make sure she expressed only a desire to return to the path of virtue in future.

Given time to reflect, Rose cast her eye over her surroundings here inside the Spinning House, the place where they locked away profligate and disorderly young women, calling them "wayward", "light in character" and much worse. How such words – so cheaply used these days – stung her now as she strove in her mind to hold them at arm's length. This was the place where the university confronted lust, Rose supposed, during a time when even reasonable people were calling licentiousness one of the great social evils of the day, though sometimes they identified such opportunistic female behaviour as a result of another evil, that of the "troublesome poor". This place, considered Rose as she tried to make sense of the trouble she was in: she had heard it was a repository for "the fallen", who must be quarantined with rigour and thoroughness in a town containing such an unnatural proportion of young men. This Proctor and his assistants, men they called "bulldogs": they were on a mission to purify the streets, as she understood, nothing less. Like everyone else, she was aware that the Spinning House had started its life as a bridewell – a house of correction for minor offences. It had been charitably built by the local carrier Thomas Hobson – he who lent his name to the familiar phrase "Hobson's choice" which in time became a general way of indicating that you must take what you are given, since there will be no other choice on offer. Originally, Hobson's choice meant that he did not allow his customers to select the horses that they would prefer to draw the carriage they were about to hire from his stables. *You must take what you are given* – the irony of it was not lost on Rose. Wasn't this just what her gaolers had pronounced, in effect? Nowadays, the Spinning House was used exclusively by the university for the purpose of ridding the streets of those young women of the town who made a bob or two by "corrupting" undergraduates. If, like Rose, you were able or inclined to earn your keep legitimately it was most likely as a house servant, or a college bedder (providing you were old and/or plain looking), or by waiting table in the many inns, tea houses, shops, stalls and dining rooms in the town – all places frequented by young university men. For a local girl, there was scarcely any getting away from the presence of young male persons, one way or another. And some, it was common knowledge, were more forward than others at making something of such proximity.

A residue of spongey brick dust crumbled away at her touch. Draughts of invisible cold crept towards her from both an insecure window and the ill-fitting door of the day room on the other side of the corridor where she had first been deposited.

A pregnant girl squatting on a wooden bench nearby worried away at her blistered arm and surveyed Rose without much enthusiasm. 'What's 'e charged you with, then?' she inquired. 'I'm in for "laying hold of a gownsman". Pooh,' she cackled. 'It's the young gentleman's fault – he weren't quick enough, ha ha. It's all the same, though, ain't it? I reckon I'll get a week in here this time. It had better not be longer or they'll be having to call a midwife.' Her sigh turned into a groan as she gave up on a response from Rose, who was at a loss how to enter this line of conversation. 'Cheer up, ducks,' finished her companion. 'Shouldn't be long 'til dinner, anyway.'

Shock, and a further sharp drop in temperature had annihilated Rose's appetite, along with any accurate sense of time passing very slowly indeed as the day proceeded. She had heard tales about what went on in this unusual prison – who hadn't?

'My old man's next door,' the girl told her some hours later, indicating with a thumb the adjoining Police Station after the two were handed their bedding for the night: two damp blankets and a damp quilt apiece. Her voice, coming out of nowhere, suddenly shrunk the silence in the bare, cell-like room they were to share. 'They say you can knock out a message on the wall if you're in the bit of our exercise yard which backs onto theirs,' explained the pregnant girl. Her lethargy, along with a tight, sluggish cough, suggested that she probably would not be attempting this herself. 'Anyway,' she finished, 'there may be snow on the way.'

'I believe there is.'

'And do it settle?'

'Lord only knows,' sighed Rose.

This was the extent of their conversation. With self-preservation increasingly uppermost in her mind, Rose began to confront the coldness gripping her innards with its bony hands as, with the passing hours, her predicament began to feel like a curse. It had the two women exhaling a grey cloud with each breath they made and Rose feared that it would soon have the power to render her as feeble as the poor creature in front of her. She had never before felt cold like it. Evidently the least shred of energy – such as it was – must be conserved in a place such as this. Fallen women had died there, it was said, from natural causes as well as syphilis, the clap, congestion of the lungs and the toll taken on their guts due to the insanitary conditions. In the dreamless dankness of early nightfall at that time of the year, Rose felt herself to be in danger of such a fate.

Only the dimmest light from outside penetrated the Spinning House shortly after three o'clock in the afternoon. The girls – there were four of them by then, none inclined to talk much – were provided a tin plate each containing tough chunks of scrag end of beef and hard potatoes. Despite not having eaten since seven o'clock that morning, when the first hour of her chores at the lodging house in Warkworth Terrace were done, Rose urged her portion on her companion, who tried, but failed to make much progress with it. In due course the remnants were collected by a small person with a twisted body and removed without comment as this person slammed shut the hatch through which it had been passed with a resounding clack.

*

Yes, yes it was true: Harry Hobbs had waved towards Rose Whipple: towards her general direction, no more, as he now recalled. He was actually waving at Arthur Moody, of course, natural sciences scholar of Downing College, and Harry was currently ribbing Arthur about his failure to reciprocate his greeting that morning over their second, or third or possibly fourth glass of port in Arthur's generously proportioned rooms in Warkworth Terrace. 'You need new spectacles, old boy,' Harry teased, the right side of his face aglow from the heat of the fire. 'I tried to catch your eye this morning but you cut me. I think I shall take offence.'

'Talking about spectacles,' Arthur said, turning aside Harry

Hobbs's taunt for the moment, 'what did you make of it? Prideaux and the woman? Farquhar could have put it in one of his plays, don't you think?'

'Well,' said Harry, 'that gaudy madam showed she was a sport, I suppose. She could have been in trouble if she hadn't dashed off, so near to the Police Station. Admirably brazen, I'd say. That's my verdict, if you want it. I don't blame her for making the most of it. You have to see the funny side.'

'The Proctor will not let it go, though,' surmised Arthur. 'No, sir, he won't, though he won't get far with it, I'm guessing. She has spunk, I'll give you that, to outrun Prideaux *and* the Proctor. Aye, she does.' And some of Arthur's other guests that evening – they were the habitual Downing crowd, lounging easily on two arm chairs and a three-piece sofa so worn down that its seat resembled a basin (they called it "the seat of learning") – found this such a fine bit of whimsy that the nonsense of it brought tears to their eyes.

'But that wasn't the end of it,' Sidney Beaumont, a theology student in receipt of a pauper's bursary, chipped in. They turned towards him for more. 'Didn't you see?'

'Those with eyes to see,' muttered Harry with a wink at Arthur, in order to keep his own joke alive – mutual joshing at each other's expense regularly set the tone of an evening that was destined to lazily go nowhere, as usual, thanks to the provision of Arthur's generous chiffonier, whose mirrored back magnified the supply of alcoholic refreshment lined up ready for use.

'Ha, ha, Hobbs, ha ha,' Arthur Moody responded, picking it up. 'But I think there is something you might have missed yourself, and now it strikes me less out of Farquhar than Ben Jonson, in my opinion.'

'Go on.'

'Well,' Arthur proceeded, 'just as the Marchmont woman was galloping away another spritely diversion was unfolding in precisely the opposite direction.' Arthur, like Harry, was a member of the university drama society and prided himself on a newly acquired ability to create a bit of suspense out of the meanest material.

'I think I know what you are going to tell us,' Francis Travers piped up, but Arthur Moody waved him away.

'There was a girl on the pavement,' Arthur continued, 'and she was on the same side of the road as I was. Not far from where I was standing, in fact. You can picture me, if you will, not quite opposite where you, Harry, must have been standing, and – yes – I admit I failed to notice you. But I was close enough to mark that by then Prideaux and that brazen woman on their horses were hotly – and vainly – being chased by that new Proctor on his bicycle.' He paused for the effect of this extra snippet of information to take shape. 'Yes,' he continued, 'gown flying, nostrils on fire like the very griffin itself. Tally-ho! But then – blow me if he didn't change course suddenly and set his sights on a poor girl who was doing nothing but pausing to watch, just like we all were.'

'The Proctor must have known when he was beaten, then. Couldn't possibly catch la Marchmont, so must make a grab for someone else or lose face?' suggested Francis Travers.

'Exactly. Precisely my point. And then' – Arthur could not hold himself any longer from delivering the *coup de grace* – 'he took *our maid* by the arm and whisked her away. That's what *you* missed, Harry. But wait a minute. Wasn't it in fact *you* who hailed her in the first place, which she then proceeded to reciprocate? Some might call that a contract in the making.'

'But that is absurd!' Harry shot back, colouring. 'I waved at you, none other.'

'And so the curtain fell,' resumed Francis, with a flourish. 'And justice was seen to be done – of the proctorial variety, of course. To the effect that if the trout slipped the net then the minnow would just have to do instead. I put this to you: is *that* sporting behaviour?'

They considered this.

'Pretty girl,' reflected Arthur. 'Our Rose.'

'So that's who you had your eye on. No wonder you had no time for me,' said Harry.

'No, no, no, dear boy. Regard it as merely one of a *shower* of observations. Girls do not interest me. Here, have another glass.'

A heap of spent coals from Arthur Moody's well stacked fire shook itself down, sending out a chorus of sparks. To stoke up the inevitable moment when lugubriousness set in, reducing all conversation to inconsequential fits and starts, they happily passed the port once more.

'Did anyone bring an umbrella?' wondered Harry eventually, spotting the evening's accumulation of snow already lining the outside of the window sill. For certain rather uncomfortable reasons

Harry was living in College during this, their second year, unlike his friends, and would very soon need to gather his greatcoat and make his departure from the unnaturally silky cauldron of Arthur Moody's room if he were to beat the curfew, set at 10.00pm by all the colleges. 'I say, I do believe it hasn't stopped since morning,' he added, moving towards the window and drawing the curtain back a little more to reveal barely an outline of the road outside. The pathway next to it, and the whole extent of Parker's Piece – on the opposite side of which was Downing College, his destination – was under a deepening cover of unbroken whiteness in the gaslight, almost unrelieved by the mark of boots, although soon he would be able to follow a single bird's triangular footprints in the fresh snow, right down to the main gate of his college.

'Well,' he concluded, as he prepared to make his way. 'At this rate we shall all have to dig our way out tomorrow morning.'

*

Along the darkness of the main conduit into the heart of Cambridge, just past Downing College, stood the buildings which, earlier that day, had brought a sardonic smile to the face of William Travers, newspaper proprietor. Together with much else in the vicinity by that hour, the Fountain Inn was unusually quiet that night, as were both the Police Station and the Spinning House. The Baptist Chapel only opened for Sunday service so the quality of its own silence may not have been as notable as that of the other three. Perhaps the weather decreed that crime might take time off on such a night, so conspicuously did it fail to linger in doorways and back alleys where it usually found willing participants as it busied itself about their dissipation and groped for their goods. The landlord of the Fountain was heard by his single customer to compare his house with a mortuary at a time when it was usually teeming. Meanwhile, prisoners, man and boy, had long been locked away for the night in the Police Station. So had the women in the Spinning House.

It turned out that there were some half dozen souls held inside the Spinning House that night, and Rose Whipple was one of them. Matron had written her name in her big Record Book and there, unfortunately, it would remain for as long as records were kept pertaining to the dreadful place. She knew that this meant that she would never be able to entirely erase her present sojourn, even if, as she trusted, she would be released the next day when they would surely discover their error in apprehending her.

Rose lay on her side, crouched on top of a bed in a cell that at length contained three others. One, a very young girl, let out a sob of despair from time to time. It wasn't her first time, she told Rose before they tried to sleep, so she would certainly earn a period of imprisonment which she could not afford. Without her earnings her family, she said – including an invalid father and a sick brother – would not be able to manage. It was desperation that had led her to the streets, though she could not bring herself to use the word, preferring to describe it as "offering favours". Rose, making a show of listening when required, tried once more to take in the unprecedented reality of her situation, clutching the two thin blankets she had been given earlier and frequently shifting her body to accommodate the corrugations of a rough mattress laid across the uncompromising ruts of an iron bedstead. No candle was allowed in the cell – whose flame might have mitigated the stiffness of small hands cupping it in turn for its meagre warmth. Wide awake, she stared upwards at a single small window, outside which snowflakes floated downwards like sullen moths. A suggestion of frost had long since sent its fingers across this mean window, both inside and out, and soon enough it would form a solid, grey-green cataract to further underline her isolation from the world beyond.

She fell to brooding as she considered her plight and the company she had been obliged to join. Somewhere beyond this particular cell, she was aware that one prisoner had been isolated for harbouring an infectious disease. Another had been placed in solitary confinement for "misconduct". As far as Rose could glean, this was to do with the rumpus she had set up on the street when apprehended during the afternoon, crying and moaning so as to attract a crowd of curious onlookers.

Earlier, Rose had watched enviously as one girl had secured her release from the Spinning House on account of having a suckling child with her and, according to her own account, being dangerously ill. Once outside, with a snigger aimed at the Spinning House, she lost no time in handing the child to a waiting accomplice, putting Matron in a foul mood for the rest of the day. Is it any wonder they lose patience with such women, wondered Rose?

She had a vague idea about what, in general, brought such girls to such a grim destination. Occasionally there were reports in *The Mercury* of some of the more colourful incidents. Such reports talked of girls who were deemed "light in character," often being picked up by the Proctor on the equivocal charge of "walking about out of their proper line of way". They were "unnatural"; they lacked "moral purity". They were "night walkers" or "profligate and disorderly women". Such bad things to call a young girl, Rose reflected, making them seem less than human. Rose had also overheard snatches of conversation between the landlady and her friends in the lodging house in Warkworth Road where she worked, referring to such "lewd behaviour" as a blight on the face of the town. She recalled an argument once breaking out between two of the lodgers in Warkworth Terrace, when one of them – Mr Moody it must have been – loudly declared that sexual excitement was dangerous to the heart and nervous system, therefore these girls were a menace on scientific let alone moral grounds.

By and by a framed notice containing a quotation came to her attention, affixed to the wall adjacent to her bed. It read: "*Neither fornicators, nor idolaters, nor adulterers, nor effeminates, nor abusers of themselves with mankind, nor thieves, nor coveters, nor drunkards, nor railers, nor extortionists, shall inherit the kingdom of God.*" What was there on earth, then, to relieve the harshness of such pitiless judgement? She felt it bearing down on her, along with the cold.

She remembered that last Christmas, *The Mercury* reported the post mortem of a girl who had died after spending just one night inside the Spinning House. She had been put in a cell with one other, the pair of them hugging each other all through the night to preserve the last vestiges of warmth under their two wet blankets. It might have been the very cell Rose presently occupied, for all she knew, a proposition which filled her with dread. The Vice-Chancellor's court held there the next morning had decided to discharge that girl, and she returned home, visibly ill. But by then she could barely move her limbs and her skin was dry and hot. A doctor called by her family prescribed purgatives for her costive bowels, Rose recalled. He laid a blister on her neck, ordered a footbath and recommended opiates for her pain. But his help came too late. Day by day she declined, and by early in the New Year she was dead. The post mortem examination discovered a healthy uterus but an enlarged ovary on the left hand side. It contained a foetus.

Rose had also imbibed stories of how mistakes were made, like the notorious case of the party of joyful young milliners on an outing who the Proctor spotted playfully calling out to all and sundry from their carriage as they trundled by. It turned out to be sufficient to get them arrested. It was also common knowledge that a respectable lady – by no means the first – had run into similar trouble recently by merely being seen talking to an undergraduate of her acquaintance. It was as if no-one was safe anymore, reflected Rose. Not if they were female, anyway.

None of this was of the slightest consolation to her. As the night wore on she tried to cover her ears against the concerto of rattling, wheezing and snoring issuing from her neighbours, along with the acrid smell of the chamber pot. And all the while the cold continued to hollow out her heart.

In the end it was a sense of shame that kept her awake, expanding in her imagination until it simply overwhelmed her. She thought of those implacable men, those university people, who strode past her day by day as though she was invisible, or beneath their contempt and of no value whatsoever. Was there ever anything so cold, so disdainful, as a clever man's certainty? As far as she understood it they were the ones who *owned* morality and could bend it as they chose. That summed it up, really: the futility of expecting any sort of justice. It cowed her, made her feel shifty. She reminded herself that she was not, and never had been, involved in soliciting, nor was there ever a chance that she would be. She knew herself to be a fundamentally good person, respectful of the law and of the way things were for people of her class. Yet she began to feel herself *implicated to the core* in the hazy sense of *badness* that existed in this building. During her short, relatively straight-forward life – she was nineteen years old – she had been at ease with herself as a member of an honest, if poor family, knowing right from wrong and later pleased to do her work at the lodging house with a diligence which had been deemed reliable and praiseworthy. What flaw was there, then, what weakness, what crack in her character had led to this disgrace? There must be something. She took her mind back once again to that morning, lighting upon the spontaneous wave she had made towards the young gentleman across the street she knew only as Mr Hobbs, a friend of the lodgers where she worked, who appeared to be waving at her. Was this it?

Young Mr Hobbs could not be blamed for anything, of course, though she found it strange, if he had been intending to be familiar with her. Had a violation or defilement taken place, by any measure? What boundary had been breached to create such a visceral tear in the dignity that had until then defined her? It had to be her fault. But for the life of her she could not fathom why.

*

Elsewhere, shrouded in snow, Cambridge slumbered.

At perfect ease with himself, the Reverend Dr Magnus Algernon Demetrius, Proctor, known by some of his victims and *all* undergraduates during his reign as "The Madman" (not least on account of the rather thoughtless combination of initials bequeathed to him by his parents) had for some hours been in a state of dreamless sleep. The fire in his commodious bedroom had been built up with skill earlier by a college servant in such a way that its embers would still be glowing when morning came. It was guaranteed to take the chill out of the air, permanently. Just as it was meant to do.

In his set of rooms in Downing College, Harry Hobbs, chided by Herbert Basset, the Downing Porter, for cutting it fine once again, piled his great coat and a couple of cushions on top of his bedding for good measure and set himself a small measure of pondering before he slept. He had one term and one year to go before he left the place, this son of a land owner from Suffolk. At this stage in his Cambridge career it was by no means certain he would graduate – he had failed his first year exams by not taking them seriously enough. After scraping a retake over the previous summer he had agreed with his father that he would remain living in College during this, his second year, with a view to sharpening his attitude. It seemed strange that it must have been not much more than a year ago that, as an impressionable nineteen year old riding in the Travers carriage towards Downing College for the first time, he had been wholly charmed by reading Wordsworth's own sensation when that poet came up to Cambridge himself, memorising the lines as though they were his own:

'I was the Dreamer, they the Dream; I roamed
Delighted, through the motley spectacle;
Gowns grave or gaudy, Doctors, Students, streets,
Lamps, Gateways, Flocks of Churches, Courts and Towers…'

Harry himself, a genial fellow in the eyes of his wide acquaintance and quite a Romantic himself, certainly knew how to dream, although after a fairly unrestrained upbringing under broad Suffolk skies he had lately become prone to a certain restlessness. What was it all for? These tedious essays. More constraints than he had ever anticipated.

That night, his thoughtful college servant left a grey stone bottle containing freshly boiled water under his sheets, for which he was most grateful. Slipping into the oblivion that follows a well-oiled evening in good company, he briefly startled himself with one last picture presenting itself in his mind: the fleeting image of a girl being led away by MAD Demetrius, the notorious Proctor, that morning. He had barely registered it at the time, being more taken up with the amusing humiliation of his tutor – the main spectacle – let alone noticing who she was. Why would anyone think he would wave at a housemaid? He had waved at Arthur Moody, not her. Doubtless he would have forgotten it altogether had not Arthur brought it up. There was something about this image that was vaguely troubling. But the power of too much alcohol all too soon overwhelmed him and he, too, soon drifted into peaceful sleep.

*

In the Travers household, Alice's slumber was as rhythmic as her customary comings and goings about the house and beyond. She lay serenely in the dip of a feather mattress, eyes closed and a hint of a smile on her face, dressed in a white lace nightcap she had crocheted herself which matched the frill on her long-sleeved nightgown. Glancing her way, her husband appreciated that smile and associated it with her unquenchable optimism even though she was asleep. She had described to him the tingle of hopefulness that came over her when the prospect of helping to organise a celebration of vast proportions for the townsfolk on Parker's Piece in honour of the new century was first raised. She believed – or so she told him, with rising certainty – that it must surely usher in a period of civility and peacefulness as the 1800s gave way to the 1900s: she would have it that people of good will, like themselves, would no doubt make it so. Tonight, her arm lay lightly across William's shoulder in such a way that he was reluctant to move, such pleasing comfort and reassurance did it provide. He remained awake for some time, enjoying his wife's closeness and careful not to toss about and disturb her. There were certain items he had planned to give thought to when all else was done for the day – he often stored them up in this way. But for the comfortable breathing of Alice tucked up beside him, he might already have taken himself down to his study to potter for a while with a single candle to light his way so as not to disturb the houschold. Sleep did not always come easily to him, so his wife's tranquillity was a great source of his own sense of well-being, rubbing along harmoniously with his own persistently even temper, which many of his acquaintances had sought fit to praise as both laudable and necessary qualities in a newspaper man of some prosperity and standing in the town. But it was true that certain issues were playing on his mind lately, one of which had been exacerbated by Prideaux's excitable visit that morning. For one thing, he wanted to work out the correct and palatable way of reminding his daughter, Aurelia, that she must make sure to take great care when walking out nowadays – indeed, she should probably not be walking about outside on her own at all. Not for the time being, anyway. It wasn't pleasant to think about imposing a curfew on her. It gave him pleasure to think she was just at an age when she ought to be delighting in a certain degree of freedom, and when she was on display he was proud of the figure she presented. Equally, though, he had no desire to stain her mind with the unsavoury matters nudging him towards such a standpoint. Aurelia, it was certain, would demand precise reasons for any curtailment of her movements, and to equivocate would not be a viable alternative, he knew that – she would wear him down in the end. Eventually he came up with the familiar solution he applied to most household and all family matters: he would consult Alice as soon as they awoke next day and leave what must be done, and in what manner, entirely to her judgement. She was his muse and his most trusted ally in most matters requiring personal decisions, particularly the more delicate ones. Almost before this soothing thought was concluded, he, too, was fast asleep.

*

Oh, joy, perfect joy, was Aurelia Travers' first reaction the following morning on gazing out of a window. She was kneeling high on the window seat in her mother's salon, a comfortable room situated on the first floor of the house on Park Terrace, so that she could observe the brand new scene stretching across Parker's Piece.

Perhaps there would be an exciting siege? Who could tell? It was plain that the snow had not ceased falling for close on twenty-four hours. A few clumsy flakes were still tumbling downwards as far as the eye could see, adding to a deep, bulbous carpet of whiteness already formed outside. It effectively de-familiarised all she could see by causing once sharp corners and stable objects to merge into one another, distorting chimneys and making giant mushrooms of trees. Snow cleanses, she decided, therefore its pristine freshness and concealment might be taken as a sign of grace, surely. At the same time, the unusual sight of so much snow felt mysterious to her, given how it changed things. More than that, it augured a period of difference which she, in her desire for her senses to be roused and her untrained intellect to be mildly engaged, found most exhilarating. An even grey cloud cover now hung low from horizon to horizon above the roof tops, giving the sky that was visible from her vantage point the appearance of an impenetrable dirigible, an alien thing sitting on top of the town. As a result, the near darkness indoors, despite it being little after ten o'clock, meant that Bernadette had been told to light the oil lamp on her mother's table before Alice came down.

Aurelia was aware that someone had already called on her father downstairs. A caller often dropped by after breakfast with something he felt was important to impart before William Travers donned his silk top hat and morning coat and made his way down to *The Mercury*. This was a busy household, despite Aurelia being the only child still living there. Francis Travers, their son and her brother, was a second year undergraduate at Downing College and had earned his independence as one of the Warkworth Road lodgers by this point. Men were often to be found in huddles, talking in her father's home office downstairs, and just as often there would be women involved in civic responsibilities up here, in Alice's own salon on the first floor of the house. Aurelia rarely took part in conversations in either location because people were all too often engaged in discussing matters of public interest of one sort or another, which were not the most appealing of subjects as far as she was concerned. If she happened to pass the respective doors of her father's and her mother's business the blur of men's voices seemed to resemble the sound of coals settling in the grate of a mature fire, while those of the women culminated in murmurings as light as a feather duster being flicked around the room. What an amusing thought!

Rather, she longed to put on her velvet winter cloak right away and go outside to investigate the altered situation, perhaps to make fleeting contact with others never encountered before as one might do when extraordinary things were happening. But her mother had instructed her at breakfast in vague but final terms that this was not to be.

Aurelia was eighteen years old and occupied the not unpleasant lull between youth and marriage. She was not sure whether this was a desirable state to be in or not, but lacked the vocabulary to describe her anxiety of being unable to predict what might come next. Never mind. Something would turn up. It always did, in her world.

' … so we might take Aurelia with us?' came the voice of her mother, about to enter the room.

'Take me where?' Aurelia called out, with delight.

'Well, I thought that perhaps you and Hope might take a basket each of provisions from the pantry over to Barnwell to Bernadette's family later when cook has finished her baking. They will be pleased to have something warm and nourishing in this kind of weather, no doubt. If the snow stops, and if the pavements are navigable, that it. I shall join you.'

'A wonderful idea. I'd say.'

'I must do some work with Hope this morning, Aurelia. After lunch, then? As long as the sweepers have made some progress outside, mind.'

'I can hardly wait.'

Aurelia was unaware of the short, strategic conversation that had taken place between her parents an hour earlier, during which her father ran over with Alice the events of the previous day as they had touched on Prideaux's unfortunate experience and a poor girl in the street who had been taken by the Proctor when he failed to catch the courtesan, raising some of the likely consequences. It seemed prudent in the circumstances, he had suggested, not to allow Aurelia out unaccompanied, adding that there was more brewing than he cared to talk about in greater detail just then. Aurelia had not been privy to her mother's slight frown, though Alice agreed with him, nevertheless. And she had no idea that the proposed outing with her mother's assistant was the result of a discreet compromise Alice came up with after William retired to his study. Alice was a peace-maker by nature, as well as being involved in a number of local committees of townswomen concerned with improving the conditions of poor families living in the Barnwell slum, where Bernadette's family had their home.

'Good. I shall tell Hope directly, then,' Alice said. 'But this afternoon it must be, no sooner. Until then, I really do need to do some work. Ah, here comes Hope. Now run along and find something useful to do, Aurelia.'

Hope Bassett had been living with the Travers for the past two years, since she was seventeen years old. She was the daughter of Herbert Bassett, porter of Downing College nearby. Her father, a solitary man and a widower, prided himself on having an acute appreciation of the vagaries of human nature. He saw it all from his porter's lodge, and frequently aggravated himself with anxiety about the darkness of the human soul – especially when it belonged to a young man. Hope was his only daughter, just as Aurelia was the only daughter of William Travers, whom he had known for many years – since William was a young student at the College himself, in fact, while he was a young man learning his trade. With this long acquaintance the basis of an unspoken bond between them, Herbert Bassett was satisfied that Hope's appointment in the Travers' household would guarantee her a position of safety. He had agreed to it at once when the opportunity was offered. But safety? From what? Two things, he reckoned. Naturally, there was the predatory nature of the young men who inhabited the town in such gross disproportion to respectable young women like his daughter, which could easily place her in jeopardy. But even more worrying to him was Hope's own dangerous beauty, to her father's way of thinking. Thus his desire was simply that that this precious child should be rendered unreachable. At least until those looks, that bearing, that incandescent face (Where did she get it from? Not from him, surely), began to lose their bloom.

Now, Hope Bassett glides meekly but purposefully into Alice's salon just as Aurelia flounces out without a word to her, mightily pre-occupied by that afternoon's promised outing. It is a space whose solidity is enhanced by a series of comfortable, rounded chairs, two weighty sideboards, a pair of carved writing desks with an amount of history embedded in their indentations, and a deep brown curtain suspended from brass rings overhanging the door to keep draughts at bay. Hope herself never wears anything but muted, indeterminate colours covering her very strictly from just below her chin down to the ankles, her arms to the wrist. She is tall, and walks with a slight stoop, her head slightly bent, the result of listening to people shorter than herself as much as the careful hand-writing she does at Alice's behest most days. Such a bearing does not invite scrutiny. In fact, her whole demeanour appears marked by studied self-restraint. There is a particular reason for needing a person like Hope in the house, known only to William and Alice. The fact is that Alice has never properly taken to reading and writing, although she makes up for it by intelligent attention to detail, a good memory and a keen ear for the nuances of conversation. It isn't that she is illiterate, exactly, it is just that letters seem to transpose themselves between the page and her brain in a confusing fashion, making reading and writing irksome and time consuming. Although Hope Bassett no doubt has some inkling of Alice's condition, there's a tacit agreement that reference should never be made to it and Alice has always been quietly indebted to Hope's compliance in this matter. For Alice's feelings can be invaded by wrinkles of shame when she thinks of herself as the possessor of such a peculiar disability.

Beckoned in by Alice, Hope moves towards her own desk and looks up expectantly for her daily instructions. Meeting her eyes briefly, Alice never fails to marvel at the girl's unusual poise, given her background. Even more so at the symmetry of her features, which complement the luminosity of her face. How on earth could such an ordinary girl possess such grace, such sublime features? If Alice were not motivated by unselfishness, she – like many others passing through this household – may have felt somewhat daunted by the glow emanating from this young person.

For her part, Hope herself rarely looked others in the eye, though with Alice she seemed to be at ease. In her own way, like Alice and very many other women of the time, she was a keen accumulator of knowledge by careful, almost cunning watchfulness – and by preserving Aurelia's discarded school books for her own interest. But all this was done obliquely, privately. And if Aurelia sometimes felt curtailed in her own home and longed to break free in little thrusts of rebellion which wobbled and went away quite quickly, Hope appeared not to be thwarted by impatience. Instead, she gave the impression of being utterly self-contained.

Meanwhile, taking refuge first in the kitchen until she was shooed out by cook, who had much to do that morning, Aurelia wandered through the ground floor until she finally picked an apple from a fruit bowl set out in the hall and tried skipping up the stairs two at a time towards her own room on the second floor, without tripping. Here, with nothing better to do, she positioned herself once more at a window over-looking Parker's Piece, envying the few young school absconders who were already dragging behind them home-made sledges and tossing snowballs at each other. At times like these, she considered, it would be nice to be like them, rather than someone with the obligations of a daughter of people of importance.

She was just in time to witness, on the street far below, the odd sight of a young woman lurching crazily through the snow along what ought to be the pavement running past the house. This figure was clearly in a state of agitation, her hair speckled with white flakes, her arms clutching her waist to keep warm when they weren't flailing awkwardly. Oh dear, just look at the poor thing: outside in all that snow with neither a coat nor a muffler.

This is not wise, thinks Aurelia, who knows very well that a chill can rapidly turn into something far, far worse at this time of the year.

*

Harry Hobbs, too, peered out of his college window, with a gasp at the sight of such unusual sameness laid out before him across the newly whitened orderliness of the great court. But his set of rooms was a comfortable one, on the whole. He had the use of a sitting room furnished with a pair of heavy dressers containing his many books, several chairs, and a table covered with an orange coloured chenille cloth for him to do his work on. All this was set upon a patterned carpet and enclosed by dark green walls. His adjoining bedroom provided hanging room for his clothes, a porcelain dish and ewer on a stand, and his narrow bed. On long winter nights as cold as the one just past he tended to sleep in his heavy woollen dressing gown tied round the waist by a cord with a golden tassel, a gift from one of his five older sisters who made it known that they missed him dreadfully while he was away at Cambridge. His breakfast and lunch he generally took in these rooms, delivered by kitchen boys on trays covered in green baize.

A college servant came in while Harry was still sitting up in bed to gather his thoughts, and began by preparing the fire. While it sparked into life, the man pulled out a metal bath from under the bed and poured a niggardly two inches of water into it. Then he placed two tin cans containing more tepid water ready by the fire. Harry kept two bowls in his room: one for washing, the other for shaving. Both were permanently blackened on the underside because he was in the habit of dashing out of bed as soon as the man closed the door behind him, placing one or the other on the open fire while he returned to doze for a precious few extra minutes. A little later, a bedder would trim and fill the oil lamp he used to illuminate his reading. In these and sundry other ways, he appreciated that his needs were well catered for.

At this stage of his university career, it was incumbent upon Harry to do his generous father the honour of achieving a good pass in his exams at the end of the current academic year in preparation for his third and final year. A "pole" degree, without honours, would be perfectly alright, of course, had he been a sportsman. But despite his athletic build – he was tall and lean and moved with poise and agility – the thought of afternoons of the kind of physicality those hearty rowing men and footballers undertook had little appeal. 'You have left it until five minutes to twelve, boy,' his father had reminded him with some gravity after the debacle of failing his first year. Harry regretted causing his father concern, seasoned all too obviously with that dear man's disappointment in his only son. A concerted dash of endeavour must be made now – no question about it.

Fortunately, John Hobbs seemed willing to carry on paying Harry's college bills. Gratified by a recent confirmation sought from his old friend Prideaux, who happened to be Harry's tutor, that his son was indeed attending lectures, this generous gentleman had responded by sending Harry a box of wine. Harry was also the possessor of an allowance of £50 to keep himself in clothes and other necessities, thanks to the patronage of his father, and this was in addition to his tuition fees. He was no poor student in receipt of a meagre bursary, like his chum Sidney Beaumont, an undoubtedly clever chap, a theology scholar and one of the Downing crowd who lodged at Warkworth Terrace along with Arthur Moody and Francis Travers. Poor old Beaumont's pa was a country vicar with a peppercorn living, meaning that Sidney must maintain himself with embarrassing frugality. It sometimes pained Harry to watch how his friend squeezed himself in order to get by. Out of affection for Sidney and with what he felt was appropriate sensitivity, Harry managed to slip his friend the odd guinea by getting him to study the racing form at Newmarket on his behalf. This country town no more than a dozen miles from Cambridge was a prohibited destination for undergraduates where, from time to time, Harry, Arthur Moody and Francis Travers allowed themselves a clandestine flutter on the horses, though betting was strictly off limits – even *The Mercury* refused to speculate on winners, on principle. But, Lord, a person needed the odd diversion to balance all this work, sighs Harry, bracing himself to leave his bed. Or not. Could he plead later that he was snowbound? Of course he couldn't – all he had to do was cross the great court to keep an appointment with his tutor. Aaahhh … be off with you, man, and be done with it, he instructed himself.

*

Rose Whipple was released from the Spinning House that morning, after learning that her case had been dismissed on the grounds of the flimsiness of the evidence against her, taking into account her status as what they called a first-timer. When this news was imparted it was accompanied by a stern warning from Matron in the voice of the righteous that she should pay attention to mending her ways or it would go worse for her the next time, make no mistake about it. The door of the Spinning House was briefly opened for her to leave, then slammed shut behind her. She stood for a moment in the street, blinded by the white glow of the fresh snow. It remained icy outside although the snow had ceased falling, and the skin of her hands seemed to have hardened after a night of extreme discomfort. With parched lips and stiff limbs, she tried to wrap her arms around her body, given the absence of any substantial outer garments. There was nothing for it, she reckoned, but to set off without delay and make her way back to the place towards which she had been heading twenty-four hours previously, innocently enough: the lodging house in Warkworth Terrace where she worked. There was no telling what reception she would receive after being absent without permission for a whole day and a night. But let's not fret about that yet, she told herself. The sheer effort of getting there must be her first challenge. It was soon obvious that the only way to progress in her flimsy shoes was in a kind of fitful stagger, trying to avoid falling down altogether. There were iron railings in front of some of the houses on Park Terrace which she was grateful to cling onto from time to time, abandoning any thought of decorum.

Just then, it happened that making his way along the treacherous path towards her was Francis Travers, son of the newspaper proprietor, who lodged with other Downing students at the house in Warkworth Terrace. As far as Rose knew, he was a pleasant enough young man who worked reasonably hard, as a result of which he'd earned his freedom after his first year by being allowed by his parents to move out of College and take up his own independent lodging nearby.

'Rose, Rose, here, let me help you,' called Francis Travers, recognising the missing maid at once. Having made his offer – a genuine one – he was wise enough to take a furtive look around him in case there was a proctor about, who could be counted upon to misconstrue such neighbourliness.

'Whatever have you been up to, Rose?' Francis couldn't stop himself from asking as she paused in front of him, unwinding her body with care until she stood precariously in an upright position.

As if he didn't know.

With a reluctant grimace instead of a reply, she took his arm and allowed herself to be escorted the short distance it took to reach Warkworth Terrace, where he left her at the foot of the road.

Some minutes later, William Travers spotted his son out walking, or rather stumbling towards him, kicking snow out of his way as he went – Francis had by then resumed his original course into town for his morning lecture. After sharing observations about the weather, Travers suggested that Francis might like to join his mother, his sister Aurelia and himself for supper one evening before too long – 'Why not, dear boy? We miss you, you know' – and maybe he would like to bring a friend or two who would appreciate being warmed with a family meal on a cold winter's evening? Francis said he would indeed like that, and that he would await a note from his mother to say when it would be convenient. Between Francis and his parents there existed a mutual understanding supported by the habitual delicacy that requires all parties to think before they speak out in order to avoid treading on each other's toes. *Taking care not to crash about with the parents* – this was how Francis had once described to Harry his role as son of the Travers household. After all, it was the sensible way, on balance – as well as reinforcing the worthy cause of guaranteeing his monthly allowance. It was in a most congenial manner that father and son parted company when they reached the front door of *The Mercury*.

*

The Mercury was a daily newspaper still in its youth during those days before the end of the century – an enterprise established by William Travers well before he was 50 years old. Though no journalist himself, when he was searching for a new investment the idea of a creating a daily newspaper struck him as a worthwhile way of taking his place as a contributor to the well-being of the town. His intention was that it would serve to speak to his companions, his business associates, their wives, members of the Town Council, sundry tradespeople and professional persons, and (hopefully) a few of those more lowly townsfolk who might use it to get a purchase on the whispers and shuffles of the current era, as well as providing a running commentary on sundry deviant and unusual incidents that happened during the course of daily life thereabouts, for their entertainment. To his way of thinking, he and his fellow citizens were all in the business of planning for auspicious times ahead, despite the tremor of underlying uncertainty that prevailed as one century braced itself for the birth pangs of the next. Perhaps his sensibility of the essential spirit of what went on about him, however mundane – especially the mundane of everyday existence in Cambridge – was another prompt, a creative one, for establishing his newspaper. After all, there was much to be gleaned from the ordinary as well as the extraordinary lives of Cambridge people. And there were certainly opportunities for the reporting of a limited amount of the sort of thing they liked – a prominent hanging, say, a nasty accident caused by a wantonly speeding cyclist, a gang of poachers caught red-handed with half a dozen brace of pheasants in their possession, or the successful pursuit of scrumpers facing their day in court. All this he would provide, along with the transmission of much information essential to their understanding of what it was he considered they needed to know, even if it was published in a most unremitting way, as reports were in those days, across interminable columns and in the most long-winded detail, according to some. Tiny type and a lack of illustrations did not help matters.

Sometimes side-stepping his master's views and, in reality, providing the essential draught that drove *The Mercury*'s brand of unremarkable reportage, this newspaper's editor, Gilbert Thompson, had supervised the appointment of a small coterie of reporters, each tasked with being a watchful surveyor of a designated local patch towards which he was sent forth on Mondays with the instruction to comb the barber shops, the inns, the Court House, the Police Station, the corridors of County Hall, several coffee houses and many other lesser points of congregation where people were to be found grunting out (fenlanders were folk of few words, released in short sentences rubbing against each other like oiled pebbles) their opinions about the state of the world. And their neighbour. The bulk of the work, though, was covering, often verbatim, various county meetings, petitions, election speeches and events, however tedious, and providing a descant of generally benign editorial comment.

Would it were that straightforward, it was Gilbert Thompson's burden to shoulder most days.

For one thing, it must be acknowledged that in addition to the inhabitants of the town and surrounding countryside *The Mercury* had from the start taken upon itself to report that other great constituency firmly ensconced within its boundaries: the University. For more than four hundred years it had been grafted onto their unremarkable East Anglian settlement – and this academic institution was undoubtedly growing, in terms of its renown, the scholarship and inventiveness of its members and its authority. How the devil, though, could one newspaper capture the interests of both the town *and* the university in one publication? This was the challenge William Travers set himself, resolving that his newspaper must be inclusive to both cultures and to all, and that a professor seeking accounts of his College's latest convention and the local girl working on the drapery counter who was after lighter matters could find satisfaction somewhere in the density of its pages. That way, the business man in him reckoned, advertisers would step forward a-plenty to support the cover price, meaning that in time he could use the revenue to establish new titles across East Anglia which would in turn reflect the particular concerns and demographic of other rural centres of commerce further afield, each district represented by a "change page" spun from the main paper to tell their own stories with added coherence right back to them. There were at this point no less than four change pages in operation in a spin-off called *The Weekly Mercury*, which came out on Fridays.

He was well placed to be the founder of such an enterprise. If he was a businessman first, he was also one of a small number of local people who had gained their degree at one of the colleges, and whose interests, naturally, spanned both the town and the university. He was a man who had a foot, as he was wont to declare, in both camps: like his friend Lucien Prideaux, he was an amphibian.

'Morning Mr Travers,' one of the delivery men hailed him as he approached *The Mercury*, a distinctive figure in his formal garb.

'Morning Bill,' he replied, in kind. There wasn't a member of his staff he didn't know by name and acknowledge with exactly the same courtesy. 'Shall we get the paper out today, do you think?' he added, opening the palm of one hand towards the sky.

'We shall if I've got anything to do with it,' replied the man, stamping his feet and clapping his hands against the cold. William rewarded him with a smile and a conspiratorial wave of his walking stick.

This was how it was: he didn't interfere too much in the daily mechanisms of getting the paper printed so that they all felt safe to talk to him, whatever their rank. He was on this account alone regarded as a gentleman of the best kind, and if anyone happened to make a mistake it was typically sympathy he offered, rather than a reprimand.

Having said that, it was common knowledge that one particular proprietorial indulgence he had assumed of late was to take upon himself the role of occasional contributor to the regular "University Intelligence" column. So it was that shortly after joining Gilbert Thompson, the proprietor drew out of his pocket a piece of paper on which he had carefully composed in his own neat hand the following:

> '*During the past week the utmost activity has prevailed everywhere, and amidst all sections of University Society.*

In the mornings study, coaching lectures; afternoons devoted almost universally to rowing, athletics, football, or other open-air sport, and the evenings to indoor entertainments. The Cambridge people can no longer complain justly of lack of entertainment through the action of the University, as the theatre is open nightly, besides which there has been a plethora of balls and concerts, promoted by combinations – political or otherwise – of the county town and University.'

He waited in anticipation for Gilbert Thompson to scan this latest gem. Well, it was not news, exactly – even he recognised that – but he hoped very much that from time to time he would be able to succeed in drawing attention to certain *auspicious* aspects of Cambridge life with a little good news – people too often forgot about how gratifying that was. At the same time, he was always prepared to abide by the editor's ruling on matters editorial – it was a matter of honour and a willing concession he made in view of not even pretending to be a journalistic person himself. As usual, Gilbert Thompson had no choice but to accept this paragraph of such exceptional blandness that there must not be another to rival it in the whole history of English newspapers. It was duly done without the relief of raising an eyebrow. The two men then spent a short while discussing broader issues coming to light from near and from far, giving them a sense of the ebb and flow of important matters of the moment. Why, thanks to the wire service they had been hot on the Whitechapel murders not so very long ago.

When they were done, Gilbert Thompson rang a bell and called for Walter Magson, one of his most astute reporters, handing the proprietor's offering over to him with a tap of his forefinger against the side of his nose. Walter responded with a ready nod to a signal he knew well. There was an understanding between them that some considerable interference with any copy submitted by the governor would likely be called for. Missives from William Travers sometimes needed a simple "re-nose" to make them more lively and coherent, but more often than not they required burying altogether within a more compelling story. The editor knew he could trust his reporter to do what must be done without causing offence. This Walter Magson was a spry, rangy individual who had two valuable qualities: he had received rudimentary schooling locally, and he knew

Cambridge intimately. His top skill was to be able to make notes at an enviable speed of some 150 words a minute using Pitman's shorthand – not far off that achieved by Mr Dickens himself several decades previously, he was proud to declare. The editor had his eye on Magson for further development. There was no lack of ambition about the boy. Walter's own nose was also trained in other ways, most notably in the art of sniffing out a likely story, whether it was a cracking court case, an unexpected outrage or minor disaster. He knew what would get people sitting up. More arcane matters, though, particularly those concerning the university, held little appeal for him. Part of Walter's ferret-like enthusiasm was linked to the fact that he had been engaged for some time to Mildred Dobbins, the telegraph machine operator, and they were slowly, oh so slowly, establishing the funds necessary for a marriage to take place.

After he had doctored William Travers's copy with his usual skill Walter conveyed it personally to the composing room because this meant a chance to give a wink to Mildred in the gallery as he passed – such fleeting connections between the couple provided much needed leaven to their long working days. The next stage in its journey involved a compositor setting William Travers's copy by hand, creating a galley proof which, like all other long, thin paper galleys would take its turn under the uncompromising scrutiny of one "Mr Charles Newsome, BA, Proof Reader" according to the brass nameplate nailed to his cupboard-sized booth at the foot of the stairs leading to the reporters' room. Here, day in and day out, he stubbornly performed his solitary work, scrutinizing the narrow scrolls provided by the compositors. Reporters knew him as a terror for grammatical mistakes, which he marked up with diligence, and the vehemence of those brush-strokes of his on their copy sometimes felt to the writer to be a kind of revenge.

Meanwhile, William Travers took a turn with his editor down to the print hall, pleased to see that the majority of workers had managed to come in despite the weather – 'loyal to a man,' he murmured approvingly – just as he nodded encouragement at all who passed, receiving from each an easy greeting in return. Twenty minutes or so later, having satisfied themselves that there would indeed be one edition coming out that day, even if it was later than usual, editor and proprietor returned the way they had come, past the wood-panelled newsroom where reporters positioned themselves at desks heaped high with filing trays, discarded notebooks and a fresh pile of copy paper for the writers to use, cut from the ends of rolls of newsprint. Mounds of clippings from the previous day's paper awaited the post boy who would call soon to bear them off them to the library to be catalogued. There was a sharp smell of pipe smoke in the reporter's room, mingling with a rubbery whiff of ink, and a sturdy iron boiler managed to intensify the reek of wet outer clothes hanging on the backs of chairs which gave the air in this particular power house the humidity of a warm fog.

'Now, I'd be grateful if you would cast your eye over this, Mr Travers,' invited Gilbert Thompson in his own turn while they sipped their morning coffee, back in his office. He passed over a "Local Note" by "Argus" – who was none other than the editor himself. It read as follows: *Numerous complaints have been made of late concerning the number of beggars that infest Chesterton. These complaints having reached the ears of the divisional police, prompt steps were taken to check the evil. A number of constables paraded the district in plain clothes, and succeeded in making a haul of this flotsam and jetsam of humanities.*

Travers pursed his lips in such a way that was neither confirmatory nor overtly critical, though calling people "evil" and "flotsam and jetsam" sounded a bit stiff. Besides which, heaven knew, tempers were in the habit of flaring up at the least provocation in the town lately. Without judgement and still gripping the editor's copy he moved his head to scan other small items in the process of being pasted up. There were short pieces about a fire in a Barnwell tenement, the arrest of a habitual pilferer, an accidental death on the railway, another case of scorching bicyclists whose furious driving did so inflame passing pedestrians … After a short pause, he looked up and merely reflected: 'You know my feeling, Gilbert, that the paper should be gentle to the poor, bold on behalf of the oppressed, and it should champion the good of Cambridge at every opportunity.' He felt confident that without much intervention from himself – this was the proper way, the mainstay of their flourishing working relationship – any offending words might be … redistributed, rather than excised. And if they weren't, well, again he trusted Gilbert Thompson's judgement. He would wait and see how it went.

'Ah, there's another thing, sir,' added the editor. 'Two more letters about the volatile situation on the streets have come to us.'

'Oh dear.'

The first, it transpired, was from one calling himself "Caustic" who snarled:

> *'How long, I pray, are we to be plagued by women of evil intent in such numbers as persist today in this town? By such a blight we begin to resemble a low pleasure garden in the manner of The Haymarket or the Arcades, I vow.'*

The next took a different tilt at the matter, coming from someone calling himself "Paterfamilias".

> *'I have known ladies belonging to the most respectable families in this town, daughters and wives of professional men, men of position and family (not tradesmen or College servants) stopped and insulted in the most offensive manner, purely and simply because they were walking unaccompanied in the street and did not happen to be personally known to the Proctors and I think that in this case you ought to ventilate this subject and assist the inhabitants of Cambridge in overthrowing this system by which Clergymen of the Church of England are compelled to disgrace their cloth and bring odium on their ministers. I may add that the police of this town (one of the most efficient bodies in the kingdom) if instructed to act in a sensible manner, would be perfectly competent to keep the streets in much more decent order than they are under the proctorial system.'*

'Oh dear me,' he said again when he had scanned them. 'Well. Perhaps it is to become an issue again, then.' It had been thirty years since the last proctorical reign of terror, as it was sometimes referred to. He sighed. 'Hold these two letters for a day or two, Gilbert, and let us see what else comes in. It is not for us to inflame people's sensibilities, I think.'

The editor stared at him. 'We have a duty to shame 'em where shame is due, I would have thought?'

'Well, that might just be our excuse,' said Travers with a rueful smile. 'I have sometimes wondered about the authenticity of people who adopt a holier-than-thou attitude, you know.'

'Not me, sir.'

'No, indeed, Gilbert. Not you.'

Allowing opinions to be expressed on the pages of *The Mercury* in the form of letters to the editor were in part – he had to admit to himself – a way of buying time for the newspaper rather than sitting on the fence, when hotly diving in to an issue guaranteed to divide the readership might be seen as driven by emotions rather than good sense. Now, that would surely not be a prudent course to take.

*

A rumour, a suspicion, a snippet of suggestion – none of it needs much in the way of propulsion to set it flying above the surface of the snow in all manner of directions at twice the speed of any improper cycling that might or might not be able to take place on a snow-bound day. One particular story had certainly travelled at a furious pace towards the outskirts of the town during the last twenty-four hours, calling briefly at Warkworth Terrace before speeding onwards. This was at least half an hour before Rose Whipple paused to collect herself on the doorstep of the lodging house before venturing to ring the bell to be re-admitted. At that moment, a purposeful young woman on her way out, her arms full of books and a bag looped over her arm, opened the door and eyed the pitiful figure in front of her before standing aside to allow her in.

'Rose, my dear, whatever has happened?'

Rose shook her head. She could not find words which would adequately convey something of the truth of the matter to Cynthia Dawes, who looked so … enviably normal in her heavy coat and boots, a long scarf draped around her neck and a simple hat pulled down tightly over her ears. A lady well prepared for life, observed Rose.

'No, don't trouble yourself,' said that lady, changing her mind about the possibility of receiving a lengthy confidence from the housemaid. Anyway, she had already caught wind of the bare bones of what had taken place the previous day. She regarded the housemaid's condition with sympathy. 'You must get warm. Come in, come in.'

Rose shuffled into the hall and stood aside to allow Josephine Meadows, Cynthia Dawes's companion at lectures, to leave the house with her.

Mrs Judith Mawkins, their landlady, waited until the two young ladies had closed the door behind them before emerging from the shadow cast by a bulky hall stand. She beckoned Rose to follow her towards the kitchen, where a blast of warmth from the range hit Rose with the force of a sudden embrace.

'Let's get you out of those wet clothes and into something dry and warm first,' ordered the landlady with good sense, taking the shivering maid by the arm just at the point where she had been gripped so fiercely by the Proctor the day before, which made her wince.

'Thank you, ma'am,' she replied, grateful for the business-like tones of her employer and an opportunity to escape to her attic room in order to change her clothes.

'Ten minutes, Rose? Then there's something I need to discuss with you.'

'Yes, miss,' Rose called back, mid-flight. Pray God it wasn't her dismissal. If it *wasn't,* that would be a miracle.

*

In town an hour later, after her attendance at a lecture, Cynthia Dawes handed her books and baggage to her companion temporarily while she made a brief detour inside the draughty emporium called Eaden Lilley in order to purchase toiletries. Cynthia was, to some, a formidable young woman, in that she was not afraid to demonstrate her love of learning together with a clear-sighted ambition to make something of herself. Ever since she was a little girl living with her father, a doctor, her mother and two brothers in a Midland town not too far away, her imagination had been fired by stories she had read of the legendary Florence Avery, one of the earliest women to join the young men at lectures in Cambridge, about whom it was said smoked cigarettes. Not only that, she openly wore silk breeches on at least one occasion, causing a sensation at the Gare St Lazare in Paris where, apparently, she was to meet her *lover* and embark on a cycling trip with him through France. Of course, she was never awarded a degree – that remained an exclusively male privilege – despite her achievement in the final examinations and the fact that she had gone on to write several books on anthropology based on her exploration of primitive religion through which, Cynthia learned, she sought to establish what religion actually amounted to before it became secularised morality. (Fascinating, thought Cynthia.) And why was it, Miss Avery also enquired, were the ghosts and bogeys of pre-Homeric religion – the Sirens, the Gorgons, the Sphinx – all women?

Cynthia felt a certain urge to continue this line of research herself and was looking forward to travelling to somewhere foreign like Greece at some point in the future, hopefully. And yet, day by day most of the lecturers made it plain that women such as Cynthia Dawes were exceedingly fortunate to be taught by them at all, inviting a frustrating sense of indebtedness in return, a posture which Cynthia herself considered fawning, preferring to hold herself steady and expressionless regarding that issue. It was true that only two thirds of professors were prepared to admit women to their lectures, and she was accustomed to hearing them always introduce matters with the singular 'Gentlemen …'.

Leaving her lecture that morning with Josephine at her side, both had heard one University man remark to his companion as they passed that he couldn't tell women from each other because they were all so much alike. Perhaps, then, speculated Cynthia, there was an extra onus on a woman who aspired to learning to cut an extra dash, so to speak – to be willing to make herself controversial – like Florence Avery. On balance, she hoped this was not the case. Racy behaviour held no appeal whatsoever for Cynthia, who had decided to align herself with a female maths scholar who had recently done something quite astonishing by having the audacity to come top in the Maths tripos despite being a woman, and should by rights have been lauded with the title of "Senior Wrangler" according to custom, however embarrassing this would be to those men she studied with, let alone to those who taught her. She, too, was awarded nothing for her achievement. According to some scientists of the time whose work Cynthia had read, a woman taking an honours degree would be a dangerous proposition anyway – such activities may run the risk of future infertility and madness, evidently. But such views did not deter her.

How many times had she turned a deaf ear to the taunts and the slights which men made no attempt to keep to themselves? Give way to no facial expression, she constantly reminded herself. Appear as though none of it matters. Leap-frog the unpleasant moment. Keep before you only the clean slate of the future. In this way Cynthia suffered their splintering slights and clumsy joshing every day, pretending not to notice as she continued on her contrary adventure in a man's world. That very week she had plainly heard herself being mocked by even the Downing men lodging at

Warkworth Road, for inviting two female friends back for a jolly cocoa evening in her own room – a harmless enough pursuit, she would have thought – or perhaps it was just too *ridiculously* harmless for them?

The queue at the toiletries counter in the department store was thankfully short, but as Cynthia approached her turn, purse at the ready, an imposing woman barged heavily in front of her, knocking her shoulder.

'Oh, I say,' murmured Cynthia, caught off balance.

The woman – it was none other than that troublesome madam known as Mrs Blanche Marchmont – turned back to face her with raised eyebrows – before suddenly changing tack by making an exaggerated capitulation and offering Cynthia a lavish bow which she had no trouble in recognising for what it was: a means of further unsettling her.

'*Laydees* first,' cried this woman in a loud but unctuous voice, addressing not only Cynthia but the rest of the queue, eliciting a few embarrassed sniggers as she winked at someone further back.

'No, it's quite alright,' insisted Cynthia, with a slight frown. 'You go first, if you will.'

This only acted as a spur to Mrs Blanche Marchmont who, it was well known, despised female blue-stockings, especially those of the hoity-toity variety. Cynthia was now obliged to watch the courtesan's sudden raising of both hands to her cheeks in mock confusion, only to trill: 'Dear me, the *laydee* wishes *me* to go before her!'

Cynthia turned away and swiftly left the shop without making her purchase, refusing to collude in such a charade.

*

The sky glowered like gunmetal all that day and the temperature hovered just above freezing. 'Looks like we're in for a time of it,' surmised Mrs Judith Mawkins, the Warkworth Terrace landlady. Rose now stood before her in a dry set of garments with her second best stiff dimity pinafore tied tightly round her waist, ready for work.

'You can take that off, my dear,' said Mrs Mawkins, pointing at the apron, 'because I think you should go home now.'

'Oh, please, I can explain – '

'But I would rather you didn't, Rose.'

Rose hung her head. Then, to her amazement: 'Don't you fret, girl, I don't believe a word of it. You are no loose bit of goods, I know that. There's been a mischief done to you, I'd say, somewhere along the line. It is a most unpleasant matter.' It is possible that this was the longest speech Mrs Mawkins had ever made to her young employee. She pursed her lips and shook her head in a way that indicated that her disapprobation resided elsewhere.

Rose produced a smile of pure relief for the first time since her arrest by the Proctor, a generous smile that she quickly dampened, given her status. While it lasted, it lit up her dark eyes and revealed the willingness of her nature. But she knew when to hold her peace. She knew particularly that Mrs Mawkins's very livelihood as a University landlady depended on keeping her license, which stipulated that she accurately record the exact hour and minute anyone living there returned after 10.00pm, the time of the curfew for students as well as staff employed in her establishment. In the case of the young men, if one of them was caught on the streets after that hour and his absence didn't tally with her record, *she* would be in trouble as well as he, which was why, the night before, the landlady had rapped on Arthur Moody's door in the end to warn Harry Hobbs that he ought to be off. Not that Rose's overnight absence counted for much in the wider scheme of things, but if enquiries were made it could be a black mark held against the landlady and she would receive a caution for allowing a female out on the streets at night where she could only be up to one thing. Both Rose and Mrs Mawkins were well aware how widely it was held in those days, especially in university circles, that domestic servants and others in similar positions in the town were expressly designed for the amusement of young gentlemen, and that lodging houses must surely contain the worst kind of temptation for young students and maids alike.

'Now listen to me, Rose,' Mrs Mawkins began, keen to move on. 'I have had a message sent from your father. I'll not mince words: it seems your mother is missing. As far as I can make out she left your village for doing some shopping in the market, taking the carrier's cart into Cambridge early yesterday morning. But she never came home. He is out searching for her and he wants you to mind the little ones this afternoon.'

'May I go, then?'

'You may. But if there are drifts out there you must come back at once. There's no point in you going missing as well, or worse.'

'I will,' promised Rose.

'And I shall need you back here by the end of the day, no later.'

'Of course, ma'am.'

*

For unrecorded generations, Rose Whittle's people had been settled on the Isle of Ely, a stark, slightly raised area to the north east of Cambridge, a place that demanded a certain amount of resignation and much resilience on the part of its inhabitants, exposing them as it did to the mercy of every kind of extreme weather. The fens themselves which surrounded that town were uniformly flat and prone to screaming winds which were gradually stripping away the rich black peatlands where a cross-hatching of sluices, drains and waterways gridded the earth at intervals. In those parts water was the governing element – there was simply no getting away from it. From Ely and further afield, the rivers Ouse and Cam were conduits for horse drawn barges and steam tugs which came bringing grain, timber, bricks, the osier twigs women wove into baskets, and peat. They arrived in Cambridge in slow moving flotillas, and these same barges would return later in the day at sedate speeds of under three miles an hour, sitting considerably higher in the water as a result of shedding their loads. The fenland merchants used lighters as well – flat-bottomed open barges with identical blunt ends which could be hitched together in fives to form a "gang". One day Rose's father, an eel man by trade from near Ely, began to weigh up in his mind whether there may be a better living to be made in a place like Cambridge, rather than out on the eerie fen, since eels like slow flowing water and might flourish on the muddy river bed of the Cam flowing through the town.

Bert Whipple, Rose's father, was a sallow-skinned man with hooded black eyes and a back hunched from crouching over his eel nets. Five years previously, he made the important decision to move up river – just as the eels tended to do. The Whipples also took two geese with them, which Jenny, Rose's mother, had learned how to pluck for the purpose of harvesting good quality quills which she hoped to sell directly to the gentlemen of the university. As for the eels, it seemed they were popular in pies and stews and were regarded as a great delicacy by University people. The family arrived in

Cambridge with a single overburdened cart and soon enough established themselves in tight, ground floor lodgings on the outskirts of Barnwell, a suburb of mean dwellings and shrouded alleyways on the outskirts of Cambridge. From this base the eel man set about making the availability of his wares known to the colleges. Soon enough, the family discovered they could just about manage on the money he made, and hoped to move further into town when funds allowed, since it was a mile walk for Bert to get to the banks of the river where he set his half dozen eel baskets, secretly submerging and camouflaging them at points known only to him by the backs of the colleges.

Rose, at last wearing clothes and boots more suited to walking out, lost no time in marching with her loaded basket – home. It felt odd, now, to call it that, and it saddened her that she should have such a feeling as she made her way towards Barnwell along narrow pathways which had been freshly dug out of the snow. While her family was simple and respectable she, like many other young Cambridge women, had lately been exposed to another, less limited way of living, as well as to a different class of people altogether, thanks to a local clergyman's reference on her behalf which had secured her an independent position at the house in Warkworth Road. *Less limited*: that was partly the reason for her feeling of wistfulness as she walked, because it was true: she was undoubtedly less limited than when she had been living with her family, and this was opening up a distance between them which was not just spatial. Nowadays, she was used to immersing herself in the urban throng of people on the streets of the town who were so different from any she had encountered out in the countryside while she was growing up. It seemed to her that in important ways her life had become both interesting and sobering. Walking to Hawkins' pastry counter each morning to buy currant loaves on behalf of the Warkworth Road residents, for example, she could not help being all too aware of the crowds of students on their way to lectures, forming a melee with an edge of excitement to it along the sidewalks. And then there was the sheer variety of madeleines, Madeiras, Eccles cakes, cream horns, fancy cakes and the rest on sale when she reached the shop where, ever so occasionally, she might reward herself with fourpence worth of mixed biscuits to take home and nibble alone in her attic room later. She was used to overhearing strange and exotic snippets of conversation in the street, a few of them remembered, to be chewed over later when her work was done. Why, that very week, while she was out collecting laundry, two gowned, middle-aged men of importance walked by, entirely oblivious of her shared existence on the pavement, leaving a sharp masculine waft in their wake and some rather memorable words. 'No,' Rose distinctly heard the shorter of the pair remarking to his companion, 'I disagree with you. I think it is inconceivable that a housemaid could be virtuous: female virtue is the luxury of the wealthy.' The response was lost to Rose, but she felt herself flush, almost as though she had been personally identified and held up for prying eyes to scrutinise before being arbitrarily condemned. And yet. Her mind took a turn, as it often did when she was puzzling something out, fastening on the word "luxury" that had been used. Might that man mean *not* what she immediately took for a cutting dismissal of herself and her class? Might it be possible that he had actually been making a more sympathetic allusion to humbler women's subsistence level of pay which intensified temptation for some of the local girls? Or was this just wishful thinking on her part? It wasn't the first time that Rose, by allowing her mind to linger on disembodied chips of conversation, had unwittingly exposed herself to the arts of argument, equivocation and reasoning. But she knew little of such things.

After an hour of hard walking, she was gladdened to find her mother already returned home, huddled stiffly in a chair and swaddled in blankets. This meant that Rose was in time to peel, quarter and boil up a pot of potatoes to go with the pie Mrs Mawkins had sent, and while the pot simmered, to set to scrubbing a toddler's soiled trousers before sitting down with her father and mother and the rest of them for a shared lunch.

'I found her in the big barn down the road earlier on,' explained Bert Whipple with a nod towards his wife. 'I should not have sent for you, Rose. What happened – well, she will tell you herself, no doubt, when her teeth have stopped chattering. Thing was, the carrier's cart could go no further taking the women home again yesterday, and there were several of them sheltering in that big barn down the road by the time I got to her. Cut off, they were.' And that was that.

As she shared his relief, there was one worry remaining in Rose's mind: might her parents have caught wind of her own misadventure? Had word reached these parts yet? As they ate, she was earnestly hoping that any hint of frisky gossip regarding her may, with luck, have run out of steam before it reached this far. Since no-one sitting at the table mentioned it while they ate their meal, it encouraged her to trust that this was indeed the case.

'I heard a story as I was coming along,' she told them, brightening up. 'It happened about a hundred years ago when there was a terrible snowstorm, much worse than this. Shall I tell it?'

The children stared at her. 'Go on, Rose, go on. Do you tell it.'

'Well, there was a farmer's wife who had been selling her wares in the Cambridge market – just like you, ma – the difference being she'd gone there alone on horseback. On her way back, a frightful blizzard got up and her horse bolted and she fell off it. She started walking across a field but she could see nothing in the blinding snow. At last, she discovered a hedge where she could shelter, but it was snowing so hard that it soon buried her completely. There she squatted, getting colder and colder. All the time she sat there she could hear a church clock chime the quarter, the half and the hour. And from time to time travellers talking far off on the road. Then she fell asleep. Much later, she heard her husband calling out, too. She tied her red handkerchief to a stick and managed to poke it through the snow, trying to wave it. But no-one saw it, or heard her crying. That night, a man in her village dreamed about a big hare buried in the snow drifts at a certain bend in the hedge. *Two days later* he found himself at the very spot and saw that red handkerchief – still waving.'

'So she was saved?' croaked her mother.

'She was. But only just. He called for a horse and cart and they managed to pull her out, but her legs were frozen and her skin was raw from where they tried to peel her stockings away later.'

'Aaah.'

'She lasted a few months. But her toes dropped off. It was the frost bite.'

'Oooooo. Lord.'

A respectful hush fell while they took this in. For just a few moments, it was as though this eel man and his family, including Rose, became as one in their shared horror at such a tale, their set faces suggesting that the precipice they themselves faced – the lip of ever-present poverty – was never far away.

'Are you sure you won't stop a night or two, Rose?' asked her mother, shaking her head. 'Only stories like that make you want to be at home, don't you think?'

Rose agreed, but she assured them that her workplace was a good enough home to her now and so she must be getting back.

After the previous day's ordeal, Rose hoped that nothing worse could come down upon her just yet. The awfulness and disgrace of that night spent in the Spinning House, she reckoned, might be made to strengthen her in time, if she managed to bear it out. The first thing to do was to put the matter behind her, she decided as she paced on back into town – to fold it away with the kind of discipline that will overcome unwanted feelings, pressing all memory of it firmly down inside that dark drawer in her psyche marked forgetting, trusting that would be the end of it. With this in mind, she experienced something rising up from her core. It announced itself as the quality of perseverance, a gift which it seemed she might indeed possess. It had been bred in her from the beginning of her hardy life out on the fens, and supplemented by the immoveable strictness of her father. A random tableau vivant suddenly composed itself in her mind that went like this: butterfingers drops a metal plate in the kitchen; it bounces loudly on the tiles; it is picked up, bent but unbroken, and tossed back to the shelf where it belongs. Well, I, Rose Whipple, may be such a plate, she reflected. Not without pride.

Unsurprisingly, given all that the previous twenty-four hours had thrown at her, a sudden weariness fell upon Rose as she measured her footsteps. She was aiming to arrive by late afternoon, as required, and was already relishing the thought of warming herself up once she was back inside the lodging house.

It was probably just as well that she missed seeing a brand new landmark silhouetted high against the twilight as she entered the heart of Cambridge. Had she been more focussed, had the light been sharper and the day less burdened by untoward happenings, it might have caught her attention and taken her mind back to the perils of the day before. But unbeknown to her, there it rested, fastened to the highest pinnacle of a certain College chapel – a favourite climbing destination for enterprising young students seeking to defy both gravity and the relentless regulations they were subject to. Here, fitful movements of wintry air caused it to flutter in a desultory way from time to time. It was destined to be treated with much ribaldry during the coming days, and was vigorously applauded by many who passed by. The attachment in question? A once resplendent red velvet hat, its sorry looking white feather plucked to a state of near baldness by the icy breeze. Firmly fixed for all to see, it became a provocative echo of a memorable incident and proved something of an engineering problem for vexed college staff eager to remove it, during which time it repaid many times over the effort made to put it up there.

*

Unlike his friend Lucien Prideaux, William Travers found himself warming to young people on the whole, and was generally at ease with them. On the other hand, Prideaux's own instinct was to hold such creatures at arm's length because he found them unsettling and suffered a recluse's fear of the bolder of them. But Travers found their conversation entertaining and their healthiness attractive. Moreover, in relation to women, while Travers was a gracious host, Prideaux – were he to find himself face to face with one of the species at a convention or in a drawing room – would produce a fixed smile, rather wider than it needed to be, before seeking to extricate himself. The only female exceptions to this were his lively god-daughter, Aurelia Travers, who charmed him with her chatter. Oh, and that paragon, her mother.

'Concerning proctors,' Aurelia was idly wondering aloud on the night of the promised supper party at the Travers's house on Park Terrace. 'Could someone tell me what is it exactly that they do? I spot one almost every time I leave the house these days.' Aurelia's voice created a tinkling complement to the sound of cutlery on plates around a week later as she made this tentative appeal to her fellow diners. It was the sort of question that her godfather, had he been invited, might have relished tackling, but Alice Travers had decided that he might prove too awkward a guest if she included him as part of a deliberately youthful evening. So there were eight of them gathered on this occasion – Travers *père et mère*, their daughter Aurelia, her brother Francis, his Downing friends Arthur Moody and Harry Hobbs, the student Cynthia Dawes whose lodgings were also in Warkworth Road, and Hope Bassett. Four men and four women, then, calibrated by their hostess with sympathetic imagination around the heavy oak table in the dining room. Each guest had been included for a simple reason – that they would supply charm and light diversion on a dark winter's evening.

With this in mind, following the invitation offered by his father on the day of the snow and given carte blanche by his mother, Francis had accordingly summoned his friend Arthur Moody in order to repay some of that young man's legendary hospitality at their lodging house. He took Harry along in order to buoy himself up – you could never tell when a fellow might need the support of friends, Francis considered, especially when dependent on the parents for the many items a young man required, all of which required funds. Besides, Harry was a family friend as well: his father had been an undergraduate at the same time as William Travers and Lucien Prideaux. Cynthia Dawes, the female student who was his landlady's niece, hadn't deserved to be ribbed about inviting her friends for cocoa, she certainly hadn't – Francis regretted his own part in such discourtesy. So in a show of goodwill he persuaded her to join them as well. Since they were short of another female, and as the ambience was to be determined by the young people, Alice Travers decided to extend a rare invitation to Hope Bassett, who normally took her meal alone upstairs or in the kitchen with the domestic staff when there was a party going on in the house.

Seven faces looked up in unison from their plates as they absorbed Aurelia's question.

'He is a custodian, an overseer, a watchman, a seeker after truth, a pillar of university probity – something like that, isn't he?' offered Francis, with a grin.

His father frowned at him.

'Proctor – the title derives from the word 'procurator', I believe,' said Harry, coming to his aid. 'Someone who provides something. You know, a person who oversees the affairs of others, perhaps.'

'As opposed to a "procuress",' Francis leapt in, unable to stop himself – 'who also provides, in her own way.'

'Enough, Francis!' said his mother.

Hope, who understood something of the Proctor's role and the part it played, obliquely, in her coming to reside with the Travers family, was listening closely without appearing to do so, curious to hear any answer which may be forthcoming. Opposite her sat

Arthur and Francis, with Aurelia in between them. Hope herself, together with Cynthia, bookended Harry, with Alice and William facing each other from the top and bottom ends of the table. This was manoeuvred by Alice so that Hope would not directly face Harry, since it was obvious to Alice that the exceptionally pleasing looks of both these particular two young people were likely to ignite a passion in one or the other of them. Or in both at once, which would be far worse.

'Ha,' continued Francis when no other response was forthcoming. 'The Proctor is there to be the bane of a young man's life, that's what. Sometimes I think they would keep us in strait-jackets.'

'That's not quite fair, Francis,' said his father. 'They have your interests and safety at heart, you know.'

'Why do you ask, Aurelia?' This was Alice, her mother.

'Well, I overheard you talking about a "proctorial reign of terror" not so long ago,' said the girl. 'That's what you called it. And I heard there was a completely blameless girl who was arrested in the snow storm last week by the Proctor. Does this mean that someone other than the town constables is able to arrest people nowadays?'

Francis, Harry and Arthur managed to share a discreet look. Harry felt himself blushing and took out a handkerchief to disguise the fact.

William Travers sighed. 'Look at it this way, my dear,' he offered in a summary sort of way. 'Young men away from home are deemed … vulnerable.'

'Vulnerable to what?' persisted Aurelia.

'Vulnerable to young women,' Cynthia could not restrain herself from declaring, in as neutral a tone as she could manage. 'Would you believe it?'

'Like you and I, perhaps?'

'Well, possibly not,' said Cynthia.

'Well, then … ?'

No-one, it seemed, quite had the stomach to help Cynthia out.

'Oh,' Aurelia said with a shrug after the pause that followed, sensing currents running deeper than her question had intended, rather regretting that she had brought it up. And suspecting that she was the only person at that table who was not privy to some mysterious secret.

'Look,' Cynthia felt obliged to add, out of respect for Aurelia's disadvantage. 'You mentioned just one example of proctorial power, Francis. That girl, you know,' she added, addressing Aurelia directly, 'turned out to be a housemaid at our lodgings, actually, known to Mr Moody and Mr Hobbs here as well as your brother, incidentally. My point would be this: that if anyone was vulnerable it was *her*, but only because she was in the wrong place at the wrong time on this occasion – nothing more. And because her class lacks, shall we say, the defences that you and I might call upon, she was made an example of. That's all there is to it. Happens frequently, I believe.'

'I feel that unfair shame preys upon the vulnerable sometimes,' murmured Alice. 'I have met many a girl who has been publicly exposed and it seems … unkind, to me, when they are pilloried out of hand. As though "shame 'em" is the way to cure weakness or the stain of their poverty and its unfortunate legacy.' In the thoughtful silence that followed Harry experienced a sharp stab of pity for the housemaid Rose. He took little part in the conversation after that.

On their way out of the house an hour or so later, Francis teased him for being unusually subdued. 'Just thinking, old boy,' said Harry. But there was a small worm working away in his mind. After pushing all thoughts of Rose away for the past week, he began to confront what may have been his own part in her downfall for the first time, with that indiscriminate wave of his hand. It disturbed him rather that he did not have the first idea of how – let alone *if* – he should set about making amends to the girl in view of what had happened to her. It was not in his nature to be callous, even by default – on the contrary, it was his way to get on well enough with pretty much all those who made up the mottled brew of undergraduate society in his day: the sybarites, the old-fashioned romantics, the would-be revolutionaries, the aesthetes and the athletes as well as the aristocrats, the scions of foreign potentates, the clever chaps, the bon viveurs, the rakes and the bohemians – and, of course, those ordinary fellows he called his friends – that is, the lodgers at Warkworth Road, in the main. It appeared to be generally accepted that Rose Whipple had been wronged, he reminded himself as he walked alone back to College later that evening.

*

Snow aside – and this latest episode dissolved as quickly as it had materialised, its inconvenience lasting no more than three days in all – if there was one other great leveller in Cambridge that year as it continued to unravel it was the extended freeze which followed the snow, meaning that people had an opportunity to dust off their wooden skates and make for the river whose customary stink was temporarily trapped beneath a stiff plate of ice. The Cam froze easily, being both slow-flowing and relatively narrow, and the first Sunday of that year's deep freeze in late February saw much activity down by the river. After church, young people of all ranks took to the towpaths, encouraged by the sight of quite a crowd gathered there, all eager to start showing off their moves.

One of the first to glide out was *Mercury* reporter Walter Magson, swaying from side to side with his nose in the air in perfect unison with his partner, their arms firmly braided behind their backs in the traditional pose of skating pairs. In other circumstances, such a way of going on might have been construed as intimate and therefore inappropriate, since Walter and Mildred were out unaccompanied, despite their being officially affianced. But it was not so when they were locked together for this particular purpose. What a gift a bit of ice was to long-term lovers enduring a period of seemingly endless waiting until funds, accumulating at such an achingly slow pace, would allow them to marry. No matter the cold, no matter how public the place, the ice gave them a rare opportunity to savour each other as they spun forth, interlocked and without fear of disapproval, each wearing a smug smile to disguise the private trance that bound them together as they headed nowhere in particular, gripping each other closely, thanks to this God-given, weather-induced interlude.

Earlier, Walter had turned up at the cottage near the river in Chesterton where Mildred lived with her parents on the off-chance that she might rise to an impromptu invitation for an outing on the ice, just the two of them. He was right about that – she was on the settee waiting for him, clutching her skates and attired for the purpose. There had been fumblings in the past on that piece of furniture, but only on rare occasions when Mildred's parents were out – a nonsense on his part which she had slapped down. She knew what was what. She would not "give in" to him before marriage. They would just have to wait until there was money to live independently as a couple. Where she lived was close enough to Barnwell for her to have female acquaintances who *had* given in – and look at where it got them. One girl had purportedly gone to stay with her aunt for some months, only to arrive back home just as her mother (also unseen during that period) produced a baby sister – or so the story went. Another had married one of the undergraduates, which at first had felt to the waiting Mildred like a piece of unwarranted good luck. But it didn't turn out to be so, not really. In return for not disclosing the young gentleman's name to the Proctor who had caught them holding hands, the student had been obliged to abandon his studies. He took the young woman in question to Margate to live, far from anyone who had known either of them. In this way he remained unnamed and un-shamed, but they were never heard of again. Well. Slinking off like that – it was a high price to pay, in Mildred's opinion.

Later that day Walter would use his good mood as well as his powers of observation to file a Mercury report on the imminent arrival of a group of young racers who had earlier set out from Ely to travel the river along the winding, ice-bound twelve miles separating the two towns. 'Look, here they come!' came the cry – and the happy pair made a dash to the bank to let them scythe past.

Amongst the first batch of skaters to cross the line was a Trinity man followed closely by none other than Arthur Moody who, in the end, hadn't enough breath left in him for one final spurt. Red-faced and steaming, Arthur collapsed by a college boathouse on the finishing line where a trestle table had been hastily assembled on which jugs of hot punch were on offer to the racers.

When it had all died down Harry Hobbs, who had come down to cheer his friend on, found himself idly skating downriver away from the bustle and the shouting. Muffled, gloved, dressed in a Norfolk jacket with a wide flat cap to keep his head warm, he'd dressed hurriedly earlier, pulling on the plus fours he'd normally use for shooting back home on the estate in Suffolk. After a short while it became plain to him that he had strayed into an area which was out of the way of the colleges. Evidently this was where poorer folk lived, and he found their gleefully expressive capers quite a pleasant diversion as he steered round them. Skating on the Cam was undoubtedly one of the few relatively classless activities available to all, he reflected. Extraordinary, really. Apparently, all it took was a plate of ice to turn the river into a free for all. Those young skaters carving arcs round each other began to charm him, especially with their spins and boisterous zig-zagging. Deprived of a partner of his own he moved idly to the tempo of his own thoughts.

Skating was as liberating as the horseplay he sometimes indulged in with his sisters, it struck him, especially during the summer when they were able at harvest time to romp about freely in the fields and play elaborate games of hide-and-seek in the copses. His sisters: how he adored them, and how they cherished him in return. He was aware of how precious he was to them all: the only boy and the youngest of the brood along with Kitty, his twin. When he was little their ruthless tickling often felt like a form of torture, taking him almost beyond laughter, but the games they played on him relentlessly, even to this day, always ended up making him smile with affection. Since he had grown up with no mother – she had died during the burden of giving birth to Harry and Kitty – those girls, his best chums, were just about his only source of reference when it came to understanding what young females were all about. The result of this was a kind of innocence that, far from inhibiting him, allowed him to be at ease in the company of the opposite sex, and caused such girls that he came across, in turn, to feel safe when they were with him. Not that his experience so far was anything beyond passing acquaintance, but nevertheless … a picture of William Travers's daughter Aurelia crossed his mind. He had met Aurelia once more since the supper party at Park Terrace and discovered that she possessed a sense of fun akin to his own. He reckoned she would get on with his sisters, just as he did.

And then he saw her.

Rose Whipple, also unaccompanied, was wearing a colourful hand knitted bonnet and skated slowly, dreamily, with a straight back, her hands tucked inside a muffler and her dark hair resting on the collar of her coat. For half a minute she was the only floating thing in his sights. He watched her form an experimental circle, the swish of her blades leaving small ridges of ice crystals in her wake. His instinct was to call out. But he didn't. Instead, with a determined grin on his face he positioned himself to graft himself onto her as she approached, in such a way that when she glanced up sharply at the sound of someone nearby on the ice – startled out of a reverie of her own, perhaps – he was on hand to lightly catch her by the waist and spin her onward, up-stream. As to where they might be heading, he gave no thought. It was enough to have entered the moment with her – *her* moment.

Neither said a word until they had travelled some hundred yards, at which point she reached out to snatch the fronds of a weeping willow growing out of the bank, bringing her face-to-face with him. 'You shouldn't have done that, Mr Hobbs,' was what she said, shaking her head. He did not know how to reply. He didn't know whether she was referring to what he'd just done – spontaneously pairing with her on his skates – or to the incident the other week, that bad business. He couldn't tell whether he should apologise for either – or both – or for just being a university man, an intruder.

When it seemed as though he was going to attempt to say something, she slipped one hand out of her muffler and placed a warm index finger on his lips. Then she made her escape, back towards where he had come upon her, her long brown burlap skirt glowing against the dying winter sun. Harry watched her go, marvelling at the black branches of a group of trees that appeared to have been finely stencilled onto the sky.

*

Should he place himself at the back of the queue for the tram into town – or not? That was the question. The *only* question. No wonder that vehicle was late arriving at the station – it was a Saturday and the poor, blinkered horse was clearly struggling to pull its overloaded, double-decker car onto the station forecourt. The newspaperman from London granted this minor dilemma less than two seconds' deliberation before giving up on transport altogether and setting out at a rapid pace on foot down the long Station Road.

Those he passed would not necessarily suspect that this furious walker was the editor of a London newspaper of some repute and sometimes shocking content, the epitome of modernity in its style. Or that he was an adventurer with a waking brain perpetually firing off in all directions, whose main mission was one of tirelessly crusading on behalf of the moral degradation of the innocent, the disenfranchised and the disempowered – wrongs best exposed, in his opinion, through the power of the press. To be sure, this particular dishevelled stranger with bulging eyes and bushy beard – who appeared to be entirely unaware of his fellow incumbents on the pavement as he pounded past them – had not so long ago travelled to Russia, where he had managed to secure introductions not only to the Tsar but also to that fellow whose novel was currently being spoken about in the salons: Count Tolstoy. It didn't take long to discover that both he and the aristocratic Russian writer had certain world-changing ideas in common, including an interest in promoting the new universal language of Esperanto. It was this, amongst other things, that he promised himself to exercise shortly with his friend William Travers, proprietor of *The Mercury*, who was an Esperantist himself. And it was towards the Travers house in Park Terrace that he was heading.

*

What's this, now?

Bernadette would inform cook later that it seemed as though the whole world had come a-calling on Mr Travers this day, placing her in rather a pickle.

At the plummy sound of the front door bell, Bernadette peeped through a small window where she spied a substantial person outside the front door of the house, stamping his feet and swaying from side to side in apparent impatience. She opened up, ushered him in. Oh, and there was Mr Hobbs, too, at the bottom of the steps, wearing an expression of enforced nonchalance and gazing further down the road as though something of importance lurked there. What did he want? What did either of them want? She hadn't been told of any appointments that morning. Master out, mistress out with Miss Hope, only Miss Aurelia about, though not yet to be seen. So she must deal with all this traffic herself.

Bernadette leads the first visitor to William Travers's study and indicates to him she will be back, bringing another. Harry. She makes an effort not to let on that she is catching whiffs of perspiration and soot from the railway emanating from this first gentleman's un-pressed suit, garb she has never seen on a visitor to the house before.

This London man announces himself to her.

'I will tell Mr Travers you are here, sir, the minute he arrives home,' she assures him. 'He usually comes back about now. Will you be wanting refreshments?'

But the great editor's eyes were glazed, a seal on other, higher thoughts, and he appeared not to have heard her. Instead, he fixed his attention on a copy of *The Mercury* lying on Travers's desk, though she waited a moment before withdrawing, just in case. Harry's admittance had so far passed unnoticed by the London editor, and although the undergraduate made a tentative attempt to open a conversation, it fell on deaf ears at first.

Bernadette scurried off to find Aurelia.

Unlike the maid, the thing Aurelia found most disconcerting about their visitor was not his odour or his slovenly appearance but the way he turned to stare at her with eyes brimful of undisclosed meaning, eyes the colour of undiluted lemon juice.

'Sir, won't you sit down?' she suggested.

He nodded, flipped the newspaper back on itself and took his place in William Travers's own chair rather than the one indicated by her, thus making further communication awkward from the outset.

But she tried.

'Have you come from afar, sir?'

'From London, young lady,' he replied, with half an eye on her and half on a speedy survey of the room. It was if he couldn't sit still, she reported to her mother later, and his manners didn't stretch to the effort of engaging her *one little bit*.

'Is my father expecting you?'

'He never expects me, young lady. I come when I come.'

'Very well. But I believe he will not be long.'

Aurelia surveyed the card he gave her.

Harry was given one as well and he studied it intently. An awkward silence engulfed the assorted party.

'I have been baking a cake,' she informed this strange man.

'Indeed.'

'You mix flour, butter and sugar, you know, into a kind of paste. To keep the mixture light you have to beat air into it, otherwise it will go flat when it is cooked.'

He peered at her as though the activity she described was either the most illuminating or the most deranged of pursuits.

Wary that she might be boxing herself into a corner, she found that she couldn't stop: 'The icing, of course, is an art, you know. I have tried piping, but cook scraped it away.' She gave him a tight, questioning smile, followed by a shrug of the shoulders, hopeful of rescue.

He frowned, unforthcoming. Harry's instinct was to be sympathetic on her part but he was unsure whether to intervene or not.

'Yes, I am determined to perfect my piping!' Aurelia sang out – at which they both turned their attention gratefully to another knock upon the front door.

Bernadette again.

'There's another gentleman, miss,' said Bernadette. 'A Father, it is.'

'Whose father would that be?' inquired Aurelia. The house was indeed becoming bewilderingly busy.

'He says he has no appointment but that he has come to pay his respects to Mr Travers, miss. He is Father James from the new church.' Well, well, thought Aurelia. It was reasonable to assume that Bernadette had made this latest caller's acquaintance already, being a Roman Catholic herself, and that her own father would no doubt be on a list of prominent people the priest desired to introduce himself to, as a newcomer.

The undergraduate and the church man were accordingly introduced to the great London editor who interrupted his pacing only to allow this to be achieved, at which point Aurelia judged that it was time to call for coffee to be brought. This accomplished, she felt she would be able to retreat.

Just then, her father burst in.

'Aha!' he exclaimed, approaching the London editor first. 'What a pleasant surprise. *Saluton, amiko!'*

'*Kara homom mi esperes trovi bone?*' offered the other. 'I am on the way to Norfolk, Travers. Since Cambridge is on the way, with an hour or two to spare I could not let an opportunity pass to see you. But no matter, if you are busy.'

Apart from the London editor and Aurelia, who was used to her father amusing the household with his Esperanto, the other people in the room – Harry Hobbs and the Catholic priest – stood by. The unexpected presence of the priest caused Harry to smile to himself, reflecting how droll it was that such a one was making what he supposed was a courtesy call on the owner of the local newspaper. He recalled that a leading Roman Catholic had lately been reported expressing his misgivings about University towns, calling them centres of infidelity and worldliness, dangerous and hostile to both Christian faith and morality. How would that sit with the apparently benign representative of Catholicism in front of him, he wondered?

'And Harry, yes, Harry, good morning to you, too,' William Travers was saying, after greeting Fr James. 'Look at this gathering! I cannot believe that so many good things arrive at once.'

'Unlike your trams,' muttered the great editor, but with that the ice was broken.

With apologies and some bumbling, the two newspapermen prepared soon afterwards to depart for *The Mercury* – just as Bernadette arrived with refreshments, followed by Aurelia with a plate in her hands bearing a cake that had evidently been rescued and adorned with a rash of glacé cherries.

'It'll probably taste like biscuit, I'm afraid, rather than sponge, but … Oh. Is everyone leaving?'

'It smells delicious,' said Harry, seizing the opportunity to linger. As soon as the clerical gentleman departed he and Aurelia would have the room to themselves.

The priest, who had already stood up, paused to relieve Bernadette of her tray which he placed on a table nearby. She didn't know quite how to respond, so she made a little bob and reached for his hand in order to kiss it. 'Bless you, Bernadette,' he said, and placed both his hands on her head in the lightest of gestures.

'And Miss Aurelia, please, Father,' said Bernadette, blushing.

Before she could respond, Aurelia found the man's priestly hands on her own head in blessing, a gesture which was observed with wry amusement by Harry. This was accompanied by a murmured prayer for her wellbeing which sounded both more natural and more kindly than anything Aurelia had ever heard from a religious person (the Travers, of course, were Church of England). Those hands: how warm they were, how sure, considered Aurelia. Being touched by this particular stranger felt oddly comforting – mesmerising, even. How strange Catholics were. Fr James was then able to indicate that he, too, should be on his way, that this had been an impromptu call and that he hadn't expected Mr Travers to receive him anyway, on this occasion.

'But please do come again,' Aurelia urged him, just as her father had done.

She followed him to the front door, then returned to Harry who, like the other two visitors, had himself turned up on a whim.

*

'I take it you read my article, Travers? It was entitled "Another Girl

Arrested in Cambridge". I trust you approved? It is a bad business, indeed. It made startling reading, if I say so myself.'

'I did, yes. It is well that these arrests are reported beyond our town, indeed,' replied William Travers with some care, for people had been gossiping about the recent apprehension by the Proctor of a local businessman's daughter, and the unholy row that followed that. 'But I fear that such a … sensational … approach might stir up a polarity of feeling if it were done here.'

'Sensation? But of course it is a sensation. What are you saying to me, man? That your own newspaper is *not* in the very business of sensation? Because if it is not, then it is doomed.'

How excitable the man could be, thought William Travers, observing how he flared up at even the lowest point of ignition. Nonetheless, he was prepared to hold his corner regarding this matter.

'A newspaper sensation, by its nature, relies upon people's baser instincts, I believe,' he began. 'I would like to think *The Mercury* aspires to speak to their nobler portions.'

Without giving any sign that he had been listening, the great man continued: 'Sensation, my friend, is the stuff of life, I assure you. Even pedants have senses, you may be sure of it, and I firmly believe that in themselves sensations are like – what shall we say? – sparks generating currents leading eventually to the intellect. Cause a sensation and you generate the first flash of an engagement, a curiosity. Do you say you do not want that?'

By then they were leaning side by side on the railings of the gallery above the print hall where completed pages of *The Mercury* were being lined up for the production of its second edition of the day.

Travers had never troubled himself much with whether or not his newspaper "engaged" its readers in this way. Its cover price was reasonable, advertisers were to be relied upon and it was slowly expanding its range, in a regular sort of way. That was sufficient to suggest it was readable, without further intervention from him.

'How many competitors do you have?' the great editor probed.

'Oh, possibly three.'

'And what would you say to me if I let on to you that the man at one of them, "*The Muse*" I believe it calls itself, is about to buy a big new rotary machine so he can print thousands more copies at each print run? And if I tell you that one day soon his front page is going to be a sensation in itself? Let me show you how.' He took out a furled up copy of *The Mercury* from one of his pockets along with the stub of a pencil. With quick, nervous scribbles he set about re-fashioning it, supplying Travers with a running commentary of his method. Travers indulged him, aware that his friend had been to America not long since, where newspapers were being put together in a new, rather flashy manner, in his own opinion.

'They call me a muck-raker, I know,' reflected the great editor as he worked, 'but I think I can honestly say that I am in the business of changing the way this country is run.' He repeated this for good effect. 'Travers, I *change* minds, not merely report doings. This is the mission of the modern newspaperman. The newspaper is the only Bible people read nowadays, believe me.'

'Are you suggesting we must set out to pander to low under-standing or no understanding at all?'

'Certainly not. I am talking about the noblest of causes that is incumbent on men of the press: to be in a position to think and write and speak up for a multitude of people. God is calling us, Travers, he is calling us to be his chosen few, his soldiers in the battle *against wrong*.' William Travers bent his head thoughtfully. 'Lord, oh Lord,' he went on, 'he calls you too, Travers, be in no doubt about it. And the only way to hold people's attention is through words that will set them on fire.'

Travers tried to picture the sort of fire that might be created in a professor's room, let alone in his own kitchen. With considerable misgiving, he compared it with what he saw and heard when he passed by The Fountain Inn on his way home to Park Terrace.

At the same time he recalled an occasion recently when his footsteps echoing down the long hallway between the front door and the nether regions of the lower ground floor of his house – containing the kitchen, pantry and store rooms of various kinds – had failed to alert anyone who might be expected to be working nearby, as they normally did. Instead, when he entered the kitchen he found both cook and the maid Bernadette side by side at the big table, wholly engrossed in that day's copy of *The Mercury*. 'No, no, don't let me disturb you,' he'd cried out, unable to disguise his pleasure at such a sight. 'Carry on,' he urged, gratified to see that a point he often made was being put to the proof in his own household. His point was this: that his servants were quite capable of reading the news, which signified that they would also be able to acknowledge its veracity with interest, never mind that it was in the main a summary of the doings of the local ruling classes, as opposed to sallies into the unsavouriness that went on behind certain other closed doors – the stuff his friend from London appeared to be so keen to expose. So he merely smiled at his energetic friend and kept his peace, for he, too, believed he knew his readers. It was a complicated and heterogeneous following that *The Mercury* claimed to have in Cambridge, but the newly literate would not be put off by six columns of pinched text on the page. Here was the proof: evidently, cook and Bernadette had learned to navigate their way through these columns – perhaps not quite as the burghers of Cambridge and the University people did – but these two women in his employ had seemed perfectly content to at least search for the odd item of light relief on the plains beyond the middle pages that might be expected to speak more closely to them. No, his friend had not convinced him. The key to a committed readership was simply regularity. The paper was a site for all that was necessary to inform, celebrate and question, if you knew where to pin it down. And Bernadette and cook certainly seemed to have mastered it.

'This is where I must equivocate,' he told the great London editor, finally, 'though I thank you for your thoughts on my behalf, I really do. But we have two distinctly different readers here in Cambridge. One is learned, the other not, on the whole. I pride myself on adopting the middle way of appealing to them. If not, I will lose either one or the other. Do you see?'

'Then you will lose both,' his friend concluded, without a moment's hesitation. 'I hope for your sake that will not be the case.'

But he wasn't quite finished.

'Of those two readers, whose side are you on? Give me an answer. Is it the august institution grafted on to your town, or its put-upon denizens, who must surely be the majority?' He liked Travers but he was tempted to regard his friend's affability as foolishness and somewhat less than realistic in the context of running a newspaper. In fact, he feared it was sure to turn out to be a fatal handicap and bluntly said so, adding that, in his opinion, for anyone to be so lukewarm about what could be turned into an *issue* was an abomination of his membership of the journalistic trade – all of it mentioned as a friend, and not to provoke, he was eager to add.

William Travers looked thoughtful as the two men prepared to leave the print room after watching the press run starting, one superstition they both shared.

'Mercur*eeee*, Mercur*eeee*, come and get it,' squawked one of the street vendors half an hour later, setting off to take up his pitch by the market.

Standing outside the building Travers, out of an innate sense of politeness, felt he must hail and pre-pay a cab to deliver the London editor back to the station, which was soon accomplished. Unbeknown to him, it happened that his friend was in fact *en route* to an assignation with a Norfolk lady, hence the brevity of his visit. To save the shame of his wife and other complications that may arise, the London editor's public diary would only record a humdrum visit to Cambridge that day and no-one would ever be the wiser for it.

William Travers walked thoughtfully back to his house on Park Terrace. When he arrived he retrieved the scrap of paper with the great editor's scribbles on it and carefully smoothed it out before slipping it into a drawer in his desk.

In a similarly intent frame of mind, Harry was still gripping that same person's card when he walked back to Downing from the house on Park Terrace later on.

*

In due course, the prospect of the month long Easter vacation leaves the burghers of Cambridge in one of two moods, depending on their degree of dependence on the University. On the one hand, the restoration of their streets – fast emptying of undergraduates as Eastertide approaches – can be something of a consolation. On the other, it is a time of the year that presages a brief period of low returns for any merchant or shopkeeper who lives by selling his goods to the University people.

This year, time is running out for Francis Travers, who has little time left to avert an escalating situation of his own making. His bar bill at the Eagle remains unpaid and if he doesn't settle it he knows he will not be welcome there next term, which will be an embarrassment. But this is nothing compared to the final notices he has already been served by his wine merchant and his outfitter, who are well aware of who he is. Both have lately resorted to threatening to pass this information on to his father. How has he allowed himself to be so careless? There is nothing more reprehensible than a fellow who can't honour his debt to a tradesman. He feels genuine sorrow for Perkins, a stationer, whose leniency towards university students (including himself) is leading to the man's bankruptcy. A blast of disgrace is gathering steam at the heels of Francis Travers, and he knows he must seek other avenues with some urgency if a crisis is to be averted. How recklessly stupid, though, getting in deep with a gambling group at another college in an attempt to recoup some of his capital. He is not proud of that miscalculation.

*

At Mrs Judith Mawkins' lodging house in Warkworth Terrace, rooms are almost ready to be thoroughly swept and sealed until the return of their incumbents a month hence.

Cynthia Dawes has resigned herself to a few quiet anonymous weeks with her parents in the Midlands over Easter and is leaving a locked trunk containing belongings she is not taking with her by her bed, which will soon yield to a stripping by Rose Whipple, who will systematically work her way through each floor, top to bottom.

Sidney Beaumont has purchased a third class railway ticket back to the family parsonage in Buckinghamshire – thankfully, it is not too far away.

Arthur Moody's father has persuaded a surgeon working at St Thomas's Hospital in London to allow his son to be a theatre assistant during the vacation, a prospect which the undergraduate finds utterly exhilarating.

Harry Hobbs has three more nights in Downing before he catches the train to the small station in Suffolk where his father, by prior arrangement, will be waiting with a pony and trap to take him home. There is but one more engagement: his attendance at a play at the Arts Theatre. Harry has received an invitation from Mrs Travers to join the family once again for this outing and is rather tickled to find himself being taken up by them in this way.

*

'Miss Dawes,' offered Harry on his last day in Cambridge as he ushered her through the portal of the lodging house on Warkworth Terrace. 'We are heading the same way, I believe. Indoors.'

'Mr Hobbs.'

'Harry, please. We are sufficiently acquainted by now, surely?'

'Oh, well, Cynthia, then, if you must,' she muttered, with half a smile.

Since being in the same company at the Travers's table for supper earlier that term, a comradely feeling had sprung up between the two of them whenever they chanced to meet.

Cynthia was ferrying home with her an armful of library books which she dropped onto the hall stand before he helped her to remove her cloak.

It was that time when the afternoon began to sag: around four o'clock.

Harry brought no such load with him. He had long considered himself finished for the day by the time he headed for the lodging house in a speculative mood, hoping one of the men who lived there might be prepared to waste a couple of hours with him before it was time for him to dine in hall for just about the last time that term. He was feeling unsettled, partly because he was irritated by his own laziness. 'I do not believe I am cut out for endless reading and examinations, you know,' he remarked, eyeing Cynthia's books.

'Really?' she said.

He had already confessed such feelings to Aurelia Travers, who was most sympathetic. Such jolly pleasantness that she undoubtedly possessed couldn't fail to speak to the essential loneliness of a single man like Harry. Those darting eyes had, he reckoned, a flirtatious look about them when he found himself in her line of sight during the theatre evening which he had duly attended with the Traverses. It rather warmed him to think that someone – that *she* – might appreciate him. She was a good egg, he decided.

As he removed his overcoat Rose Whipple appeared from the kitchen, bearing a coal hod. 'Shall I light a fire for you now in the parlour?' she enquired of them, glancing at each in turn. 'No-one else is in,' she confirmed. 'Would you like tea?' Harry smiled at her (he had not forgotten their moments on the ice) and replied: 'Why, thank you, Rose, I think we should'. It was odd, passing Rose from time to time in the course of his daily routine. Absurdly, he sometimes felt he was on the verge of a blush when they came upon each other like this, which must be disguised with levity of one sort or another. It may have had something to do with a recurring suspicion that a connection existed between them – which, of course, it did not. But he realised that she had let him off lightly in the matter of the fateful wave he had seemingly enjoined her to make towards him on the day of the local courtesan's ludicrous game with his tutor. He appreciated that it would have been easy for Rose to name him and shift any blame his way. But she hadn't.

Tea seemed like a good idea, and they watched while Rose knelt down and nimbly twisted pieces of old newspaper into coils that would nurture the kindling she then assembled in the grate. In her expert hands it wasn't many minutes before its spitting progress turned into a roaring fire so that the room quickly lost its stiffness and the cold smell of a sooty chimney gave way to the more pleasant odour of polish coming from the furniture.

'I'll go and fetch a tray then,' said Rose. 'I shan't be a minute.'

Harry stretched out his long legs and crossed them at the ankle, unwinding his college scarf and reclining comfortably on an easy chair with his hands behind his ears. Cynthia's head was back-lit in the window seat where she sat opposite him, in such a way that he could barely make out her features in the cosy gloom of late afternoon. The softness of the dying light outside made her appear more compliant, softer, perhaps, than her usual demeanour would suggest.

'What shall you do when you finally leave Cambridge?' she put to him by way of conversation when they had settled, though Harry received it in the form of a challenge.

'Well. There's a question,' he said, preparing to fob it off. 'How about you? Shall you teach?'

'Which is, of course, all that can be expected of me? No – don't worry,' she said, 'I take no offence. But I do have a bigger plan.'

'I am intrigued. Please go on.'

'Well,' she began, in two minds whether he was an appropriate confidante or not and deciding that, on balance, he probably was, despite the cocoa evening ribbing. Harry Hobbs had a sweetness about him and she couldn't quite imagine him being as deliberately cruel or dismissive as so many of the other men of her acquaintance when confronted by a clever woman. So she told him: 'I have a desire to travel.'

'How delightful. Where? And for what purpose?'

Since she would not have been entirely surprised if something so boldly offered rebounded in the form of a sneer, she was immediately grateful that he seemed interested enough to take her ambition at face value.

'Well, I would like to visit Egypt, and perhaps Greece, and maybe involve myself in the new archaeology that is starting up there,' she said, warming to her cherished plan. If only he knew how much this remained in the realms of fantasy as yet, and how precarious it all was.

Without hesitation, he said: 'What a fine idea. I'm afraid I know nothing of the subject, but I rather like the idea of going abroad myself one day.'

'*Do* you? Is this your own plan?'

'Oh, no, I wouldn't say that, exactly. I do like the sound of an adventure, though.'

'So – what of you?'

'Well,' he began, straightening his back as a preface to adopting a more serious demeanour. 'I have lately had a mind to try my hand at journalism.'

'Oh! Goodness me. I can't visualise you as a "hack" at all. But perhaps you have something more learned in mind?'

'Well, I met the editor of a great London newspaper recently. At the Travers' house. It was only for a few minutes, but I managed to mention that I had had a few of my efforts published since I've been at Cambridge. He gave me his card. He invited me to call on him one day, before he left. I have long admired a new sort of journalism which this London man is pioneering. It's not literary stuff, but neither is it froth. And it's pretty advanced compared with what we read in *The Mercury*.'

'Tell me more.'

'I suppose you could call it a kind of campaigning, though some call it trouble making. Setting out to make widely known things that are not at all right.'

'For example, the way young women in Cambridge are apt to be pounced upon by the proctor if they are not careful, dare I say it?'

'You might indeed say that. It's the way he sets about his journalism, I think, that intrigues me,' Harry continued. 'Picking up where Dickens left off, I suppose. Though not as floridly. What he seems to go for is more fundamental than mere reporting, though. Do you know that he once took himself off to live in a workhouse in order to be able to describe first-hand the iniquities of such places?'

'Should you like to do that?'

Harry tried to give an honest answer.

'I think I might like to be able to make a difference one day,' he told her.

'Well, good for you, Harry Hobbs. So you are a man of conscience?' Maybe this was said with tongue in cheek, but if she was teasing him it was with some affection.

'I should hope so.'

At that moment Rose nudged the door open with her hip, entering the room backwards, and placed a steaming brown tea pot on an occasional table.

'Get yourself a cup too, why don't you, Rose,' invited Harry. This brief exchange with Cynthia Dawes had woken him up. It was the housemaid's time off at the dead end of the afternoon and there was nobody else nearby to see them sitting down with her anyway. Cynthia nodded her approval.

There had been a unanimous, if largely unarticulated feeling in the house of support for Rose ever since she had been held in the Spinning House. It was surprising, Rose thought as she drew up a chair for herself – and not in an unpleasant way at all – how each one of the undergraduate lodgers had become a little more thoughtful in their attitude towards her, principally by seeming to notice her at all as she went about her business. Francis Travers, for example, had brought back a cream cake for her one day after his lecture. And Arthur Moody was clearly taking care to leave his room in a tidier state before he went out in the morning. Cynthia herself wished sometimes that she didn't appear as such a remote a figure, and made an effort to smile brightly at Rose whenever they passed. It all helped Rose to feel easier with them. And maybe with herself as well.

And so it wasn't so very odd that afternoon to watch her fetch a cup for herself, and for the three young people to then pass a blameless half hour warming themselves in front of the fire while playing a few lively hands of whist using a pack of cards Cynthia drew out of one of the drawers.

They were laughing at some move of the cards when Mrs Mawkins put her head round the door to see what was going on. Rose instantly took the landlady's arrival as a cue to clear away the tea and return to her quarters. It didn't take long after that for

Cynthia to follow her, bearing her books upstairs.

Mrs Mawkins, who had paused on the threshold following both women's departure, then said good afternoon to Harry. He was left alone in the room but showed no sign of moving, asking instead for her permission to await his friends, which she granted. From the doorway she continued to survey him until he felt her gaze on him.

'Be careful, Mr Hobbs,' she told him, enigmatically. 'Of raising expectations, you know'. Before he could puzzle her meaning and attempt a response she left, closing the sitting room door behind her.

2 – EASTER TERM

He cocked a keen ear towards the smothered call of the cuckoo, that reliable harbinger of a new season. How could a young person not succumb with gratitude to a sense of well-being on a day such as this, blessed with clement weather at last after a rather stiff winter? The very air seemed to tremble in anticipation of – well, everything out there and yet to be discovered.

It was a morning in May and Harry Hobbs was strolling, much absorbed by the light meanderings of his mind, along Trumpington Street, a watery bane of cyclists and pedestrians alike with its steady stream of fresh water travelling along artificially wide gutters on each side of the road in imitation of much reduced Venetian canals.

He had set out earlier for his usual walk along Regent Street as far as the Catholic Church before turning right into Lensfield Road then cutting back along Trumpington Street. His plan was to approach the town centre again via Pembroke Street. The route would finally lead him along Downing Street towards his rooms for a period of enforced reading. But not yet. A generous slice of the early summer sky gave the impression of soaring towards the royal blue of the universe in a sustained intake of breath at its own splendour. It made him ponder for a few moments the puzzling matter of time – time, that is, when it displays itself vertically like this, rather than in its familiarly horizontal, chronological way. *I saw eternity the other night* … well, no, not the other night, actually, but during the summer before coming up to Cambridge, which now seemed such an age ago. It was when he and Francis Travers, fresh out of school, had purchased knapsacks and ventured on a walking excursion – a week spent tramping along the isolated walkways by the dykes of the fens. One night, it was so hot that the two of them, foot sore and sticky with sweat, decided to pass the night in the open air beside their tent. Unable to sleep, this son of a farmer lay on his back for a long time staring at the sky, bewitched by the unfathomable grandeur of it. Reminded of this, he summoned to mind the poet's next lines which he'd learned as a schoolboy…

> *'Like a great ring of pure and endless light,*
> *All calm, as it was bright;*

And round beneath it, Time in ours, days, years
Driv'n by the spheres
Like a vast shadow mov'd; in which the world
And all her train were hurl'd …

To an earthbound fleck of dust like himself – an anonymous fledgling in the scheme of things – big, vague impressions were but idle speculation. They were an indulgence granted to young people in his indeterminate position, he felt. But thinking about time – Lord, it was a heady business. Today, it tempted him towards a notion that his time, his era, this portion of time his life happened to occupy, was rippling with notions of change, even as he was striding back towards College. Good Lord! It was conceivable, for example, that the internal combustion engine may make the horse entirely redundant one day. That Roman Catholics might be accepted as equal members of the University without a blink. That women could be awarded degrees – *and why not*? Ah, but following this skein of thought he found himself baulking at the idea of the female sex being granted the vote. Universal suffrage – that was another thing altogether. Where would it lead? To women in parliament? Gracious! He pictured rooms now peopled exclusively by men, smelling of metal, dust, tobacco, Macassar oil and the coarseness of paper. Of *hardness*. He was familiar with the grumbling of smoke-roughened voices. The harsh talk. The unrestrained expletives. Oh, and the orificial eruptions which punctuated those male gatherings that women knew nothing about at all – why, he'd indulged in a few of those himself in the privacy of Arthur Moody's rooms at Warkworth Road, without a second thought. So no, the notion of a woman nibbling at the fringes of all that didn't seem quite right. And yet: '*Why not*?' repeated a voice in his mind sounding exactly like that of Cynthia Dawes, someone who was always ready to challenge a fixed proposition. Just as well you don't have to answer that one, Harry Hobbs, he told himself.

He raised his face once more towards the columns of warm watery light hanging between buildings on either side of the road.

Then – talk of the devil: dashed if it wasn't Cynthia herself coming towards him – on her way, perhaps (this conscientious scholar of the ancient world) to the Fitzwilliam Museum nearby where he knew she was of late painstakingly teasing the significance out of some of the rather fine Grecian artefacts displayed there. She was evidently unaware of him – was unaware of anyone as she strode along, a slight frown of concentration on her face. Absent-mindedly, she toed a frayed newspaper page hanging limply half way across the watery gutter whilst running one hand along the iron railing of the nearby hospital.

'I say, look out, there!' Harry called out as Cynthia drew near, reaching out to offer her a steadying arm so as to prevent her losing her balance on the edge of the pavement and tripping into the stream itself. Almost immediately, they both became aware of a bawdy woman bearing down upon them with a young acolyte linked onto each of her arms, who looked determined to take possession of the entire width of the pavement. As these young women shoved past them, one of them gave Harry a provocative wink. He dropped his arm abruptly from Cynthia's elbow and raised his forehead lest any gesture he might make may be misinterpreted.

'Oi, don't you look down your nose at me, gownsman,' shouted the common woman, to a rattle of giggling from her companions. 'You may be sure that I consume fruitier than you for breakfast every day.' This last was uttered with an air of superior merriment, in the manner of a bird of prey making a half-hearted swat at a passing fly as the female party strode by. Both Harry and Cynthia were glad to be spared the bother of a further altercation.

'Oh, these women,' muttered Cynthia, dusting down her skirt and re-arranging her hair. 'They are enemies to themselves, I often think.'

'No better than you might expect,' agreed Harry who, nevertheless, reserved a modicum of admiration for such indefatigable cheek.

They walked on a way together, discussing the forthcoming examinations. And one other issue: the apparent disappearance of Francis Travers, which neither could account for. Harry suppressed a yawn as he listened to her – not from lack of interest, but because it was the time of year when the grinding progress of the grocers' wagons at first light around 4.00am extended as far as Harry's College rooms, brought on by the town's retailers who were set to remain open until it got dark. As a result of the early light, he tended to get up early, in a leisurely fashion, and after breakfast in his rooms it was his habit to set out for a walk on the streets to while away the time until his morning schedule began. That morning he had overslept, meaning that he had already missed his lecture.

'Where are you off to, Cynthia? To The Fitzwilliam?'

'No, to Deck the Chemist,' she told him, 'where I shall purchase some refined lemon juice for a *fruit punch*, which I and the girls will enjoy over a light supper, I am thinking, to celebrate our progress, since nobody else will.'

'Or even a *negus*?' he teased, intending to relieve the weight of this injustice.

'Will you never tire of making fun me? *No*. We don't drink alcohol and you are very well aware of that fact,' she answered him, in the same spirit. It was so easy to smile at this particular young man. 'But whatever has happened to Francis? I don't believe he has moved back home, has he?'

'No, he has not,' Harry told her, with the authority of one who has taken to visiting the Travers household regularly on an apparently casual basis, though not necessarily to seek out Francis Travers.

A group of women on tricycles pedalled by in the sunlight, followed by an impatient trio of undergraduates on bone-shaking "safety" bicycles, their hard-rimmed tyres grinding against the gritty surface of the road. 'Ouch,' muttered Harry, and Cynthia wasn't sure whether he was referring to the unforgiving vehicles' suspension or the possibility of hostilities breaking out between the two groups of cyclists – though it didn't matter much either way. A kindly breeze brought their way earthy smells from Coe Fen and Sheeps' Green as a gentle heat began to form, causing those riverside meadows to breathe in the sunlight. The lazy mist hovering low over them was vanishing fast.

Shortly after this, they parted company.

Since it was later than usual, Harry decided to change course at the last minute, to wander in a roundabout way towards the river. Still in a buoyant mood, he spared a moment to idly peer down at the crowd of washerwomen from the parishes of St Botolph and St Mary the Less taking advantage of it being a Tuesday, when Laundress Green was free from grazing animals. Some of them were setting up a shout for space on the Green to hang out their large items of washing. He was amused to spot a dog chasing its own tail with much confused barking at a vast white linen sheet which responded with its own call, similar to that of a yacht's sail being snapped back and forth, followed by a curious groaning sound. Then, as if in response to his mood, from a high college window came the muffled *a capella* notes of a madrigal he knew well:

'Now is the month of Maying
When merry lads are playing,
Fa la la ...'

Harry felt the sun on his left hand cheek and hummed along gladly.

'Each with his bonny lass
Upon the greening grass,
Fa la la ...'

But his complementary descant ceased when he spotted Francis Travers, his back slumped against a wall up ahead, evidently going nowhere. How the devil had he ended up there? Harry hurried down with no more than half an ear to the remnants of the melody that pursued him:

'And to the bagpipe's sound
The nymphs tread out their ground,
Fa la la ...'

What he beheld took him aback. Coming up close to his friend, it took no more than a glance to register an unmistakable opium glaze about Francis's eyes.

'Is that you, Harry?' muttered the much reduced figure in front of him. At least he was wearing his gown, Harry registered. This suggested that so far, at least, he had avoided being noticed by the University authorities.

'What's up with you, old fellow? We haven't seen you for a while.'

'That's because I don't come in until late,' grunted Francis. 'In secret, if you want to know. Up the back stairs.' A dangerous risk, reflected Harry, though he made no comment. If Francis were caught there would be repercussions – and not only for Francis but also for his landlady. This was a serious business. He must be pretty far gone to not care about that.

'Will you walk along with me a little way?' Harry offered. 'I'm off to call on Prziborsky for a shave.'

Francis stroked his chin, which bore some days' worth of stubble and rustled at his touch like iron filings being probed. 'No money, dear boy. Sorry.'

'Then let me treat you. Here, up you come.' He tugged his friend by the arm and slowly began to steer him in the direction of the heart of the town. Their first stop was a visit to Bacons the Tobacconist where Harry treated himself to a colourful box of Russian cigarettes. Seeking to humour his friend, he made a little nod and a grimace to Francis in order to draw his attention to the familiar "Ode to Tobacco" pasted on the wall as a tribute to this establishment, once penned by a Fellow of Christ's College, which warned of

> *"How they who use fusees*
> *All grow by slow degrees*
> *Brainless as chimpanzees*
> *Meagre as lizards … "*

'That's us, I suppose,' Francis managed.

In Petty Cury, that busiest of thoroughfares, they made their way through the usual weekday pandemonium of wagons, horse drawn carts, street vendors and bicycles, quickly finding themselves sucked into the clamour of merchants, shoppers and students. At one point, Harry was obliged to push his sluggish friend under the awning of a shop for the pair of them to avoid a purposeful cab which had clipped the basket of the old onion seller on the corner of the market, setting it tumbling their way.

Prziborsky's narrow shop was at the forefront of a group of unnaturally thin buildings dividing the Round Church Street from Ram Yard. A short sojourn here was regarded by some young men – Harry and Francis amongst them – as a very pleasant respite to some of the more onerous demands made on their time.

The barber stood back with outstretched arms in a sign of recognition, waving the pair across the threshold of his establishment. But Mr Travers, it seemed, had not paid his last bill in this establishment, so Harry – all in the course of a discreet meeting of eyes – gave the barber to understand that he would be paying for a haircut and shave for both them, in addition to clearing any arrears run up by Francis. This established, Harry was sent to recline in Prziborsky's throne of a chair whilst Francis, sitting next to him, was left in the hands of an assistant. They could chat to each other via the mirrors in front of them and when Francis showed no reluctance to talk about himself the barber fell silent, garnering the nub of their conversation. This was short, since Francis muttered his words gruffly in a tone of aggressive embarrassment. The gist of it seemed to be that he had run up a gambling debt with a syndicate of well-off men and that opium had become his way of taking the edge of his increasingly unpalatable situation once it had gone too far. It was an all too familiar tale, thought Harry, one steeped in banality and the hateful weakness of Francis's shame that he was now obliged to witness.

'It's gone too far, you see,' Francis concluded, adopting a careless voice.

Harry made a quick mental calculation. 'I could run to two pounds. Would that help?'

From the depths of his humiliation came a snort of derision from Francis.

'I could ask the other fellows to chip in as well.'

'Spare me a scintilla of pride,' said Francis. 'I'm afraid I owe much more than you can guess. Look, I really don't want to talk about it anymore, Harry. But thanks all the same.'

'What about your father?' Harry persisted.

'No, no, *no*. On no account must he know. On absolutely no account at all must he find out. I will deal with it, don't worry, dear boy.'

'How?'

'There will be a way.'

But Harry feared this was the remains of the opium talking. He resolved to mull the matter over more fully once he was on his own.

For a while, they lay back, listening to the rasp of the barber's knife.

'You know, I am off to London in a few days' time,' Harry announced after a pause long enough to enable him to change the subject. 'With permission from Prideaux. Though I must say he didn't seem too happy to give it.'

'Oh?'

'There is a man I met at your father's house before Easter. Here, take a look at this.' He reached for a much thumbed calling card in his trouser pocket and passed it to his friend.

'An editor? What's this? Are you getting ideas about the future already? We have the grind of one more year here before then. Who, anyway, would wish to be a hack?' Francis held the card at arm's length, as though he took Harry for a fool.

'Well, *I* might,' said Harry. 'Why not?'

As he prepared himself to be divested of Prziborsky's warm towels, a joyous line or two sprung into Harry's mind, penned by the boy Wordsworth, his favourite, as that teenage poet turned into legend the momentous day he arrived in Cambridge a hundred years earlier along the stage-coach route which had its terminus very near to where they were sitting:

> *'Onward we drove beneath the Castle, caught*
> *While crossing Magdalene Bridge, a glimpse of Cam;*
> *And at the Hoop alighted, famous inn.'*

Was it only eighteen months since Harry, too, had savoured his own sense of excitement, feeling like a small god as he rode into Cambridge from the station? Once, he thought to himself, I felt *joy*. But a person couldn't expect such feverish charm to last.

Nearby, indeed, still stood The Hoop, and after Harry had settled up the two friends lost no time in heading directly there for a bowl of pigeon pie each and a jug of beer.

I am right to go to London, he decided as he parted company with Francis: I am ready for life. Nothing would dampen his desire to investigate whether there may be an opportunity one day to place himself under the guidance of a great editor in the hope of a making his own way.

*

Sometime later that same day, three people alighted from the hansom cab William Travers had thoughtfully laid on to collect them from the station. Awaiting their arrival in the lobby of the University Arms Hotel, conveniently sited at the end of Park Terrace where it met the main road, were Harry and Aurelia. The hotel reminded Harry of the hulk of a very large ship: palm trees and dark marble floor tiles set the scene in the main reception area. It was a grave, muffled sort of place. But nothing could dampen either the anticipation or the elation of the visitors when they at last arrived for a two-day stay. First Kitty, Harry's twin sister, then Beatrice, the eldest, out-paced their father in a rush of spontaneous joy at the sight of an adored brother. Then Kitty turned to Aurelia with an affectionate embrace – they had attended Miss Frencham's academy together once, as school-girls. Beatrice saw fit to gaze at the twins while this was taking place, waiting until it was her turn to be acquainted with Aurelia, who she also hugged warmly, a gesture that appeared to startle the girl. 'I am so, so pleased to meet you,' Beatrice beamed, with the whole-heartedness of a generous spirit. She was eager and trusting by nature – Harry knew her kindness well and he watched her with tenderness. But, oh dear, Beatrice was chiding herself (as she often did when her feelings got the better of her, which they always did) – am I too gushing?

'Steady on, Beatrice,' advised her father, as though he could read her mind. 'Don't overwhelm the girl.'

'Oh, please,' Aurelia responded gamely. 'Not at all. I, too, am delighted to see you. Our paths haven't crossed directly but I have always been aware of you, being Kitty's friend from school.'

John Hobbs – who chose these two of his daughters to accompany him on his first visit to Cambridge since he had been an undergraduate himself – had been interested to hear of his son's developing intimacy with the Travers family. It was enough to prompt him to make a positive response to the latest of the occasional invitations sent by his old friend William Travers over the years, though all other correspondence between the two of them had more or less fallen into the fallow during the twenty or more years since they had been close friends at Downing together. But now, in the hotel where they would stay for two days, Harry's father was preparing to discretely appraise Aurelia Travers. Was his son's friendship with this pleasant looking young person becoming a serious matter? Surely not, he hoped. The boy was too young and too easily led from his studies. There was little doubt in his mind at this point that Harry would come home after his finals next summer, just as he had done himself in his own time, and that the university experience would eventually shrink inside his memory to become a little more than a rite of passage, as it had been to him and to his own father before him.

John Hobbs was a taciturn man, his nature formed by loss. Harry and Kitty had grown up in the shadow cast by the death of the mother they never knew. There was for both of them a sense of absence in the place of a mother, who was always more of an abstraction than an entity. Maybe a sense of indebtedness, too in the knowledge that their own lives were the price of their mother's. All the children his late wife had left him with had long learned to hold themselves in a little in their father's presence, to experience John Hobbs under the familiarly wistful shade he carried with him as he carefully performed his parental duties, which he did with habitual kindness and a passive gentility. They had learned not to intrude and not to expect much in the way of intimacy. As it turned out, though, both Harry and Kitty were turning out to be as gregarious by nature as their father was withdrawn.

It certainly seemed to all those present at the hotel, when notes were compared in various quarters later on, that Harry and Aurelia "got on". It was true that Harry had been encouraged to visit the house in Park Terrace again after the supper party last term and he had duly done so again this term, usually once or twice a week, around mid-morning, as it suited him. Just passing … *thought I might drop in.* In between visits, he was surprised by a feeling of lightness, but also the sense of a quest – for what, exactly, he couldn't put his finger on. It wasn't as though he was in love with Aurelia, he judged. But what was love, anyway? Yet – it surely had to have more of a passion about it, didn't it? Nevertheless, for a man who got on with girls quite naturally, getting on with one particular girl was proving a rather pleasant pastime. They laughed a lot together. She had a wonderful sense of fun, just like his sisters, and it seemed to make way for a certain familiarity, if not a perfect creative balance between them. *Perhaps I should marry her,* thought Harry without a great deal of conviction, watching her talking easily with his relatives. *She wouldn't be hard to live with.* Both families, according to the signs, would be pleased. It was a good feeling, the thought of being able to please the people he valued.

Just as the young people fell to talking amongst themselves William and Alice Travers arrived and suggested that they all proceed to the hotel's lounge for afternoon tea.

What a pity, Alice thought to herself as Harry made the introductions all over again – that the *boy* should be so debonair and his sisters so sweetly lacking in grace. How unfair that *he*, who needed it less, had cornered the market in attractiveness.

As soon as his guests were settled William Travers excused himself, explaining that he must be off to *The Mercury* to settle a matter which had just come to the attention of his editor. 'We shall have time to talk at supper, John,' he said. 'And Lucien is looking forward so very much to seeing you tomorrow. I long to hear about farming in Suffolk.'

'Not much to say about that,' his friend replied. 'But I'll try.'

'Oh, come now. It has been far too long since we have seen you,

John. Of course there will, I'm sure of it.'

But he wasn't. And there were other things pressing on his mind. What he had that morning learned at *The Mercury* was affecting him more than he anticipated and it was not a matter he was prepared to explore in this setting. The fact was that two girls had been discovered dead in the Spinning House that week which he felt was terribly sad, and surely quite unnecessary.

*

A watering van whose operative had an erratic aim was already displacing dust on the tram lines by the time Harry set off for the station for his trip to London. In quick succession, it caused a nervous horse to rear up, a couple of cyclists to swerve and several women unfortunate enough to be in its wake to gather up their long skirts (one of them let out a hoot, the other a sharp 'I say!' in protest). There was muck on the road that day, lots of it. To complicate matters, a number of overflowing ash boxes had been placed higgledy-piggledy on the pavement awaiting the refuse cart, and meddlesome boys had deliberately tipped several of them over, releasing smouldering cinders which rose up to form a denser cloud, glittering in the sunlight and leaving flakes on the clothes of a few passers-by. Leading his horse at a walking pace, the chief dustman, wearing a sensible sacking shoulder cape, sent out a curse towards the source of this affront and raised his whip in their direction.

Harry prided himself on being somewhat sprucely dressed for the occasion that awaited him in London later that day and patted his clothes to dislodge any debris that might have settled on them. He negotiated his way past various minor street episodes, hardly registering them. It was, he considered, a fine walk to the station but it would take him at least twenty minutes at this rate. This distance was no accident. The University had been horrified by the idea of a railway line reaching Cambridge, fearing that it would attract more foreigners and an unwanted influx of the uneducated public. Above all, its concern was that students would surely be tempted to use the trains to reach bad places: race courses, fairgrounds, theatres and brothels (as though there weren't enough of the latter already available on their doorstep). Hence the need for Harry to obtain a formal note of permission from his tutor for this trip to London during term time. Without it, he would not be allowed to travel.

In due course he was swept along by a thickening crowd, mostly men in top hats or bowlers ready for work in the City. A tram nearing its destination trundled past them at the walking pace of the horse who pulled it, labouring with a full load at that time of the morning. For the first time since he came up to Cambridge, Harry realised that he was departing the town with a sense of purpose. Not quite an ambition as such, perhaps – more a keen feeling that he, too, might be not too far away from … well, exercising a talent. Much as he loved home and all the familiar smells and sights of the Suffolk estate, he felt fairly sure by then that he would not be burying himself there. At least, not for some years. He conjured up for himself an office not unlike the reporters' room at *The Mercury*, the only newspaper whose nether regions he had visited so far. In this new, imaginary place he would have a desk of his own and be the possessor of a well-stacked spike on which to fasten old copy and notifications. There was some satisfaction to be gained from the image of himself with his shirt-sleeves rolled up. Yes, to be able to engage an actual readership, an audience – a following, even – of unknown people interested in what *he* had to say. Or, in Harry's case, the manner of saying it – this, he felt, was the strength he was keen to demonstrate to the great editor in London. Well, well, well … we shall see, he reminded himself periodically in mounting anticipation of what might transpire later, until he reached the station forecourt. He recalled an item in yesterday's second edition of *The Mercury* which he had idly scanned while waiting for his exeat in the porter's lodge. It was a letter to the editor (how Cambridge people vituperated, sulked, exclaimed and huffed) – complaining that the writer's dog had been mown down by a cab driven with wanton speed bearing a man who was late for his train. *'The manner in which people are permitted to drive round this corner, at the rate of 10 miles an hour, is simply outrageous,'* spluttered the unfortunate correspondent. Harry didn't envisage himself as a writer of *letters*, naturally, but, making an association with the word, he allowed himself to conjure up one Harry Hobbs, man of letters who, if he were part of the editorial staff of a newspaper, might be able to spot an issue lingering in the margins and take it up. He began to feel sure he could do it. He started to formulate an editorial along those very lines: "Cambridge is gravely concerned by the bravura of furious cab drivers competing with university and town trikes and velocipeds, with carts, horses, mules, other beasts of burden, with the walking public and sundry men of business or trade. This newspaper is proud to make representation at the highest level to the authorities of both the town and university …" and so on and so forth, blah, blah, blah. Hmm. Was such a style a little overblown? Or was it rightfully authoritative in its peroration?

These ramblings quickly fizzled out when he awoke to himself in a queue at the ticket booth, ready to present his permission. Eastern Counties Railway had every reason to collude with the University in this respect – it could be fined a withering £5 if it let one of the young undergraduates slip through, unauthorised. Making himself ready for possible infringements, a proctor had free access to all parts of the station when trains were due – and there was one of that persuasion now, raising his nose at the shilling novels adorning the shelves while he scrutinized those beginning to stream towards the platform. Was there nowhere in Cambridge that a young man could proceed without being under surveillance? Harry instinctively strove to weave himself into the crowd, despite the legitimacy of his permission.

Just before nine o'clock he took his seat in a second class compartment. It was already occupied by two other men. He established a place for himself opposite a lady who sat with her back to the engine, gazing out of the window. In that moment of unknowing that sometimes occurs before recognition seeps in, Harry indulged himself in a completely objective perusal of her young features: the lusciousness of her skin, a soft curl of dark eyelashes, thick waves of pale coloured hair loosely gathered in a bun above her shoulder. If I were an artist, he mused, I would emphasise such pleasing features … such lines to play with … amplifying a face and form until it became more than the sum of its parts – even to the point of seeming to possess a halo.

Dash it, this must be an angel …

But, wait. Don't I know her?

Risking rudeness by peering more closely, he saw at once that it was none other than the reclusive companion of Mrs Travers, the daughter of the Downing Porter, Herbert Bassett. He had become used to sensing her presence when he visited the house on Park Terrace, especially when she caused a slight movement of air as she slipped by. Now, it seemed, they were face to face and unrestricted by the proximity of any member of the Travers household. It felt to him as though he was being presented with an unexpected gift for his journey. How, then, should he set about making use of it?

Whatever was transfixing her on the other side of the window, Hope Basset registered no interest at all in either Harry or the compartment's other incumbents who, after sharing perfunctory salutations, retired behind their newspapers. This gave Harry the luxury of one or two more minutes to absorb the vision he beheld before him until her thoughts became interrupted by the slow clunk of carriages engaging in motion as the train began to shunt towards the end of the platform, then past the cattle market and under the station bridge on the first leg of its journey to London. Her sudden awakening meant that it was he, still staring at her, who was caught off-guard when their eyes met. Immediately, he felt ashamed of such a lapse in manners, though he fancied the corner of one side of her mouth might possibly be about to rise in sympathy with his embarrassment.

He recovered himself. 'Miss Bassett, I believe?' She nodded, with a hardly perceptible nod of her head, then resumed her eager perusal of the countryside as the train gathered speed, clearly not inviting conversation.

Harry spent the rest of the journey alternately reviewing a flurry of scribblings he was in the process of making in preparation for his meeting with the great editor whilst surreptitiously monitoring the apparition on the other side of the compartment, as though she might disappear if he didn't. As for Hope, she seemed content to clutch the small book she was holding, which she eventually settled down to read.

Maybe he could be of service to her at some point? Yes, there was a neat female valise placed above her in the luggage rack. He would make sure he was the man to leap up and retrieve it for her, when the time came.

*

Harry had never been to the capital city before. As the journey neared its conclusion, he became fascinated by the increasing loftiness of suburbs slipping past. Soon enough, he guessed that they had reached the East End of London itself, a sooty area plagued by the most dreadful fogs, by all accounts. A place of beggars and robbers and people with arcane inside knowledge, no doubt. As well as all the mightily important people in the land, too, of course. What a place. The train, slowing, began to grind and yelp a little as it threaded its way through the gaunt, blackened buildings lowering over the tracks on either side which seemed to squeeze its sides like an accordion.

His destination was Liverpool Street Station and the adjacent Great Eastern Hotel which, peculiarly, appeared to be a part of the station itself, in that its great sign was clearly displayed right next to a platform. It became plain that the hotel possessed its own dedicated tracks and sidings for daily deliveries, including sea water for the salt baths it offered its residents. Harry watched a liveried cart heading diagonally across the busy forecourt, narrowly avoiding the path of a brightly lacquered Great Eastern Railway Company trolley decked out with an oak frame and brass oil caps, a stout vehicle loaded with casks.

With much to take in he almost missed helping Miss Bassett with her case and had to elbow aside one of the other men in order to reach up for it himself. Again, was that the slightest of smiles on her face?

But what a place! It felt as though he had unwittingly entered a cathedral as he stepped down onto the platform. Black wrought iron girders soared above the platforms, holding in place a long glass roof furred with soot. There was surely a sense of relief in the hoarse scream of steam released from the engine of his train as it sent out its dirty exhalation. It made the two young people reach for their ears.

'Where may I take this for you?' Harry asked Hope when they finally emerged onto a square crowded with fast walking people, all of whom seemed to know exactly what they were doing at that time of the morning.

'I am staying tonight at the Great Eastern Hotel,' said Hope, reaching for her case. 'But really, I can manage quite well myself, thank you.'

'Oh!' said Harry. 'But so am I. Please, then, allow me …'

'Very well then. Thank you, Mr Hobbs.' He had to disguise his pleasure that she remembered his name.

They strolled side by side toward the Gothic entrance door of the hotel, two temporary exiles from their customary way of life. It seemed to establish a levelling effect between them.

'And what is your business today, Mr Hobbs?' she enquired as they walked. She had a soft voice, he noticed, low-pitched, which made her sound both measured and kindly.

'I am pleased you should ask,' he felt confident enough to respond. 'I am to see the editor of a great newspaper. In fact, destiny might be calling me this very day.' This last was added in an attempt at a little light irony at his own expense to help her feel comfortable with him.

'As it may be for me, too,' she replied. But she would not be drawn further.

All too soon they must part and follow their own ways. Thanking him, she raised her hand for a porter to escort her to the grand reception lounge of the hotel, set dramatically under a high-ceilinged atrium allowing light to flow into the interior from six floors above. Harry gauged that it would be politic to release her without protest at that point but he hung back for a moment or two to watch how she would proceed.

Then he stood alone and took a deep breath. So this was the big city, the very omphalos of the Empire, its symbols first encountered in a grand station and a great hotel. He grinned with the satisfaction of having arrived, with the firm idea of preparing to create a role for himself in the grander scheme of things.

Shortly afterwards, as he prepared to hail a carriage, he spotted Hope Bassett stepping onto an omnibus, bearing a shoulder bag. He waved. She acknowledged him. And with that each of them became part of the mosaic of a different crowd.

*

In the event, it was to be a day like none other Harry had ever experienced, followed by a night in excess of his wildest imagining. But first of all, he must arrive at the great editor's establishment by way of streets bustling with frock-coated, top-hatted men and ladies striding confidently together, some carrying parasols. He travelled a short way by cab before penetrating several long alleys on foot beyond the main thoroughfare. From then on, he felt obliged to place a number of penny pieces from his pocket into the blackened hands of itinerants, while managing to side-step several gangs of boy pickpockets busy in this new area. The assault on his senses was enough to disorient him and his arrival at the newspaper offices was a little later than planned, leaving him anxious that the great editor had neither forgotten about him nor moved swiftly on to other things, in which case his journey would be wasted.

What great good fortune it had been to come across the man during that chance encounter in Cambridge last term when he had called at the Travers house one day. So impressed was Harry at the time that he had since taken the time to seek out some of the man's writings, and was struck by a very direct use of words that both shocked and thrilled him with their exclamatory tone. Here was a zeal he had never encountered before: the desire to *represent* people – not as a member of parliament or a petitioner of the law, but as a man of the press. The strangeness of this notion struck Harry as being far beyond what he had always presumed was the role of a newspaper man. What a man was this, in England, at the end of the old century? He was eager to find out.

The newspaper he was visiting was just off the Strand. Harry surmised that hereabouts was the haunt of hawkers, touts and gamblers, of women for hire and ill-clad loiterers. So this was what they called Grub Street. He passed several coffee houses, by now clutching his pocket book firmly.

Once at the newspaper, he caught hold of a copy boy racing past and was led at speed along a warren of corridors deep into the interior of the building. A newspaper, Harry's very limited experience told him, is a place where, bewilderingly, everyone always seems to be doing something else, rather fast – just as was the case here. 'Hark,' said the lad to Harry at a certain point, bidding him to stand still and feel in the soles of his shoes the tremor of the big steam press in the rat-infested basement of that place beginning to crank out a first edition in a whirr of words which, when the turmoil of the print run was done, would miraculously transcend the chaos of their processing. What a wondrous thing today's newspaper is, thought Harry,

Outside the editor's office Harry managed to dispense the last of his pennies before the boy ran off, touching his forehead. He patted his waistcoat, assembled himself and knocked.

'Enter!' summoned the great man. A smell of varnish, ink, damp earth and lamp oil tickled Harry's nostrils. It arose from the region of the editor's vast desk, submerged beneath a flurry of dishevelled papers, heaped high. How different this was from the time William Travers had taken him into the well-ordered offices of *the Mercury* in Cambridge during one of the afternoons he laid aside for visitors so as not to inconvenience his staff. There were few appointments here, Harry surmised at once – just spontaneous events, surely.

'I never had the good fortune to be at a university myself,' proclaimed the great editor without preamble and possibly with some pride, reckoned Harry. He eyed the youth standing before him to savour the effect of his words. His feet were resting on a mantelpiece and he gave out an air of proprietorship. Harry wondered whether this posture was his way of laying down his credentials. He returned Harry's smile by baring a mouthful of brown, uneven teeth. His whole appearance was, thought Harry, a little disturbing. Those keen blue eyes that seemed to probe the soul, they were as invulnerable as they were perforating … they were at odds with the stained, un-pressed suit he wore, an untidy tweed which had seen much better days.

'Remind me,' said the editor, flicking away a wasp. 'And do please be quick about it. What exactly are you here for?'

Harry begged him to recall their initial meeting and explained that he was exploring a desire to take up writing. He drew out an article of his own which had been published in a university magazine, but when no move on the part of the editor was made to accept it he was obliged to lay it to rest on a corner of the desk. Rather disconcertingly, he spotted a mouse crawling along a shelf of books above the man's head.

'So. You would like to work for me? Is that it?'

'Why, yes!' said Harry, brightening as he leaned forward in order to be closer to the great man.

'Hah!' said the editor. 'Not quite so fast, young sir. Tell me, do you know anything about newspapers?'

'I am rather hoping someone as celebrated as yourself will tell me.'

'As I suspected.'

The editor unfurled his legs and surveyed his visitor.

'Very well,' he said, weighing up the young man before him. Harry straightened his back in preparation for some sort of a test. He fancied the man had a look in his eye similar to that of Prideaux when he was planning to set a trap. Yes, he knew that look.

'Let us see what you think of this.' The great man reached for a well-thumbed document which, he explained, he had recently written for his staff, referring to it as the paper's "Gospel". He opened it randomly, at a section on female staff. 'Here's something you will not have come across, I vow.' He gave a single syllable laugh. 'I have two females working here, you know. I like 'em. They work well. Listen to this. "Woman,"' thundered the man, reciting from his "Gospel" – '"*Woman*,"' he repeated, savouring the word, '"no longer the mere ancillary of man, to be petted or enslaved at his will, is to have as independent a voice in the disposal of her life as he. Royalties included."' How does that strike you, young sir?'

Reckoning such a counter-cultural statement to be a challenge to his poise, Harry lost no time in affirming: 'I am in whole-hearted agreement.'

'You are, eh? Well let me tell you this, then,' he continued, laying aside the document. 'It is the job of a journalist to stand between those who know nothing, and it is his duty to interpret the knowledge of the few for the understanding of the many. Are you with me? That is the way it must be.'

Harry nodded his assent.

'Be in no doubt,' the great man continued. 'What we do here is interpret the aspirations of the lower, inarticulate classes to those in power. I find myself inflamed with a sense of purpose that creates the very furnace of a burning in my thoughts. Does it burn in yours, young man?'

'Avowedly it does, sir.'

'And while keeping the public informed about everything that needs improvement, you know that a newspaper should be at once lively … and *worthy* of the news it conveys.'

Worthy? What could this mean?

'Tell me, young sir, if you were to propose a *campaign* to me to take up, what might it be?'

Maybe it was fortuitous providence, he remembered much later on, but instead of stammering out something about speeding cyclists and congested streets, something else sprang into his mind.

'Sir,' he said, 'I think I have seen injustice done to a number of women in Cambridge.'

'Ah.'

'There are young women who have been arrested by the university authorities, sometimes for simply talking to a man in the street. And they may be locked away as a result. It seems wrong to me.'

'Are you telling me about injustice? An abuse of power? An

outrageous liberty being imposed on innocent people? Is this what you are telling me? No doubt, then, my friend Travers is investigating how matters stand?'

Harry sensed his loyalties being strained and decided to launch a strategic turn to the conversation at this point. No doubt about it, he was feeling, like a sudden blast, the fever of the man but he was also mindful of the position of his father's friend, back in Cambridge and had no wish to cast aspersions on the way he handled the daily news.

'What must I do, sir, to aspire to work on a newspaper?' he ventured to ask.

'Are you bold enough to gain knowledge by experience?'

'I think I am.'

'Do you desire to whip out wrong-doing? Mr Arnold, you know, once called the journalism of our day a feather-brained thing. Ha.' With a sweep of his arm he disposed of the familiar, droning, heavyweight accounts constructed by an older generation of literary men who published articles in newspapers, reducing such verbosity to a mouldering stack of memories. 'You see, I say this,' he rationalised: 'what is the point of writing *anything* if all you want to do is produce more of the same? Or write as an *intellectual*. Believe me, the time is coming when in order to survive a newspaper will have to speak not just *to*, but *for*, its public, who at present are able to give sound to very small portions indeed of what you might describe as their own voice, presented in such way that it will be amenable to their limitations.'

At that point a copy boy brought in the freshly printed first edition of the day and the editor stood up to receive it, giving it a cursory glance before handing it to Harry. In doing so, he managed to dislodge a cloud of dust from his suit which he patted down with a fly catcher on his desk. Harry took this as a signal that his interview was drawing to a close and stood up as well.

'You may take this and see what it tells you about what I have been saying if you are as bright and ambitious as you say,' said the editor, handing it to Harry. 'And come and see me when you have finished your studies, if you like. I promise nothing. Who knows what the world will be doing by then? Or myself, for that matter. You may in turn send me something *interesting* to read in the meantime.' With that, Harry was dismissed, to emerge minutes later on the noisy road feeling slightly stunned, squinting against the brightness of the afternoon.

He walked most of the way back to his hotel in a daze of clamorous excitement, pausing only for a glass of claret and stewed pheasant breasts cooked in red wine at a reasonable looking hostelry along his route. Later, he could barely recall a single detail of this journey. It was as though he saw in front of him only what was necessary in order to avoid tripping on uneven paving stones, slipping on discarded vegetable peelings or bumping in to someone blocking his way. His brain was a turmoil of speculation. He was no longer a young man trapped inside the febrile discipline of Cambridge – no, he had been given a sliver of hope to progress the idea of an independent future. What a powerful thing is hope! What a pure, what an expansive gift, when it is accompanied by youthfulness.

*

It wasn't until some while later, when he was sitting in the dining room of the Great Eastern Hotel for another sturdy meal – which he felt he had earned by partaking in such a momentous excursion that day – that his thoughts turned to his travelling companion, Miss Hope Bassett. What could it be that brought her to London? Was she there on behalf of her employer, Mrs Travers? What other reason could there be? And she was unaccompanied. Was there something in that?

His buoyant mood had not abated one bit by the time he folded his linen napkin along with the edition of the newspaper he had been presented with that morning, after duly reading it from beginning to end. Then he made his way to the foyer, intending to collect his room key.

On the way, he nearly collided with Hope Bassett as he turned towards the stairs, but instead of recoiling she appeared to be as dazed as he was himself.

'Has the day gone well for you, Miss Bassett?' he enquired.

'I would say that it has,' she said. 'And your own?'

'Why, yes, as a matter of fact – yes. Have you had your supper, though? I was about to take coffee in the lounge myself.'

'I am not hungry, thank you.'

'Then please, do please join me, if you would.' This felt to him correct, seeing that they were both adrift in a strange place. But surely her demeanour had changed since he saw her last? His presence in the Travers household had always caused her to shrink into herself, in his limited experience of her, to avoid his eyes rather than take part in any opportunity for contact with him. He put such awkwardness down to shyness, a familiar trait in single women. What he noticed at once this evening was that the reticence he had come to know her by, however sketchily, was no longer there.

They made a striking couple: he, with his hands resting on the arms of an easy chair; she, straight-backed and poised in an identical chair, with only a small table separating them. The silver coffee pot soon began to remind him of an egg-timer as its contents slowly diminished. It was a monitoring device for this unaccustomed time they were spending together. His main thought was: how could he prolong it? She, on the other hand, seemed perfectly alert, and lost no time in urging him to recount how his day had been passed. From what he could judge she seemed to be quite taken by his story.

'So now, you see, I have to think about what I can send him by way of a decent example of my work,' concluded Harry, 'and I fear that a lot depends upon the immediate impression I manage to create with whatever I can cobble together. I hardly know where to begin.'

She pondered this.

'Is it very important to you?' she asked.

'I shall have to give the task he has given me a great deal of thought.'

Her undivided attention led him to share the rather audacious idea that entered his mind on his way back to the hotel earlier.

'I am thinking,' he began, 'as we speak, about framing a short recollection of my visit to the great editor by way of an imagined interview with him, perhaps, based on our conversation. He seems to set much store on interviews.'

'Go on.'

'Well, it might attempt to draw a circle around the man, and inside it to encompass all he stands for. To demonstrate that I have understood him.'

'I see. How unusual.'

'I suppose what I am trying to say is that you might call such an interview, based entirely on our discussion, an exercise in sketch *writing*, much in the way that an artist might *draw* a miniature to represent a person, and although the end result may appear black and flat it is clear that it seeks to be a *likeness*.'

'Because it is composed as a profile?'

'You know, I couldn't have put it better.'

'I must say that this is something I, for one, would look forward to reading, if it were published,' she told him.

'Would you?'

'Yes. Without doubt.'

Could he pull such an endeavour off? Also: why had it never occurred to him that such a one as she possessed a fine mind?

'There is something else he told me,' said Harry, thinking back. 'There are two lady journalists working at his newspaper, and he is all for them. He said he believed it was wrong when working women are treated as ancillaries to men.'

'Then he is a man after my own heart.'

Harry smiled with her, before recounting the editor's words. 'He told me: "I instruct them not to bear themselves in two parts: one for work, one for leisure. I tell them not to be mannish either, or forward, too." What a fine set of contradictions such women in employment must deal with!' By then, the young woman sitting in front of him seemed herself to be the epitome of both endeavour and feminine attractiveness combined perfectly naturally in one being.

'I suppose you have a view on women's emancipation?' he asked her, by way of extending this conversation. 'I was thinking of it the other day.'

'Oh!' she exclaimed with a sudden show of feeling. 'Emancipation! What an idea. Do you not know that I am a slave? No, that is harsh. Let's say, rather, that I am a prisoner. I have no ideas to play with. What use are opinions to me?' As she told him of her current "escape", feigning a visit to an aunt who lived in London, he remembered her position in the Travers household, and the father who would go to any lengths to keep her concealed there, by all accounts.

'I shall never do such a thing again,' she said. 'Escape, I mean.'

'Thank you for listening to me,' he said, as he tried to digest this. 'About my writing.'

'That, Mr Hobbs, is because *writing* is what I do on behalf of Mrs Travers, and *writing* is what I think a great deal about. It matters to me, too.'

She amazed him.

'May I call you Hope?'

Thus it came to pass that by the time the third jug of coffee was set before them, Hope Bassett and Harry Hobbs had split asunder the impediment of being of the opposite sex. How absurdly easy it was, after all, to release that cord and move towards the plains of mutuality. Here lay not only the realm of the possible – hitherto *terra incognita* – but a sphere where freedom to explore was a perfectly natural, unwritten, instinctive contract between two young people who found themselves presented with an unusual taste of independence.

'But in what way are you a prisoner? Who could possibly cause such a thing to be so?' Harry probed, since he was feeling liberated by this shift in their relations.

'I am the daughter of a porter of Downing College, in case you didn't know it.'

'You are a wise, clever person, in my estimation.'

'I thank you for the compliment, but I can assure you that because my father is only concerned with the way I appear he fears this might be a burden both to myself and to others. Whereas, as far as I am concerned, it is burden enough, I find, to have some sort of a brain.'

'I celebrate it,' Harry declared.

'You are kind, but on the whole men do not appreciate that in a woman, despite what your editor has told you. You must believe me.'

'Well, I am with the editor in condemning a false waste, then.' She looked a little wistful at this point, and it seemed the right thing to do to reach across and squeeze her hand by way of encouragement.

'Shall I tell you what I have been doing today?' she asked him.

'Please do.'

'I have been to a new college in London. It has a Ladies' Department where a woman can study as though it were quite the natural thing to do, and where she may gain some recognition for it, which isn't the case at Cambridge.'

'You wish to be an undergraduate?'

'I do. I really do.' She paused, before deciding to confess to him: 'I want more than anything not to be obliged to … forever melt into the lives of … others. I hope this doesn't sound ungrateful. If I am offered a place I hope I may be able to convince my father that I can be released from Mrs Travers. I write, as I have told you, for Mrs Travers, but one day I would like to write for myself.'

'Then we are two of a kind,' said Harry, gripping her two hands with both of his.

'Do you return to Cambridge tomorrow?' he asked eventually.

'I'm afraid I do,' she told him. 'But,' she added, brightening, 'I may have something to look forward to now. I felt comfortable during the interview and I think I said the right sort of thing.'

In Harry's estimation she appeared to be in need of a friend. Might it be him?

'If I succeed,' she told him, 'then in a little more than a year I will be gone.'

'But not yet, not tonight, pray,' he blurted out.

'No, not tonight.'

'Then let us take advantage of these peculiar circumstances and talk ourselves into the night.'

*

Not long after these events in London, Rose Whipple earned a free afternoon to follow her own leanings down by the river. On the rare occasions she was permitted to indulge in idleness, she liked to set herself a puzzle: that of identifying, with a private gloat of satisfaction, the evidence of her father the eel man's guile. None of it would be visible to ordinary people, but she knew how to discern one or two humps in the wall disguised by hanging ivy. These would indicate the position of the iron rings he surreptitiously fastened to the river's embankment. From these were submerged the conical eel nets which he visited at night to check the contents and remove them. It felt to Rose as though she was in collusion with him when she fancied she spotted one of these.

After satisfying herself with what was known only to her father and herself, Rose fixed upon a row of pigeons perched on a branch reaching out across the river and attempted to imagine the sight they would be observing, made that much clearer from above: such a riot of straw hats bobbing back and forth along the tow path. But Rose Whipple went one step further than the birds in attempting to match the colours of their hatbands to the colleges while she strolled past a group of men bathing by the bank. ('It's a wonder they don't all get typhoid,' muttered an elderly woman passing by, holding her handkerchief to her face to ward off the thick water's smell.)

Much of Cambridge had turned out for the May races on the river that day. Cook had persuaded Bernadette, the Travers's maid to join her on her way towards the lower river ready for the spectacle of the narrow college eights gathering, and with the household empty Hope Basset ventured out as well, some paces behind them, keeping her head down. Soon, those rowing men would be jostling for position as they took their boats up stream towards the start point.

In due course, along comes Rose Whipple. Cook points towards her. Bernadette acknowledges her friend while she is still a way off. Cook mutters to Bernadette: 'She seems to have recovered after that bad business with Miss Aurelia's companion – that Mr Hobbs.' Bernadette replies with a knowing: 'Oh, what a business that was'. It seems possible that Miss Basset might have picked up something of the brief exchange. So Cook points a finger to her lips to signal the end of idle gossip between them.

Whom should Rose cheer? It would have to be Downing, of course, sporting their purple and black garlands. A busy procession of spectators' boats was busily heading past where the women stood. Rose could make out the Darwins' big boat, The Griffin, moored after its three mile journey from Newnham Grange to Ditton Fields where it was now squeezed in by other vessels. That esteemed family would be on their way to join other specially invited guests on the lawn of Ditton Rectory for tea, where two large marquees had been set up, she supposed. Then, as Rose and Bernadette held tightly to each other to avoid being separated by the gathering crush of spectators, a cry went up to signal that the races were about to start.

How gorgeous were the young people, especially the young ladies in their flowery hats and wispy summer frocks, the two housemaids agreed. How splendid were the rowing men in their singlets and straw hats. What an excitement it was for Rose and Bernadette to stop as near as they could to Ditton Paddock when the starting gun fired, eager for their first glimpse of boats scything through the dense brown waters of the Cam.

And no-one – not a maid or a don or a businessman or a tradesman, not the lowliest road sweeper or dust collector, not the rat-catcher, or the justice of the peace, nor any of the Guardians of the Poor (for they were all out today, raising a great cheer) – no, not a one of them would think to question the oddness of racing on this narrow waterway where no boat could possibly pass another – meaning that the aim was to bump the one in front, prow to stern, instead. Nor was it odd that each humble beer brewer or fish merchant of the town should be fervent about the success of a particular college, since most of them had some sort of commercial connection with the bursar of that college.

But wait a minute – isn't that Harry Hobbs of Downing College amongst the people of esteem in Ditton Paddock, he who once showed himself to be a rather fine skater? He will be with the Travers party, no doubt, all honoured guests. Rose squints across the river to try to make him out. Aha: there is Miss Aurelia, fanning herself. He can't be far, then. She senses an exaggerated movement in that region, more emphatic than the flags some of the children are waving. There is an inadvertent shove, a child losing its footing and slithering down the bank with a yelp. Oh, look – here comes a tall, elegant figure reaching down for the rescue, gorgeous in his purple, black and white blazer, a white handkerchief tucked into the breast pocket. It could be him. It *is* him, surely. Rose, jettisoning any inhibition, ventures to raise a hand in his direction. He may recognise her as he looks out over the river and dusts himself down, wearing a grin on his face – aimed, she fancies, her way. Then again, she may be imagining such a thing. No matter. She smiles back anyway.

Let's hope the weather holds now for the May Balls, the final flourish of this academic year.

*

The house on Park Terrace one June evening is bristling with anticipation, and it's all becoming something of a strain on the patience of the maids, Cook and Hope Basset. Aurelia Travers is being called upon by Harry Hobbs – there's no other way of putting it (deduce of that what you will, grumbles Cook once or twice, who believes it will all end in tears, but she is a born pessimist, or so Bernadette tells her). Alice Travers, usually self-contained, permits herself to adopt an air of nervous briskness concerning the matter. How young the two in question seem. But she and William, in the privacy of their bedroom late at night where tactical decisions are jointly arrived at have lately had the conversation that parents of daughters, especially only daughters, undertake when they believe they are on the scent of a romance.

William: What do you think he wants?

Alice: Why, William, our lovely Aurelia. Obviously.

William: I mean, is he old enough, let alone in a proper position, to think about taking on a girl?

Alice: They are young, both of them, my dear. Let's not even entertain the idea of "taking on". They seem happy in each other's company. I think we should read into it no more than that.

William: Hmm.

He doesn't share certain implications of this last monosyllabic utterance with his wife. He is a man: there are issues men do not go into with women. And he adores Aurelia every bit as much as she does. Harry Hobbs, that friend of Francis and son of one of his oldest acquaintances – he seems a reasonable enough fellow from a decent family, on the face of it. But then experience takes over, inserting itself into his instinct for reasonableness.

After a short impasse, he re-opens the conversation, prompted by those muddier matters while avoiding alluding to them directly.

William: Aurelia is barely eighteen years old. The boy can be barely twenty, if he is the same age as Francis. Neither of them have had much of a taste of life.

Alice: Of course they haven't, William. This is exactly what they are having now.

William: Exactly so. Which worries me a little, my love.

Alice: For what reason? She cannot be kept locked up for ever, you know.

William: Nor would I want her to be, but –

Alice: Then have a little faith. Think of them as playing a pleasant game together. After all, she may well forget all about him when the university goes down for the summer.

William: Hmm.

*

It is all rather strange, Aurelia often thinks as she lies awake in her own bed. For example, she has no idea why this friendship with Harry Hobbs has actually come about and even less about where it might be leading. Sometimes she suspects he finds her naïve, but he only teases her when she tries to be restrained, dignified, *mysterious*, which she believes might be an appropriate disposition when she is in his company. The truth is that Alice, as usual, has hit on what is perhaps the essential ingredient of their regular liaisons: the fact that they make each other laugh, and before long in each other's company what they love to do more than anything else is indulge in games together. Play: delight, beguile, and above all amuse and be amused. All Aurelia knows for sure is that they both have a sharp sense of humour which is used to spur on the other at the least provocation. Is that such a bad thing?

*

Summer heat expands like a warming bulb. A most gentle movement of air from time to time stirs the fullness of leaves on the willow trees by the river, causing them to crackle in their own incomprehensible language. The May races are done, and this week Rose herself, out to deliver accounts to be paid by her Downing lodgers, can't resist a glance at the lists of exam results publicly displayed outside the Senate House. This is another annual spectacle – the sight of nervous undergraduates milling in front of the boards all morning. Mr Hobbs, she spots, has scraped a third class at the end of his second year – ah well. Mr Travers, too. Now that was a miracle, given the state he was in. But Mr Moody and Mr Beaumont were in the upper second class, and she knew this would please them, being men heading for the professions of medicine and the church.

Cynthia Dawes, on the other hand, is cock-a-hoop with her own result though she will not be sharing it with a soul for the present. To be assessed as a first class student is an empty honour when it is unofficial and not deemed worthy of display. So she keeps it to herself. It can't be as bad as being that clever girl studying mathematics who once came top of the list – a first amongst firsts. Her achievement, too, was duly snubbed. In her own mind, Cynthia awards the traditional wooden spoon to all the men who allowed such a state of affairs to persist, but she understands well that to complain would not only sound ungracious but would reveal her as a fretful worm struggling for survival under a very large anthill. She is confident she can do better than that.

*

And now: *The May Balls* are nearly upon us. Such are the words on the lips of a thousand people caught up in the forthcoming week of festivities. Those fortunate enough to have invitations are about to be served by a vast hinterland of cooks, cleaners, servers, inn-keepers, merchants of all varieties of foodstuffs, wine sellers, hoteliers and keepers of the peace. College servants are already out and about, beginning to plant staves in the grounds ready for the torches which will burn throughout the night to guide the footsteps of participants. All the colleges offering a ball will be aglow with illuminations capable of casting unnaturally distorted shadows when these flares are lit. In their own way, local people tend to feel a little proud that such a spectacle identifies itself with their own town at this time of the year.

Rose Whipple, like many others of her rank, is preparing to eschew sleep on both the Wednesday and the Friday of the week of the May Balls after she has completed her normal work at Warkworth Road. This is because she has been offered extra employment by two of the colleges for their May balls. It will mean spending a marathon twenty-four hours awake on each occasion but she is young, and such a bold departure from her mundane routine counts as a rare brand of excitement. The point of it is that she will earn the precious extra portion she needs to support herself during the long months of the summer vacation when Mrs Mawkins will shut up the lodging house and travel to her sister's home in Skegness for an untroubled sojourn by the sea. But the whole prospect of this work is dazzling. Rose Whipple, no less than Aurelia Travers, is looking forward to the balls. Indeed she is.

*

Harry had purchased an invitation which now stood proudly on the marble mantelpiece in a parlour on the ground floor of the house on Park Terrace. In sloping black script on stiff paper the colour of parchment, it announced: "The Members of Downing College request the pleasure of Mr Harold Hobbs and Miss Aurelia Travers to a May Ball. Dancing commences at 10.00pm, accompanied by the Band of the Royal Artillery." A governess cousin of William Travers, by all accounts well past her prime, had been mustered for the purpose of chaperoning Aurelia and instructed to maintain a not too cumbersome watchfulness over her while at the Ball.

At a time when the household would normally be thinking of retiring, they are assembled in the parlour now, and the father of the house is in the process of removing the glass stopper from a decanter of sherry. Carefully, solicitously, he pours generous glasses for Harry, Aurelia, cousin Maud, the chaperone, and Alice before filling one for himself. That accomplished, William Travers takes a comfortable pause, with one foot on the ornate ironwork fender and an elbow resting on the mantelpiece. He wants a minute or two to survey his daughter in her finery. And what a sight she is, he thinks, with pride, a vision of womanhood in bubbling blue taffeta and long white gloves. Bernadette and Cook have both been invited to put their heads round the door for a quick view of the young couple. Harry does her proud, they agree, looking so effortlessly debonair himself. And if he seems a little nervous, with a darting look each time muffled footsteps may be heard outside the room they are in, well, it only serves as a foil for Aurelia's effervescence.

A little later, Harry and Aurelia – followed by cousin Maud and William and Alice Travers – stepped outside for the short walk to Downing College. The night was mild. A half-moon gave out its feeble light in a minor key. The streets seemed unusually quiet that night and the grass of Parker's Piece, apart from the presence of the odd nocturnal stroller, was a carpet of tranquillity.

Aurelia took Harry's arm as several overlapping bells proclaimed the hour, just as the last of the day's steam trains sounded its final whistle in the distance. A town constable standing outside the police station nodded his approval at the small party as they passed by. There was no illumination at all coming from either the church, the Police Station or the Spinning House next door, but a rumble of conversation from the Fountain reminded them that there were still a few men of the town enjoying their pipes and ale on this special night. Every so often, a whiff of Aurelia's eau de cologne attempted to strangle a stray funnel of tainted river air, for which the walkers were grateful.

'Let the festivities commence,' whispered Harry to his partner, as they joined other arrivals walking down the long avenue leading to a marquee set up at his College. From then on, the older Traverses were content to leave the young ones to their own devices and left soon afterwards, though William insisted on dancing the first "valse" with his daughter. The torches lining the College's Inner Court created extended shadow dancers skittering across walls in a melee of ghostly interlopers.

Early on, "The Gay Gordons" loosened them up, followed by "Here Comes the Galloping Major!" Not a few hair pins were shaken loose during the dancing and one or two of the men unfastened their cufflinks and stiff white ties in the heat. Harry seized the moment with zest, gripping Aurelia by the waist and swirling her round, making her squeal with laughter. This was turning out to be just their sort of romp, he fancied, and they seemed determined to make the most of it.

It was around three o'clock in the morning when Harry and Aurelia, along with a few other couples, set out on a calming drift towards the Master's Great Meadow. With due diligence cousin Maud, whose energy was much depleted by this time, shuffled along at a discreet distance behind them, disregarded and alone. And this was when Harry found himself asking Aurelia whether she might consider marrying him one day – as a purely hypothetical suggestion, of course. Even as he uttered the fateful words, he seemed to stumble. Then he added: 'May I, do you think …?' But "hope" was the word he found his heart simply would not allow him to utter. To his surprise, her smile slackened and she looked taken aback. He waited. A little sombrely, she told him: 'I don't think I am able to answer that presently,' and he worried that he had misjudged her mood. He didn't press her further but silently squeezed her hand instead, in the hope that he hadn't been insensitive. 'Shall we go back now?' she asked him, pressing his fingers in return.

'Of course. Oh, but there is a little more to come. Breakfast will be soon be served. They make hot soup in case the early hours are cool, you know.'

'Well, I would love to see the sunrise with you, Harry,' she told him with a sigh, holding his hand.

'And so you shall, dear girl.'

No-one had advised cousin Maud what might be prudent footwear for passing a whole night on her feet. Corns and a bunion notwithstanding, bending slightly forward and periodically pressing one hand into the small of her back, she was still trudging after Harry and Aurelia when he finally escorted her back to Park Terrace, ever faithful to the task that had been entrusted to her but vowing that she would never again agree to such a circuit. Feeling decidedly aged (though she was not yet fifty and had led a quiet life – uneventful, unchallenging, relatively invisible – no complaints about that) it was the thought of a stiff hot toddy once she was restored to her small house that put some fire into her last weary footsteps. The pleasure of that thought drew her forward like an invisible beacon.

Elsewhere, while the bats sweep the river for insects and owls peer down from their camouflage in the willow and the eel man slips his coracle silently into the water, sending a fan of wrinkles across its surface, the most indefatigable of the young men are heading for the bridges. With cries to indicate they realise the idiocy of what they are about to do, they are preparing to jump, fully clothed, into the felty, dark brown of the foetid Cam. At the same time, an early milk cart bearing clinking churns is the only vehicle in the middle of town, just before Cambridge stirs itself once more. It will not be long before local men and women cross the paths of the depleting band of young men and women whose brilliance the night before is destined to fade as night gives way to day and the flares burn themselves out.

'To think,' observed Aurelia as they made their way along Park Terrace, 'that these people are normally busy while we are still asleep.'

'I think we have just seen two kinds of dancing,' replied Harry. 'One frivolous and lovely, the other working away behind the scenes, driven by endeavour and curtailed by necessity. I wonder: how is it possible to weave any sort of tapestry out of that?'

Aurelia seemed unusually deep in thought and made no reply, concentrating on her own slow footsteps, her eyes on the pavement. The lingering heat, last gift of a summer night, sat lightly on the outline of the two young people.

Crepuscular first light, a time that always struck Harry as prescient, was giving way to the promise of morning as they walked slowly up the steps towards the front door of Aurelia's home. There was a horse harnessed to a cab parked directly outside and its driver dozed, his head slumped on his chest. This was the conveyance, arranged by William Travers, that awaited cousin Maud. The horse shook itself and pawed the ground in front of it when the driver was roused by Harry. Cousin Maud lost no time in bidding the young couple a hasty goodnight.

But what other sleepy shades hereabouts are stirring in the low light?

The first – footsore but triumphant, given the healthy amount of tips in the pockets of her apron – is Rose Whittle, marching along in a state of good cheer mixed with self-congratulation as she heads for Warkworth Terrace and the early morning chores that await her there.

The second is harder to make out, especially when eyes are tired and vision is apt to be distorted. Could it be the figure of a woman up there, leaning against a top floor window at the house on Park Terrace? If it is, she is so inert that to a normal eye there may not be a figure there at all – so maybe it is just the way the curtain hangs. But someone *is* there, and her presence is confirmed the moment she surrenders herself to the interior of the house, the tendril of a shadow reforming its outline with the precision of one who has no wish to be spotted. Without a doubt, it has to be the figure of Hope Bassett letting go of the curtain of her room on the third floor. Only Harry Hobbs notices any of this, and his heart is seared by it.

*

Just before the very end of term that summer, Lucian Prideaux was invited to *The Mercury* by his friend, the proprietor. As he walked across from Downing, Prideaux was not savouring the conversation that would follow. Since he was both Francis Travers's tutor at Downing as well as his godfather he found himself in an awkward position: two such roles can never be guaranteed to sit comfortably together. Perhaps this was why Travers had chosen his office, rather than the intimacy of his home to try to hammer out a way of resolving the embarrassing situation his son had finally had no choice but to place him in.

Should it be "boys will be boys" then, or something more discerning, wondered Prideaux? The latter, he decided, out of respect – not for the boy but for his father, who Prideaux had truly loved for many years, honouring his steadfast principles, his warmth and – at times – what he acknowledged as his modest wisdom.

'Thank you for coming, Lucien,' said William, closing the door of his office behind them. 'I will come straight out with it. I'm afraid I have rather lost my trust in Francis. This saddens me more than you can know.'

'Ah yes. I am sorry it has come to this, my dear friend. I was not aware of the gambling until you informed me. Probably I ought to have been. In which case, I am doubly sorry.'

'I was not aware of it myself, but his landlady called upon Alice – in something of a pincer movement, I suppose you could say' (he crossed his arms) – 'so as to alert me.'

'What was her report?'

'I cannot mince words. He deliberately violated her curfew, I'm afraid – and this must remain strictly between us – regularly coming in late at night, by her account, which I have no reason to distrust. She is concerned she will lose her license if the university finds out about it. It is dreadful behaviour. You, of course, will say nothing to the authorities?'

'Of course not,' said Prideaux, after a moment.

'He is not without merit, I believe?' pressed the concerned father. 'I suppose you could say it was a silly and rather extravagant experiment on my part, allowing the boy to take lodgings when his home – his childhood home, he would have it – is only down the road, so to speak. Alice has been placed in a very awkward position. He has let me down.'

'Indeed. It is an unfortunate turn of events. But I must tell you, William, that he would not be the first undergraduate to fall into a trap – there are a great many snares waiting to catch young men in Cambridge these days. There are evil people about, as you must know, who are out to take advantage not only of his funds *but also his virtue*. Be grateful he has succumbed to just the one and not to both.'

'I shall be grateful only if he returns to normal. Well, then. I will say it: I have undertaken to clear his debts. There was not much choice, in the circumstances, though I am far from happy about it. On condition, of course, that he undertakes never to be tempted by the cards again.'

'That is generous and, I think, the best that can be done, in the circumstances. He did not fail his exams, after all. All being well he should be able to resume in October for his final year, holding his head up after a sobering summer break.'

'Shall you speak to him?'

Prideaux pondered this.

'I think we should see what a summer away from temptation brings first. Best if he takes matters in his own hands, I would advise.'

William pondered this. Francis, though a man to Prideaux and the outside world, remained something of a boy to his father.

'You know that he has agreed to come to Hunstanton with us for early August?'

'Well, that sounds healthy.'

'Yes, Alice and Aurelia are looking forward to it immensely.'

'Will you be able to get up there too?'

'Yes I will, I think. Ha! They call it the "silly season" in newspaper parlance,' smiled William, glad to find a detour around this glum subject. 'Here, let me show you.' He fumbled amongst the papers on his desk. Why, only that morning he had approved a "Man-about-Town" item illustrating such silliness. It was deemed an opportunity for a junior reporter to flex his wings: "Let the roads be as slippery as glass, muddy as a country lane, or as clean and smooth as a ballroom floor," fulminated young Walter Magson – whose wedding day seemed to recede at the same pace as everything else moved onward – "the Cambridge cabbie regards it as his sacred duty to be as reckless as he possibly can …" His beloved Mildred Dobbins's telegraph machine would be tapping less urgently during the days when Cambridge emptied itself once more, only to allow day-dreams about such a remote event to rise up more frequently in her mind.

'I shall manage a week or two away, I think,' said Travers. 'I am pleased that Harry Hobbs has agreed to join us. He will be a companion for Francis. Otherwise, I fear, he may succumb to brooding.'

'That sounds like a fair arrangement. I shall watch Francis carefully next term, be in no doubt.'

'Yes,' sighed Travers. 'He will be living in college again.'

'And this will surely make it easier to do.'

3 – THE LONG VACATION

So the rats in Barnwell are settling for the night, and the few lights that remain in use in the colleges are gradually being snuffed out like spent glow worms, one by one: it is now a high midsummer night, and one during which the town begins to perform a rather drastic purge of much of its population in a scurry of last minute packing signaling the finale of another academic year. On the morrow, no doubt, there will be some of the usual scribble of purposeful muddle before the day hinges, but those with sharp ears will not take long to register a long drawn out sigh of depleting energy as the college people make their way way elsewhere. They won't be back until early autumn.

Spare a passing thought for endeavours of a home-grown variety taking place on the newly dappled common land at Laundress Green, Coe Fen and Christ's Pieces. Quite quickly, these places are partially obscured by small *villages* of carpets brought out from the Colleges, the lodging houses and the better homes, to be tossed over extended grids of improvised lines for their yearly summer beating, and Rose Whipple is readying herself for her part in this activity. Local people are able to keep closer to their homes now, such as the redundant lamp-lighters with their long poles resting in alleyways until they will be needed again in October. On the other hand, out streams a horde of children as though flushed from unseasonal hibernation, carrying their hoops and marbles and skipping ropes, flicking towards each other catapults loaded with horse beans and small stones, kicking an old pig's bladder for a game of street football, chipping their teeth on humbugs and shrieking as loudly as alley cats as they chase after the muffin man's bell. It is time for the travelling knife grinders to come calling, and travelling women selling their bundles of hand-made pegs. It is time, too, to hang canaries and goldfinches in their cages outside in the sunshine for a while instead of shutting them up indoors.

A blank-faced Spinning House seems to be unusually lean of business.

Dr Magnus Algernon Demetrius, the fiendish Proctor, is more than glad to put behind him the inconvenience of the malodorous river, slyly incubating typhoid and smallpox in its polluted waters in an annual surge of "Cam fever", along with his burdensome dealings with recalcitrant young persons. He sets off promptly with his haversack and walking stick at the end of term for European civilisation and Athens, specifically, thence to the distant ruins of Delphi where this classical scholar will indulge a keen desire to bring history alive once more by touching its ancient runes, murmuring his invocations in ancient Greek in the stadium where naked strength had once been a virtue.

*

On the whole, Cambridge was a pleasanter place during the summer months, decided Lucien Prideaux one day. He was planning to set out for an experimental morning ride towards the Gogs for the first time since the incident on the day of the snow storm in February, reassured by the satisfying thought that there was little chance during the summer recess of being assaulted along his route by shameless undergraduates, disreputable women or emboldened townspeople who had nothing better to do than to mock him. Therefore, he might soon take up again the book he had been writing for the last ten years.

Soon, thought Rose Whipple – whose work at Warkworth Road had become so much lighter, following the sudden departure of the lodgers – soon, there would be the Midsummer Fair, with its noisy china auctions and the spectacle of the dancing bear, the strong men, and a wild ride down the wooden helter-skelter to look forward to. And the prospect of bringing back some new Nottingham lace curtains to spruce up the rooms. Mrs Judith Mawkins was looking forward to purchasing these at the fair before she, too, left Cambridge.

How the sun beamed upon Cambridge that summer, challenging William Travers to ease his winged collar and unfasten a button on his waistcoat to give vent to the airs given off by his body. How the all but stagnant air pitched the yeasty smell from various breweries against the river's stink, the steaming horse droppings and the rotting orange peel making walking hazardous, the rank odour of the fish market in Pease Hill, and Bird and Son's vinegar works – blending it all into a ripe miasma.

Surely, though, next year, set to start in October (*everyone* in Cambridge organised themselves by the academic year) augured well, or so William Travers began to believe. Surely those most propitious decisions made but a handful of years previously, laying down that six town councillors would join with University people in dealing with matters of importance to both, would bring about better relations and a more even sense of co-operation between the two authorities. For now, though, it was enough that people were noticeably a little less fractious and prone to transgress, and reports in *The Mercury* were less chaffing. Not much need, then, for him to linger upon his friend the London editor's recommendation to take up the forthright sort of reporting occasioned by that gentleman's own regular incursions into the depths of depravity. That craze would surely not last beyond the start of the 20th century which he visualised as pleasingly clean and empty of conflict. He sometimes suspected embroidery of the facts in his friend's "exposures" with their unhealthy use of exaggerated language and tendency to huff and puff. Impure journalism, he called it, over-heated stuff, though as a businessman he acknowledged some of it may be effective in terms of increased sales in the short term. No, the sooner the family set off for the wide expanses of a cool beach bordering the North Sea at Hunstanton the better, he was inclined to agree with Alice, where, for a short while, he would be quite content, and not a little relieved to allow *The Mercury* to jog along in his absence.

While Cambridge sweltered, Hope Bassett was sent home to be with her father, as was Cynthia Dawes with hers. Many of the young women who staffed the busy inns during term time were making their own plans to depart for the countryside to help with the harvest, especially with the fruit picking when the time came.

Eventually, Mildred Dobbins entrusted her telegraph machine to a young apprentice and permitted herself to join her long-time fiancé Walter Magson (who longed for October and the return of some grit to report) for a temperate three days in the Essex village of Clacton-by-the sea, hosted by an aunt of hers who lived there. 'Stop your forwardness, Walter,' chided Mildred more than once as they prepared to leave, with the steely resolve he had to admit he rather admired in her, shoving him away when he tried to kiss her in public. Though he was all for enjoying things as they came along.

*

At last, lulled by the companionable rattle of a train bearing him towards Suffolk for the start of the vacation, and with no more irksome essay deadlines to meet, Harry Hobbs found the time to closely examine one particular incident that had taken place during the latter part of the term just ended. He was tempted to believe it was one of the most significant in his life, the more it receded and grew its own complementary wings. He realised that he had been waiting for a moment like this to unwrap it with the care it demanded, and this explained why he had not been able to confront it squarely until he found himself entirely alone and uninterrupted. He was aware that an element of fate was threaded through this most important matter of all, owing to the way it had been taken out of his hands with such astonishing abruptness. More than once he was sunk by a sudden wave of despair because there was no doubt about it now: there was nothing whatsoever he could do to reverse the mystery of his apparent rejection.

Quite simply, he had not managed to find a way of speaking to Hope Basset since their time together in London – no, not once, during the term just ended – and this troubled him deeply. Though he had waited for as long as he could for her to join him for breakfast after the night they had passed together there had been no sight of her in the hotel the next morning. He did not see her until he was striding along the platform where the train back to Cambridge stood, with little time to spare. Reclining in a comfortable berth on the branch-line train in which he was now travelling, he drew up from his memory a rapid kaleidoscope of images. But try as he might it was impossible to make any of it last more than – what – five, ten seconds? What a tantalising stroke it was, though, this picture of Hope Bassett entering the Ladies Only carriage of their waiting train at Liverpool Street Station: no more than the glimpse of a fugitive brown stocking on an ankle raised to negotiate the step … her right hand, gloved in navy blue, clutching the leather window strap for support … the mutton-chop sleeve of her silk blouse billowing briefly. The way she holds herself suggests she is either in a hurry – or most determined, even at that early point, to leave London without seeing him again, he now concludes. She glances neither to her right nor her left. Her skirt forms a triangular shape resembling the sail of a small yacht as she nimbly raises herself up by the leather window strap in a single motion, to be swiftly consumed by the interior. Five, ten seconds. Then, at their destination, he spots her slipping into a cab before he is able to call out to her.

Since then: nothing. Nothing at all, despite his many efforts to put himself in her way.

A snubbing on this level might have annoyed or embarrassed another man, but it alternately bewildered and pained Harry.

To no avail were the increased number of visits he paid to the Travers household – she always managed to remove herself from his orbit, almost as though she were on the look-out to avoid him. There were a number of other, solitary moments when he would position himself by a certain tree on Parker's Piece for as long as he dared, wary of appearing to be a loiterer. From this vantage point, he found he could glance up often at the room on the third floor he believed was hers, without being too conspicuous.

Still, he had to admit to himself that the sheer madness of that night in London defied any conventional explanation. It was as distinct from normality as anything he had ever encountered. Even now, on his way home, he could not fathom quite where to place himself in the run of it, wholly lacking tools to read its grammar. Here was a habitually self-contained young woman who mostly appeared engulfed in her own silence. And yet, one night she had spoken. How she had spoken! His impression was that a curtain had been drawn back before, in the blink of an eye, it was snapped shut even tighter, he fancied, than before.

Again, again and again … an almost invisible waiter raises up the silver coffee jug on the table between them and discretely tilts it to demonstrate its emptiness. Harry, without taking his eyes from Hope, nods. Another jug is brought, along with clean cups. In a while, another still. All the time they are talking, talking seamlessly in the hushed voices that seem appropriate in the public setting of the hotel's lounge. What the deuce did we talk about, he asked himself? Words, words and more words seemed to bounce back and forth that night in an effortless vocal choreography, the two of them seemingly locked into each other and insensible of their surroundings. This much Harry was sure of, as he began to further unravel the whole encounter with Hope Bassett. Did it matter that two or more hours or more slipped by while all around them the room gradually began to empty? 'Good Lord, it must be getting late,' he remembered saying at one point, with much reluctance but out of politeness, in case he was being over-bearing while she might be hoping to be free of him. But she made no move, so neither did he. After that, there came a time when the caffeine sparks in his brain were transformed into a general pounding in that region, he recalled, and he became aware of a thundersome pulsing of the blood around his body. It was all he could do to escort her to her room, well after midnight. There was an embrace, made awkward by being furtive. But it was wholly sincere on both sides, he could have sworn it. Closing the door of his own room behind him, he was able to bring to mind the very moment when nervous energy suddenly gave way to an all-consuming feeling of total exhaustion. But that night he retired a happy man, and fell asleep immediately.

Was the whole enterprise of talking to her in such a febrile manner an inconsiderate blunder, then? He wished he could confide in Kitty, his dear twin sister. There was no protocol for any of it. Nor did any of the novels he had read describe anything like it. Later, to his sorrow, he found he was also quite unable to put pen to paper in order to tease some sense out of those hours. Might a dalliance (if this is what it was) with a decent girl like Hope render him eccentric, at the very least? There were plenty of others who bore that description in Cambridge, all singularly odd, as far as he could be sure. Was he odd, too?

And now there were only unanswered questions to torment him. Had he in some way spoiled her, the lovely Hope? Before it happened (and ever since that night) both of them were used to being obedient to the rules of others. After all, those rules formed the scaffold on which normal, civilised existence was formulated and carried out. Unexpectedly released from these constrictions, each was wholly unprepared for those few precious hours that presented them with an unheard of opportunity for exploring what might become a friendship, albeit at a unnaturally accelerated pace. The attraction between them was a mighty one, he was sure of it, even at this remove. Could she imagine he was not honest in his affection for her? For goodness sake, there was not a thing he did not revere about her. Such a friendship, even in its earliest moments, had a sacred quality about it as far as he was concerned.

His train stopped to take on water at a small station. In the stillness of this pause, it was all too easy to re-create the quality of a great tenderness he fancied bound them, offered and bestowed in a perfect ebb and flow. It was not a quality born of good manners, nor was it filial tenderness, but the sort of loving tenderness that is like a plant in season, led by blind nature to seek out the light in the other. He had never before experienced anything so treasurable. But he had been forced to accept, early on, that running counter to this was the reality that there were few prospects of re-igniting such closeness with Hope Bassett back in Cambridge. For one thing, her position in the Travers household would be an obstacle. For another, significant others were already implicated: Aurelia, for one; her delightful parents; his friend and fellow student Francis; his own father; his sisters. Even Bassett, the Downing porter, for goodness sake. He began to perceive that all of them had a certain stake in him as his train rumbled onward and his eyes followed a grand shadow being drawn across the passing fields by its smoke. He felt mystified and alone the more he thought about Hope Bassett. How easy it was to conjure up her cheeks, her hair, the sweet sagacity he read in her eyes, a residue of her breath on another train's window.

To his sisters in particular, Harry was a young man who genuinely loved women rather than mocking their otherness – which seemed to be the form when he was in the company of men. He loved *womanliness* in all its variety, and would respond to it with affability and good humour. Mulling it over, it began to occur to him that he might have degraded himself by misusing not just one, but two young women before he left Cambridge for the vacation – both Aurelia (had he continued to see her under false pretences last term?), and Hope herself (did she consider him fickle or base for it?). What have I done, he asked himself? What *have* I done? A battle followed in his head between what was expected of him – indeed what he expected of himself – and his desire to prolong that sublime abandonment he had experienced in the company of Hope Bassett. His instinct urged him to come down on the side of remorse – while he was astute enough to recognize that this would amount to a criticism of *her* as well as himself, which of course could not be stomached. His heart, on the other hand, was telling him that surrender had been to *her*, not to "it" – to a person, not a situation, or a manual of correct behaviour. Anyway, this also was what Cambridge people did, wasn't it – break boundaries? Back and forth it went in his mind. He knew very well that it is consequences that give history its meaning, that consequences are the very freight of history as it penetrates the present. But how he wished for consequences of some sort now, to move things along. How he yearned that he might raise this very point with Hope herself.

Then, unbidden, came one more illumination of a very different kind. For, if truth were told, there were surely *three* women who might have been compromised through careless actions of his own. To Aurelia and Hope must be added Rose Whipple, surely, thanks to his own part in that unresolved incident earlier in the year which resulted in her being falsely imprisoned.

What sort of man did this make him?

*

Change. It ebbs and it flows from the nexus of veins and arteries of a university town in a curious but not entirely unpredictable tide of complementary and contradictory movements of people … it is the invisible momentum charging countless voyages out and back, threading itself through the warp and weft of its clamorous (and occasionally momentous) endeavours … This was the gist of one of Harry's less stressful penses as he sat on the terrace of a hotel in Hunstanton one afternoon around a week and a half later, quietly enjoying a glass of lemonade with Francis. In front of the hotel was a sloping greensward beyond which lay the public gardens and then, beyond the promenade, the sea. He watched a quilted white cloud move over the grass at the top of the cliff, producing its own shade below like a giant carpet being rolled out before him in a deeper shade of green. He was waiting for news from his father to let him know when they were planning to start the harvest on the farm so that he could come and take charge as he had been doing ever since he grew taller than the old man, by tacit agreement between them. *One day, my boy, it'll all be yours …*

Francis and Harry had long since taken their daily early morning swim and now they were trying to make out the wooden bathing machine with a squared number seven painted in bright blue on its rear end, because this was the mobile shed containing both Aurelia and her mother. Swimming was a much easier proposition for men, the pair agreed: all he and Francis had to do was don their woollen navy and white striped one-piece bathing suits and step into the water at a tactful distance from the women's designated area. That morning they had duly struck out against the incoming tide only to be shocked by the ferocity of its speed and the pull of the current, ending up sprinting for the shore at a frantic front crawl that could barely keep pace with it. The North Sea was a force to be reckoned with. They had been told. Now they believed it.

'Look, there they come,' said Francis, pointing.

Harry followed his friend's finger, squinting against chromium flints of light glinting from the plateau of a now calm sea a little below where they were sitting. Number seven was one of a slow procession of huts being pulled offshore either by burly men bearing chains, up to their waist in salt water, or by a shire horse brought in for the purpose. In a little while this activity would stop; then, when they had prepared themselves, the women inside these vehicles would be able to raise the canvas flap at the front end and test the temperature of the water with their toes before taking the plunge. Salty sea water: it was believed to have medicinal properties. You could hear the agitation of female voices, distantly, but they were not yet to be seen.

*

Alice and Aurelia, meanwhile, behind the curtains of number seven bathing hut, were busying themselves changing into matching rose-patterned costumes with gathered frills at the waist, their arms covered to the wrist and their bodies to below the knee. Their mobile hut, hired for the season, was one of the better ones. It was enamelled white inside, with two facing mirrors and a shelf built specially for their toiletries. A blue silk bag lined with rubber was poised on top of a small square seat whose lid obscured a supply of clean towels, soaps and perfumery in readiness for after their outing. To soften the austerity of the four walls ruffles of white muslin had been attached, trimmed with lace and, at intervals, cheerful blue ribbons.

'Shall you walk along the promenade after supper with Harry tonight, Aurelia?' asked Alice as they sat side by side on the back platform of the hut with the water lapping their legs.

'I dare say I may,' Aurelia told her. 'We shall see. He seems to prefer the company of Francis.'

'You seem to be getting along with him, don't you?' Alice ventured to probe.

'I think we do. Get along.'

'But you don't seem very …'

'Excited? No, mother, I am not overly so. I'm not sure I am ready for … excitement.' Her daughter was, Alice thought, making an

120

effort not to sound clipped. Therefore she must not be pushed on this sensitive matter.

'Well, there is certainly no hurry, dear.'

But that was just it. Aurelia could barely put it into words herself, the feeling of slight foreboding dogging her ever since Harry's unusual proposal, compounded by certain worrying rumours of his involvement with a housemaid who ended up in the Spinning House which she simply could not rid herself of. On the other hand, to be "settled" was not at all something that caused her discomfort. She knew she was not an adventurous girl; rather, she saw herself as one who had been spoiled a little, perhaps, by the close and loving relationship she had with her parents, the sweet, easy comforts of a happy home and the fruitfulness of the esteem in which the Travers family, including herself, was held within their own *mileau* in Cambridge. It afforded her much satisfaction, and no doubt she was beginning to realize how much she prized it.

'If …' she began. It was a tentative opener, and Alice forbore disturbing the fragility of what might turn out to be a confidence by supplying her with helpful words, or even by looking at her directly.

Aurelia tried again. 'He is wonderfully good fun,' she said. 'I am the envy of a lot of girls, I'm sure. He is kind and attentive. And very handsome.'

What, wondered Alice, is she trying so hard to justify, then? She continued to listen.

'I could not wish for a better … husband, I suppose. I don't want to sound ungrateful. But – mother, what is it I am *supposed* to feel?'

What an unexpected poser! Alice had never – not since she first laid eyes on him – entertained anything but melting admiration for William Travers, who – even now – often prompted a frisson in the region of her stomach when he came close to her. But you cannot tell your daughter you find her father rather thrilling.

Aurelia's foot began idly toying with the sea.

'Is it love?' was the best Alice could do.

'Ah, love,' said Aurelia, with a smile. And then – 'Oooo … I do love the sea! Come along, let's get ourselves wet!'

*

The sun in July draws a high arc across each day as it crosses the Wash, that broad estuary on the north Norfolk coast. As it happened, Harry and Francis set out to stride the whole length of the promenade that evening, transferring to the beach for their walk back to the hotel. The heat of the day was receding, along with the sea, leaving them pensive and silenced by the enervating effect of small, spent waves falling with less and less muscle as the receding tide urged them back out to sea. 'What a difference from this morning,' said Harry after a while, receiving a nod from Francis in response. Aware of his role there as a distraction for his friend, Harry had not been encouraging too much in the way of soul searching between them. Instead, he took it on himself to keep a sympathetic eye on Francis during time spent with the Travers in Hunstanton. It seemed to be working: the young man who had begun the holiday in a shifty, anxious way was now someone who was prepared to initiate the odd stone skimming competition with his friend – and win. There were some matters best not interfered with, decided Harry, and he was happy to put parentheses around his friend's lapse during last term. Heaven knows, he thought, I now have an issue or two of my own to contend with.

So without any effort on the part of either of them their conversations were naturally inconsequential and, as a result, healing for both. It was a reward of this short period of restoration that both sensed their friendship entering a richer, more comfortable phase.

'Shepherd's delight, eh?' observed Francis, pointing. A bloodshot aurora out at sea signalled the long setting of the sun. Strange, they agreed, given the North Sea faces east, but such is the upside-down nature of a place like Hunstanton, built on one side of the wide estuary, that sunset comes into view. Along with one or two stationary walkers positioned at long intervals on the beach Harry and Francis paused to relish the miracle of light that transformed sea and sky into a glowing collaboration of colour. Orange, pink and even green seemed to be tripping across the water. In response, the horizontally striped cliffs rising up to face it in layers of yellow sandstone, chalk and iron ore were suddenly ignited by splinters of dying sunlight, as though someone had put a taper to them. The two young men recommenced their stroll back to the hotel only when the spectacle began to fade, all colour drawn back into an oncoming maw of darkness.

'Are you looking forward to our final year?' asked Francis as they walked.

Harry's response was non-committal.

*

Back in the hotel, their skin aglow after the stiff air and bracing salt of the sea that afternoon, Aurelia and Alice joined a table for a game of bridge before ordering their cocoa. Aurelia had elected to be the one who would pass on a message just delivered from Suffolk for Harry when he returned and she was a little subdued to think he'd be leaving them for the harvest at home. How would she be, as a farmer's wife, she wondered, not for the first time? She had in mind a picture of a rambling manor house, miscellaneous barns and workers' cottages, and the chorale of miscellaneous animals. It didn't sit entirely comfortably with a town girl, particularly since it looked likely that four hearty females would have to be included in such a plan. How she would miss Cambridge with its endlessly fascinating menagerie of folk passing through, its intensity and its intrigues, even though much of it was held at arm's length and intuited rather than experienced.

'I think I must retire,' said Alice at length to Aurelia, with a yawn. 'Shall you come up as well?'

Aurelia was tired after their exertions and knew that she would sleep well that night. 'I shall wait a while for Harry,' she replied. 'He is being summoned home I believe.' Shortly afterwards, as she glanced towards the wide, glass-paned door of the lounge, she saw him coming towards her, with Francis not far behind.

For no known reason, the vision of Harry standing in the hotel's foyer whilst he retrieved his room key brought to Aurelia's mind the memory of a passing incident that had taken place in the corridor leading to the kitchen of the Travers house in Cambridge a few months previously. There stood Cook and Bernadette, the little Irish maid – gossiping, she supposed. They had their backs to her. It was not long after some restrictions had been imposed to curtail her walking out of the house alone. Yes, it was in the wake of that commotion involving dear old uncle Lucien, when he'd come panting up to the house in search of her father after being shamed in the street, pursued by an improper woman. Before cook and Bernadette had a chance to notice her, she stopped dead in her tracks at the whisper of a certain name … 'that friend of Mr Francis, Mr Hobbs, it was …' '… and they say he was the one who started the whole thing off …' '… such a scandal' … '…that poor girl'.

Aurelia hadn't been able to make out exactly what they were talking about until the rumour about a housemaid being taken to the Spinning House later surfaced. Then it seemed to fall into place.

She appeared startled when Harry approached her.

'Dear me,' he said, taking her arm. 'Have you seen a ghost?'

'I believe I might have,' she said, snapping herself out of it.

Lying in her bed a little later, she fancied the question she had put to her mother that afternoon had probably been answered, albeit in the most strange, roundabout way, as she formulated more connections out of scraps of Cook's and Bernadette's loose talk, and the way that they stopped mid-sentence and fell silent the minute they saw her hovering nearby. For what indeed is a girl to feel when she discovers that her lover is in all likelihood one of those weak young men who have been corrupted by the cunningness of a wayward girl?

*

It struck Rose while gazing out of her third class window in the train from Cambridge one morning in August how very different are the rolling arable fields of Suffolk compared to the boggy fenlands around Cambridge. It was the contrast that struck her, between the heavy black peat and the dry, light brown dust spinning in whorls from the surface of a shorn field the train was just then passing.

This was new territory for Rose, but she had volunteered for it, and she was not about to allow her mission to cause her trepidation.

During the course of a visit to his friends in Warkworth Road towards the end of last term, Mr Hobbs had asked her whether she might be good enough to consider collecting a letter on his behalf – a letter he had asked to be sent *not* to Downing College, since he would not be there for the duration of the long vac, but instead to himself care of the lodging house where he was familiar. Would she look out for it and intercept it? He must be expecting something important, then, surmised Rose, and she agreed readily enough to his request. Accordingly, before leaving Cambridge himself he had provided her with an open rail ticket, supplementing it with a generous tip to sustain her on her mission. Would she be so very kind as to consider delivering this missive to him *by hand* as soon as it came – as he hoped it would? If it wasn't too much trouble?

The item had duly arrived.

So here she is on her day off, on what feels like an adventure. The letter itself is tucked into a small purse inside a wicker basket containing bread and cheese and a bag of strawberries. She is determined to rise to the challenge.

An hour after setting out, a squat village of mainly thatched or flint-walled cottages flew past the window, its outlying fields a hive of industry for as far as the eye could see spread over fields marked out by squat hedgerows. Her attention was caught by something in one of those fields she had never come across before: a gigantic and ungainly hay wain, supporting an athletic figure holding a long fork standing aloft on a growing mound of corn. She followed this figure, poised precariously to receive the loosely bound stacks as they were tossed up to him, his trousers strapped at the waist and ankle to keep the straw ends from wounding his skin. Now here was another kind of farming altogether. What a business! She could also see a multitude of people tending the fields at different points in the harvesting cycle. The whole scene was being worked by an army of labouring men, while women gleaned the edges and children played under the bristly shade of the hedges.

Rose sat back to enjoy the richness of such a scene. She picked out hedges threaded through with honeysuckle and wild roses at this time of high summer, and some of the children appeared to be picking wild raspberries that appeared to be growing plenteously as well. Wild geranium, buttercup and ragged robin were at the same time being plundered for their nectar by clouds of multi-coloured butterflies. All this she relished. It fed a hitherto undiscovered hunger within her for bright things, for sweet air, heightened by a feeling of mounting excitement.

The train was wheezing along at little more than walking pace by the time it eased itself along a narrow platform, gasping for water and suddenly releasing a fierce cloud of white steam, which made her jump. A bundle of first editions of *The Mercury* was tossed out of a carriage before it came to a halt.

Rose gathered her basket, adjusted her bonnet and smoothed down the gaily patterned cotton summer skirt she had lately run up for herself.

Rose was the only passenger to step out onto the small platform that day, gripping the open window by the exit door of her carriage to maintain her balance. Standing alone on the platform, she cast her eyes up and down its length. Only a man in uniform with a flag seemed to be about, waiting to wave the train on its journey.

Then she heard her name being called: 'Rose. Rose, over here'. He was sitting on a bench on the opposite platform. 'Come over by the footbridge,' directed Harry.

She couldn't help feeling self-conscious as she set off to climb the steps leading to the other side, aware of the sound her shoes made on the steps and the fact that he was watching her. Coming down to the platform where he sat she noted that his bare arms were weathered, the hairs on them bleached by the summer sun. He sat easily, his outstretched legs crossed at the ankle, a white handkerchief covering his head and a battered hat in his hand.

'Here, sit down a minute, Rose, and gather your breath,' he invited, patting the seat. 'What a pretty dress.' She blushed. He had her at a disadvantage, being a gentleman and not one of her regular acquaintances. She had no idea how to address him in this place, so she held her peace and made an attempt at a dignified poise, in the form of a straight back and a smile which was not quite a smile. Was this appropriate? It would have to do. She had a sinking feeling that this meeting was going to be very short.

He came out with it at once. 'Have you brought it, Rose?'

'Of course I have, Mr Hobbs,' she said, reaching into her basket.

'Wait a moment,' he told her, placing his hand on hers. She blushed once more, hoping that it wouldn't be visible to him. Now she truly felt awkward.

'I have been wondering whether, since you have come all this way, you would like to join some of our families who are working yonder?' He indicated with a wave of his hand a field almost adjacent to the station. 'They are about to have their lunch and they have told me that they would welcome my messenger from Cambridge.'

She had no idea how to answer him.

'There is a train back at tea time. I have checked. Do say you will. I am so grateful to you for bringing this to me, Rose.'

She nodded her assent.

He took her by the elbow and they made their way to where a party of working men, women and children were sitting on the ground before a square rug spread out on the ground. She was embarrassed to notice that they were ready to eat, yet they were clearly awaiting her arrival. She sat down with them, instinctively opening the contents of her basket to share with them whilst once more offering the letter to Harry. This time he took it and stuffed it into a deep pocket in his jacket, feigning indifference.

'There now,' he said to her, in a tone of satisfaction. 'I shall go up to the big house and come and collect you when the time comes.' Several of the men touched their caps as he left.

So that was how it was to be, thought Rose, and felt a fool for fleetingly looking forward to more of his company. Left amongst strangers, there was a vacuum for her to contend with, but she recognised that this was his way of showing gratitude for her exertions on his behalf, admitting to herself that he had kindly planned a little treat for her in advance, in the hope that it would please her. He had chosen well: the people were softly spoken and welcoming ('no fuss, dear, and we don't stand on ceremony here') and she found herself absorbed easily into their company. She knew enough of country folk to be able to penetrate their taciturn façade and was content to listen to their news about the harvest supper they were looking forward to, now that most of the corn was in. They offered her beer which had been stored under the hedge to keep it cool – or, at least, from being too warm. She took up a tankard and in a little while lay back, as they did, and fell into a doze for twenty minutes or so.

They were woken by the creak and crank of a loaded wagon drawn by two shire horses whose shiny flanks were running with sweat. 'Roit, then, *toim* to git back to wuk,' a foreman called out. The women set to packing away the dregs of their lunch and the woollen rug was rolled and tied with string. As though on cue, Harry could be spotted making his way towards them on foot. Rose could see that she was not the only witness to meekly register the pleasure of beholding him. She felt a necklace of goose-pimples wind itself around her neck.

'Are you ready, Rose?' he called. 'Let me take you back to the station, then.' She noticed that the bulge in his pocket was no more, suggesting that whatever his letter contained it had been taken out and no doubt read. His expression gave nothing away as to the contents – *but really, girl, why should it?* Having brought it all this way she longed to ask him whether it contained good news and she found herself hoping very much that it did. But it was not her business. With the sun at his back, the penumbra of his blonde hair glowed and his smile had a shine to it as well, in her opinion. Still, she knew him well enough to appreciate that radiating geniality came as second nature to Harry Hobbs. It was what made Rose, his friends at Cambridge, his sisters and the people who worked on the farm all note to themselves from time to time that they would be prepared to do a very great deal for such a person.

In no time at all they reached the platform. There, he thoughtfully waited with her for ten minutes or so until, taking her by the arm, he put her on her train, thanking her once again for her trouble and wishing her a safe journey back to Cambridge.

Clouds were gathering by the time she set out to walk from Cambridge station the mile or so back to Warkworth Road. It felt to Rose as though the summer might be thinking about turning soon, that in small ways – a small posse of prematurely dry leaves rattling on the pavement, certain birds on the move – it might be starting to reign in the thrust of its fertility.

But there was still some time to go before October, and the new term.

4 – MICHAELMAS TERM

Following a few dry runs during the Long Vac, on a morning when the autumn was ripening pleasantly Lucien Prideaux made a significant decision.

In sum: he could see no reason – apart from cowardice – for not resuming his early morning ride *during term time*. As if to prove a point to himself about the entitlement to dignity belonging by right to a man of his position, he would therefore follow exactly the same path due south that he had enjoyed before. With a brief shudder of disgust he brought to mind that perpetrator of his humiliation on one cold day back in February before resolving to dwell no further on the unfortunate business.

But to thwart him on one early autumn morning of the new academic year, an institution about which he, amongst others, sometimes felt uneasy was soon horribly, publicly, *intrusively* in evidence. Turning back at the familiar boundary stone just outside Cambridge, he caught sight of it coming towards him on foot from the direction of the open countryside. He could not avoid fixing his attention upon one of his colleagues, striding briskly side-by-side and in perfect step with – his *wife*. The pair appeared to be in the midst of a lively conversation. 'Why, halloa, Prideaux,' hailed the approaching academic, who wore a dog collar. The man seemed rather satisfied with himself, noted Prideaux, mildly irritated by this disturbance. In his estimation there was a degree of smugness in so bold a greeting. As many had warned, including himself, the decision to allow Fellows of the University to marry would drag along in its wake untold implications. And so had proved the case, in Prideaux's opinion. Lucien Prideaux duly raised his hat to the married pair in the poised, mannered way he reserved for people he did not entirely trust, tilting his head and offering a thin smile, careful not to meet the eyes of either without slowing the rhythm of his own progress. In a serendipitous moment as they passed by, he recalled attending a recent reception and hearing a single female voice from the new women's college at Newnham piping up in an octave higher than the throng assembled there: 'Newnham will be a *beacon* for the university,' with the shrill zeal of the subversive. For a moment it had cut through the soft murmur of conviviality. You could have heard a pin drop.

But oh, the wives, the university wives … he fears their influence. They seem to be either reasonably (if erratically) educated, or well-versed in the politics of the day – or both. Their salons were said to produce lively conversations of a forthrightness hitherto unheard of in Cambridge. How correct John Knox was when he talked of the "monstrous regiment of women". Now they were here. In Cambridge.

A bit further on another institution was about to rise up and head his way from just beyond the crest of the Gogs. Alerted by its sound, he had to squint to make out what it was as it rushed towards him. It threatened to enter his orbit so swiftly that evasive action was called for and he kicked his reluctant horse so that it mounted the verge. ('You, my friend, are not far from the knacker's yard,' Prideaux muttered as the wretched animal gave out a rubbery blow of its lips.) But see this: downhill were speeding two young university men, seemingly fused together on one of the new tandem bicycles, their bodies forming a perfect reversed "Z". At an insane rate, the vehicle shot past Prideaux and his horse. He was astonished by the odd whirring sound it made – quite unlike the clatter and screech of hard-rimmed bicycles that flew about the town at a fraction of the speed of this one – which, he was in time to perceive, sported a pair of the latest pneumatic tires. He fancied he recognised one of the riders as a young man named Rolls who was already gaining a reputation at the University for his engineering wizardry. They were clad nattily in Norfolk jackets with roomy trousers tucked into their knee socks, as though they meant business. On their feet: patent bicycling shoes, flat and athletically narrow. What a sight!

But wasn't such innovation all the rage nowadays? His friend William Travers was one of a handful of significant townspeople who had been connected to the telephone exchange and Prideaux had been treated to a demonstration of the amusing stand-up device by a gleeful Travers during the summer just passed. Relentlessly, roads were being transformed by tar, rolled and flattened to provide a seamless surface, and there were plans afoot to construct a sewage system to serve the town which would surely have a purifying effect on the river in due course. Therefore some of this progress, he did concede, was probably in the right order of things.

A blissful fifteen minutes of silence formed its invisible canopy over his head as he resumed his ride. Today, as of old, he was quite without cogitational ambition. On the contrary, he relished the welcome peace of a period of idle solitude, just like he used to, his synapses set at a restful coasting pace and challenged only by recalling some of the words with which, during a rather silly conversation with Travers and the delightful Mrs Travers, the three of them had sought to define the collective persona of town folk, to be followed by another set for those attached to the University. Were they *that* different? Were they *actually* a separate race? This was the question they were set by Alice Travers in a light-hearted mood. Travers and Prideaux were amphibians, after all – entitled to call themselves members of both camps. How remarkable was that? Were they not able to come up with a recipe for lasting peace and accord?

It was the University's turn for scrutiny first. 'We are singular, sage, lofty,' began Prideaux, who at this point in his life identified himself as significantly more University than Town. 'And, I grant you, occasionally devious.' Oh, the machinations, the crafty dealings that informed the whispers and shuffles of academic life.

'Although betimes, what shall we say, earnest? Oh, and pious, certainly ...' from Travers, a townsman if ever there was one.

'And brilliant, eccentric, prone to japes and tricks,' Alice Travers gleefully contributed, with the trace of an echo. She was thinking of the celebrated female maths scholar whose success passed entirely without accolade, which thought led her to her son Francis who was unlikely to be troubled by much in the way of academic honours, earned or not, but would complete his course at Cambridge, all being well – whereas a person like Hope Bassett, that loyal and perspicacious girl, had no chance whatsoever of reaping any rewards as a result of her intelligence, in any setting at all. From time to time Alice experienced a stab of discomfort when she noticed Hope's grave, all-seeing eyes, taking everything in and invited to partake in so little. On the whole, she rather doubted anything would come of Hope's fancy to take up a University place in London, though she understood perfectly why studying at Cambridge would be all but impossible for her, given her father's immoveable stance regarding his precious child. All in all, though, it seemed a little far-fetched for the daughter of a college porter to entertain such an unusual ambition.

'But we are also fen people, you and I, Lucien,' Travers proposed, opening the batting for the Town.

'Very well: taciturn, stubborn, inward looking.'

'Oh, Lucien, you are harsh,' Alice piped up. 'Call us stoical, humorous in a wry sort of way – call us long suffering, if you will.'

'And generous,' added Travers. 'I think generous, yes. And, by Jove, rather loyal by nature. If a little staid. And God-fearing as well.'

Alice clapped her hands.

'You have mentioned but one characteristic the two camps possess in common,' Prideaux was quick to pounce. 'Our religion. Be it dogged or inspired.'

'Or undertaken in pursuit of power and authority,' Alice was moved to slip in, regretting instantly what might be construed as critical forwardnesss. She mitigated this with a speedy postscript: 'I am referring to the hierarchy of subjects, I mean. The way that Theology is privileged above all others.'

'As it should be,' said her husband, who was well aware of the merciless competitiveness with which his dear friend contended during his working life.

On his homeward journey on horseback that morning, the word "piety" came into Prideaux's mind as he recalled this conversation … it *should* be a binding quality, surely. And there was another thing he remembered as he appealed to his horse to consider breaking into a lumpy trot. It concerned his god-daughter. On a not too distant warm August afternoon, when neither had been much occupied, he had been persuaded by Aurelia to accompany her on a stroll down to the mill pond. On that occasion, he recalled, she had been minded to seek from him some knowledge. He presumed her interest was prompted by her friendship with Harry Hobbs, who had taken her as his partner to the May Ball. He presumed she was becoming a little more serious, and he put this down to a desire to be more of a conversational match for the undergraduate.

'Please tell me something, Uncle Lucien,' she began when they had settled at a table set up outside a café

'What shall I tell you, my dear?'

'I have been reading in the newspaper today' (he guessed there was only one she followed – *The Mercury*) ' – about an incident during which – I believe it was occasioned by a recent gathering of two groups of young men who confronted each other near the Corn

Exchange – fighting broke out and arrests were made. Why do you think this – what shall we call it? – rivalry? – keeps occurring?'

He smiled at her naivety.

'My dear, suffice it to say that it has always been the case,' he said, 'from the earliest days a number of centuries ago when the university began to form its own unique graft upon our modest town. I do not know whether I, or anyone else, can accurately tell you why. Perhaps it is human nature. Perhaps it is that when enough young people form a sense of allegiance with their tribe then their assumed status seems to require protection, or assertion of some sort. Look, there is even rivalry between those undergraduates who hail from the south and those who come here to Cambridge from the north, from Wales, Scotland, England north of the River Trent: you know, they call themselves the "Boreales", as opposed to the "Australis" from places like Kent or Devon.'

She nudged him back on course. 'But the undergraduates and the young men of the town? Why do they brawl?'

'Well, it has always been the case that ancient University rights and privileges may somewhat rankle as far as those who, after all, were here first are concerned. For myself, I believe it depends upon how such neighbours are policed. You must bear in mind that the University has an international standing, as against the rather enclosed nature of our town. This in itself must merit due recognition of its status, which, I think, is not always forthcoming.'

'Are we to worry?'

He considered this. Would that youths of both complexion jetting around the town looking for trouble as in days of old should never make a return, turning the narrow streets of Cambridge into a low stage for seditious behaviour.

'And another thing,' said Aurelia while he pondered. 'You know, Mother worries about the girls being taken to the Spinning House these days.' This caught him by surprise – as though there might be some connection between fractious youths of whatever hue and the altogether different issue of the doings of some females of the town.

'Oh, but you must not fret about such things, my dear. Think, if you will, that they have been removed for a small while from the streets for their own safety and the well-being of their souls.'

'Mother wonders *why* they are transgressing in the first place, you see.'

'I do not think there is anything we can do about that,' he snapped.

Though he indicated that this was the end of the matter, his own private observation was that some things just won't go away, especially when polite conversation precludes further probing. It was a rather unsatisfactory conclusion to their little talk, but surely Aurelia was quite used to that. She would just have to accept his equivocation as payment for preserving her innocence. And yet, this was plainly only a partial truth, because preserving her *ignorance* would be closer to the mark. Strange it was that such an enquiry should privilege ignorance as a ransom for purity. But there it was.

And now, as he and his querulous horse approached the outskirts of the town once more he shook his head with retrospective pleasure at the memory of Aurelia's acquiescence. He mused that all must be well in the world when such girls inhabited it. And yet. Something *was* brewing this very term, something he feared would not go away. Something of consequence, he suspected, though he could not put his finger on what it might be. There had been occasional whiffs of unease already, seeking an outlet in lecture theatres, along the towpaths of the river and in some of the households with which he was familiar. It seemed to be generated by a malign spirit in the air lying in wait to ensnare the unwary:

> *"Light thickens; and the crow*
> *Makes wing to the rooky wood:*
> *Good things of day begin to droop and drowse,*
> *Whiles night's black agents to their preys do rouse."*

Moreover, he concluded, as he dismounted in front of the Downing stables: "whoever touches pitch becomes dirty". This, after all, was Bible wisdom.

*

No, it wouldn't go away. Lucien Prideaux was right about that.

One grizzling October afternoon, chilly and wet, the Proctor made a foray almost as far as the edge of the infamous district of Barnwell where, with the help of his assistants, he rounded up two young undergraduates who had no choice but to submit to his jurisdiction and be reported to their college. Soon afterwards, double that number of girls were made captives, simply for appearing to be hanging around in the squalid doorways of Union Row, a road with a bad reputation in that part of town. So it happened that Eva Dipper, laundress, compulsorily enjoyed her first bath in a month once the door of the Spinning House was slammed shut behind her (the water wasn't quite what you'd call perishing, she told her sister on her release a week later, but it fairly shrivelled the skin and made her bones feel as though they were retreating unnaturally inside her lean body). Vi and Effie Wren, enjoying an afternoon of respite from their early shifts at the Eagle, were next to go in (silly girls, neither of them yet eighteen, giggling to cover their embarrassment at the spectacle they made), accepting with a toss of the head the ticket for their clothes given them in return for the coarse uniform provided by the the Spinning House. They were deemed light in character when Matron recorded them in her Black Book. Then it was the turn of petrified, wide-eyed Mabs Mabbett, whose cracked voice prematurely shouted out the responses at evening prayers, as though her mind had been unhinged by her arrest. All she'd been doing was testing the weather outside her front door prior to a visit to the market, holding up her fingers to gauge the chill in the air – not soliciting any young man.

'What a cull!' observed Matron to the Keeper of the Jail next door when the opportunity arose.

A blunt man, he was quick to retort: 'Mark my words, girl, I reckon it's all going a bit too far'.

No, it would not go away.

The Spinning House "court" sat in its usual exclusive fashion whenever the need arose, always in camera, meaning that most confinements slipped under the radar of *The Mercury*'s daily reportage unless there was an open fracas in the streets – as when Minny Mantle was nabbed. Dressed in men's clothes, the minx was heading towards a licensed lodging house where she hoped to ply her trade from the inside by pretending to be a student. Caught in the act after ten minutes of further stealth on the Proctor's part, both she and a hapless young university lodger were dragged out of the house and led away. While he cowered in shame, she (a tall, malnourished woman with the dough-pale features of a fen dweller) chose to take a stand when brought face-to-face with the Proctor, making an insolent grab at a nearby garden railing to thwart him in his mission. While he admonished her, she began a crescendo of interruptions and had to be manhandled all the way to the Spinning House. That day, the spectacle of her rebelliousness sent a vigorous skein of gossip as far as *The Mercury* in the unhealthy atmosphere that hung over the town. Time for Walter Magson to wire off a timely comment.

'*Has not the time come,*' thundered "Scornful" in the pages of a London newspaper a day or so later (thanks to Walter Magson's quick thinking, since *The Mercury* wasn't having any of it) – '*when public opinion ought to be brought to bear upon the question, in order to procure the abolition of this iniquitous power, doubly hateful because directed at a class which, God knows, stands far more in need of loving exhortation and advice than of harsh treatment and imprisonment?*'

'Oh Lord,' sighed Alice Travers at breakfast as she read this, hugging tightly to her body a handsome violet and rose coloured lambswool shawl recently presented to her at the conclusion of her term as leader of the local Society for the Protection of Fallen Women. Alice had walked many a mile through Barnwell on a mission to reach out to the Minny Mantles of the town in the hope of persuading them to learn needlework, to spin and sew and modestly sell respectable wares – instead of themselves. She was a little bruised and saddened at this point by her almost total failure to wean a single young girl in that poverty-stricken den of iniquity from the wantonness of prostitution, though she would never stop trying. In addition, she was dismayed by the short term expedience of those pursuing the seemingly easier trade by preference. At this point she has come to believe that she understands a little about the nature of desperation, and the hopeless quality of persistent, unending hardship. As well as the folly of such misplaced opportunism.

*

Without a doubt, it will not go away.

It was on one mature autumn morning, whilst strolling down the avenue towards the Downing Street main gate, that Harry was almost brought to a standstill by what felt to him like an entirely new sensation, though it had visited him with some power on occasions the previous term, and again during the long vac. He had other things on his mind, so this time it caught him entirely unawares, feeling like an unexpected shove from behind from something or someone unknown. It seemed to arise out of a sudden compression of air in his immediate vicinity, squeezing him in a determined way, yet it was not at all unpleasant. In fact, such a feeling struck him as a gratuitous bonus, given the burdensome and all-absorbing nature of his studies. Then it faded as quickly as it had surfaced, before he could grasp the sense of it, leaving him with a curious sensation of having been *possessed* by something or other.

How could this be?

It was not until he was returning to his room after spending a couple of aimless hours in the library that he recalled the sheer force of that earlier feeling which left him in such a soaring frame of mind. It was only a matter of time before a certain word began to form in his mind. He pictured the two syllables of this word shimmering across the whispering grass of the Master's field as he gazed towards it. Seconds later, it seemed to collude in a mysterious way with the shadows leaking through a high window in the Porter's Lodge when he dropped by to collect any messages that may have been left for him in his absence. But above all, he came to realise – with a stab of dangerous excitement crisping into mild apprehension – that it was intimately bound up with a recurring memory of light shining on the abundant hair of Hope Bassett, the Downing Porter's daughter.

That word was *longing*. He marvelled at the strength of its hold on him. And no – it would not go away.

Ah, Hope. (And thoughtless hope that should catch him out with such a wildly hopeful feeling.) All hope, cruelly cancelled before there had been time or opportunity to mend tender roots, brutally severed by what he had at first concluded must be some brand of unfathomable wisdom coming, as it did, from that delectable prisoner in the house on Park Terrace. Though it had wounded him at the time, and subsequently, he no longer had any intention of actually confronting the humiliation she had tossed his way on the day they returned in isolation following their diffuse missions in London. Girls were lovely, but they were odd creatures, he argued to himself, not for the first time. And this one, he suspected (this truly lovely one), seemed to be worth so much more than a creature like himself. How he longed for her, though. But no, girls were probably best encountered with a little light teasing, in his experience to date. After all, hadn't he all but engaged himself to the imminently more accessible (suitable?) Aurelia Travers, an amusing enough companion and one who would find as natural and warm a welcome within his family as he had within hers?

As he traced these considerations, Harry found himself struck by yet another wave of pure yearning for Hope Bassett – she, and nobody else. By then he had entered his rooms where he flung himself down on his bed and clasped his hands behind his head.

The next time it hit him was when he left Downing later that day, after evensong and a well-cooked eel stew in hall. He hurried past Fred Bassett, who happened to be standing squarely in a thoughtful mood under the arch of his Porter's Lodge, surveying the quad. There was something not right about letting his imagination get the better of him in this man's presence. As a consequence, he could not meet Bassett's eyes, barely nodding as he sensed, by a slight shift in the man's stance, that he was making a mental note of Harry's impending absence that evening.

*

At *The Mercury*, meanwhile, one telegraph operator allows herself a bit of innocent fretting, as she regularly does. Another autumn is fast descending towards winter, yet will it not ever reach a conclusion? How long must a girl be made to wait? She is beginning to feel it wouldn't matter, surely, if they had the simplest of nuptials and took up a room in her parents' house? But no, Walter will have it properly done. Mildred Dobbins stares critically at the coloured glass she wears on her ring finger, bought by her ambitious (but impecunious) fiancé. He had lately brought urgent copy back from yet another incident on the street, dashed off spontaneously in a trice. It will only take one big story, he likes to tell her from time to time. Keep your spirits up, girl, he assures her, sending his enthusiasm up towards the teleprinter. He needs a sustainable sort of splash which will be taken up by the London papers in a big way. So he passes it to his beloved to tap out. It is up to him to be resolute on behalf of Mildred when she flags, especially when the wires are quiet and she sits at her bench and sighs so, longing to see daylight.

*

One other who is resolute enough to be saving her pennies is Rose Whipple. There is a velvet pouch in a drawer of the chest of drawers in her room in the attic stuffed with coins and a few guineas gained in tips from the May Balls as well as from the envelope Mr Hobbs pressed on her for delivering his mail in the summer. This is what she privately calls her fortune, modest though it is. It pleases her to draw it out from time to time, to weigh it in her hands, to tip it out and view it, to marvel at its substance, and to satisfy herself that it *is* growing. She is proud of her parsimony, her good husbanding of scant resources. This small nest egg prompts her to take extra pride in the proficiency of her work, humble though it is, for this is its main source. To her annoyance, such pride was lately placed in jeopardy when Mr Hobbs, visiting his friend Mr Moody, caught her in the downstairs corridor ferrying a huge mound of fresh washing towards the kitchen for ironing. He intercepted her, making as if to relieve her of the load. Her reaction was to clutch it even more tightly. 'I can manage, sir,' she was moved to insist, increasing her pace. He had surely touched a sore spot. Absurd as it may appear to him, her fortitude regarding the skivvying that was her livelihood was one of the very few certainties in life to which she clung. Those humble attributes – the hardness of her muscles, her readiness to get up hours before anyone else every morning in order to set the household in motion, her reserved but generally cheerful demeanour, the effort put into each task as thoughtfully developed as any undergraduate's studies for his degree, by her reckoning: these qualities surely provided justifiable reassurance that one day she might expect to receive a first class "character" from her employer, and perhaps move on in a higher capacity to a bigger establishment? Rose would therefore hold her head up as she went about her business. Nobody should be allowed to take that from her.

*

'What does the weather do this morning, Bates?' enquired Harry Hobbs from his bed one morning in November when his man backed into his bedroom at the unfriendly time of 6.30am with steaming water for his wash and shave.

'It is damp, sir.'

Damp? This could mean all manner of things. In Cambridge, there ought to be as many words for damp as the Eskimos have for snow, thought Harry. But he was accustomed to the man's frugality with words. So he would have to ascertain for himself what the man meant by "damp". A whispering drizzle? A snivelling wetness that guaranteed fallen leaves would be soggy and slippery underfoot? A persistent moist spindrift? Raising himself as far as the bottom rim of his window, a matt curtain of grey mist outside confronted him. It would be cold, chilblain-inducing damp, then.

'I wonder, Bates,' he enquired, 'if you would be good enough to convey a rather urgent message to Dr Prideaux for me – directly, to make sure it is in his hands – after you leave your duties on this staircase? I am not well, you see, and shall not be able to join him for my tutorial this morning.'

Bates surveyed him with silent neutrality.

'Very well,' acquiesced Harry. 'I will not compromise you.' But he drew a short intake of breath, almost as though he might actually be ailing. 'Please pass me ink, pen and paper and I will write a note which perhaps you would be good enough to leave at the Porter's Lodge. As soon as you can.' The burdensome fact of the matter was that the essay he was due to read out to his tutor simply hadn't been accomplished. There was another one outstanding as well, but Harry calculated that he might dash off both, if left entirely alone for a bit. Anything rather than put himself in the position of having to make another fatuous excuse to Prideaux and beg for another extension. Their meetings were on the whole prickly affairs. Despite the good will he applied to them, Harry always came away with a feeling of being pummelled by the encounter, squeezed into a smaller version of himself by a superior mind. It was not pleasant to squirm in front of that demanding figure.

Bates formed an expression of both complicity and disapproval by raising his eyebrows in a way neither disapproving nor censorious but foregrounding the sense of a question mark. He placed the bowl he was bearing on a chair, then started to delve into the haphazard heaps of rough notes and books spread over a number of surfaces, as requested. When this failed to yield the requisite tools he foraged amongst a wilderness of loose papers tumbling from improvised folders, one of which leaked a trail of single sheets on which – Harry shifted himself abruptly to gather it in before Bates came to it – it appeared a poem might be in the process of being drafted. It had been spun out to no more than three or four lines, each one subject to much amendment before being put out of its misery with a firm cross through it before another version was attempted.

Harry pointed this way and the other, hoping to guide Bates towards one of his pens and away from his poem, the result of his brain finally giving up the ghost on essay writing the previous night when he was still being attacked by any number of fanciful impressions arising from his *longing*. So far, however, his efforts at rhyme proved as disappointing as his failure to keep up to date with his work. He conceded that others were better at it than him:

"The heart less bounding at emotion new
The hope, once crushed, less quick to spring again."

Today, impending winter threatens to harden the earth, causing chaffing at the heel, and there is to be little relief for Harry from his longing. But neither is his ambition to be a writer entirely quashed on this crepey white morning with a hang-dog look about it. His note to his tutor is despatched. He vows to order lunch in his room and will knuckle down to spending an inordinate amount of time re-arranging his notes before making one last push of concentration on the manifest dullness of the task in hand – namely, the completion of not one but two cobbled together essays.

Pleasantly surprising himself, this is exactly what he does.

His spirits buoyed, he is ready to risk emerging from his room for some welcome recreation. He has an appointment that evening with several fellows who make up the editorial team of a droll university publication so abstruse that it defies interpretation. This inter-mittently published vehicle is the distraction of a bohemian group whose editorial meetings are an excuse for much languishing, spiced with choice wine and cigars. Harry has his own piece to offer tonight, a state of affairs which usually feels fairly satisfying and serves as a justification for holding his head up. Spurred by pleasant anticipation of a convivial evening after leaving his work out for Prideaux, his mood is not unlike the relief that sometimes comes with a major voiding of the bowel, it strikes him, with some satisfaction. He shrugs off the purlieus of Downing with a surge of relief. In renewed hope, and never one to waste a journalistic opportunity, he has in his pocket that which the great editor recently rejected: his attempt to write up an "interview" with the man. Will they like it? Will a student magazine suit such a piece better?

"Dear Mr Hobbs," that editor had written, in a short, handwritten missive, his spiky hand failing to acknowledge Harry's effort, expectation, and – surely – originality. *"I thank you for sending me a sample of your writing. I cannot imagine why you might have believed that to interview <u>me</u> without my being aware that such a thing was taking place would be of much interest. It is true (as you record) that I, a member of the press, have made it a practice of mine to enter into the stories I am investigating from time to time. But I did not invite you to*

do the same, and I regard it as somewhat impudent." Reading this devastating opener while sitting alone under an oak tree on a hot summer day while the harvest was being robustly enacted all about him, Harry had felt himself burn with embarrassment. If only he could have explained, given the man his own justification for such a piece ...

But the letter continued.

"*To be fair, young sir,*' conceded the editor, '*since you have asked my opinion and express an ambition to join my trade, I will say this to you. You seem to have a sharp eye (even tho' at my expense). I like that. You may contact me again when you have acquired some experience and concluded your studies. That is all I can say at present.*'

What "experience" might that be? After much thought, clinging to these sparse words and with William Travers's approval, he had passed a rather odd day at *The Mercury* after returning to Cambridge for the new academic year. Here, he managed to get in the way of a number of busy people, all of whom ignored him. He would have *done* something, only nobody seemed to see any point in him as they rushed past. A provincial daily newspaper certainly appeared to be a well-oiled machine, he was bound to conclude after passing some hours trying to appear vaguely involved. He observed that each component was locked into a defined purpose and that there was indeed a sense of precision about the whole procedure. This was the gist of what such an "experience" suggested to him at the end of a somewhat confusing day. There was a certain nervous excitement about the whole business of getting a newspaper printed, he reflected when he left the place with some relief, hurrying past the black delivery vans and managing to persuade himself (almost) that he had just been, albeit in a superfluous way, part of the sense of urgency that spilled out from the great press of *The Mercury* onto the streets outside.

As a result, when he re-read the letter that had rather knocked him back a couple of months previously, Harry was able to derive a little battered hope from it. To have received a personal letter from a great editor was, perhaps, something he could allow himself to allude to – casually, of course – when he submitted his "Interview with a London Editor" to that evening's crowd.

So it was with a bold step he set his course through a moonless evening on the streets of Cambridge.

That same evening, curtains were drawn and fires well stoked at the Travers house on Park Terrace by the time Bernadette had dealt with matters pertaining to various rooms before all was considered settled. Her final mission took her towards the top of the house where Hope Bassett had her quarters. On her own initiative, she came bearing a restorative cordial to replace Miss Bassett's untouched tea. Bernadette was familiar with that lady's dreadful headaches, episodes which seemed to grip Hope's head as tightly as did the stays around her abdomen, and she had no alternative but to retire when one of them overcame her.

Bernadette tiptoed in. Standing by Hope's bed, she whispered: 'Should I turn the lamp up, Miss?'

Hope peered at her through narrowed eyes as though seeing her for the first time before replying: 'No, thank you Bernadette. I really can't bear the light.'

So Bernadette kneeled by the bedside. After placing her right hand on the patient's forehead she began to stroke Hope's hair. 'Thank you,' whispered Hope, after a minute of this.

Very gradually, the little maid sensed Hope's tense body beginning to unfurl, though she had no way of knowing whether this meant she was merely falling asleep. She would not venture to ask if this was the case, for fear of interfering with the sense of peace that her simple act of solace appeared to be achieving. Instead, careful neither to alter the pressure of her hand nor to relieve her knees, Bernadette drew from her skirts a simple wooden rosary and began, with the deftness of regular practice, to pray her way through the beads. After twenty minutes she slipped the rosary back into its pocket and glanced towards the window. It was a Friday and soon, when she was free, it was her intention to pay a visit to her parents and the younger children in their squat dwelling in Barnwell, not so far away. She strained her neck to check what it was doing outside. All she could see in a crack between the curtains was a vertical oblong of dense darkness – a quality which seemed to have descended prematurely that evening. Ever so gently, she removed her hand from Hope's head, tenderly laid a cover over her and tip-toed over to the window. For once, the shadowy form peeping out from behind a curtain in the room on the top floor was not that of Hope Bassett. While she hovered there Bernadette was in time to hear the click of the front door and make out the figure of William Travers. How peculiar, though: before he reached the pavement he was entirely swallowed up by the black spectre of a gathering fog, its earlier cirrus insubstantiality fast becoming impenetrable as several thousand domestic fires thereabouts started blazing indoors.

Before Bernadette turned away from this scene with a private 'tsk' to herself (knowing at once that it would not be a good night for being abroad, not in such foul weather) she made out another figure heading the way she herself intended to go soon. It was Rose Whipple, and she was carrying a basket. Rose, she guessed, would be wanting to use her Friday evening off to visit her own family, just as Bernadette was determined to do, in defiance of the weather.

*

Harry Hobbs passed a genial few hours in the grand set of rooms of a larger college, as he knew he would. He turned down the offer of an opium pipe but let himself be persuaded to drink at least a bottle of a rather rich claret that was lying heavily on his stomach now. No bohemian himself, he was one of those rare, fortunate people who never felt out of place in whatever company he found himself, and he had certainly found the evening a pleasant diversion. Early on, they rejected his interview with the great editor with amused disdain. ('What the deuce is this? Is it meant to be entertaining, dear boy? Sorry, old fellow. What sort of writing is it meant to be anyway?') Never mind. Harry shrugged, stuffed it into a trouser pocket and accepted another glass.

Outside on Trinity Street, after he finally left them, a very different sort of weather enveloped him at once – the fog was now a dank, furry substance, thickened by soot. It was shortly after nine o'clock by then, so he must set about heading back to Downing, post haste. Warmed, and dazed by a combination of that heavy wine and the harsh roasting in his throat of too much tobacco, he didn't notice at first how cold it had become. The thick substance he found himself attempting to walk through felt as though it might freeze at any moment, and it was inducing almost complete darkness all around. He came upon what could be Sidney Street – not quite the route he had intended. Had he veered from his course? He was struck by how unusually empty the road was – strange, at that time of the evening. A wraith brushed his arm, followed by several shadows gliding by like disembodied bits of drapery. They turned out to be people, while a slow moving shape apparently floating along a little way off like a barge through grey foam was in fact a carriage, its wheels invisible. It was disorienting … even the tap of his shoes on the pavement sent out only the dullest sound.

Harry was aware that a perfect smog is likely to form when winter fires lit inside row upon row of terraced houses poorly sealed against the sulphurous gloom all send out warm smoke – only for the colder air beneath to be trapped. He was obliged to slow his pace significantly, challenged by the uncertainty of his bearings. He thought he might have crossed the river at Magdalene Bridge – but only because the path he was treading formed some kind of a hump.

It was at this point that troubling things began to happen. A dormant waggon seemed to be in his path, a black shape that turned into four figures in a huddle. Did he turn left when he should have veered right to avoid bumping into them? And what was this? An unfamiliar wall appeared ink-stained, close up.

The minutes passed.

With no idea whether he was heading south any more – this was the direction he sought – he plodded warily onwards. What alternative was there? Perhaps he would eventually walk himself into daylight, he thought, grimly. It occurred to him how precariously he was situated on this black night, and how quickly a pleasing evening can turn into the confused state he now found he was in. He became taunted by flashing apparitions of disappointed sisters, the mockery of a famous editor, a profoundly disgruntled father, the disapproval of William Travers (a man he liked and admired), a disappointed Aurelia – she, whom he had continued to visit this term but without any further reference to seal the understanding he might have given her reason to expect. They all took an exaggerated turn at tormenting him with unnaturally elongated, accusing faces as glum as the ghostly concentration of darkness all around him. A muffled cough broke his reverie. It seemed ownerless, until something – a body, maybe – placed a hand on his shoulder then vanished.

He swung round, only to collide with another figure, whose merchandise tumbled to the ground.

'Rose!' he exclaimed. 'What in heaven's name are you doing?'

'Hush, sir. I have had leave to visit my family and I am on my way back.'

145

Just then a peevish whistle sounded three times.

The dense air seemed for a moment to form several whirls in the gloom nearby where they stood, set in motion by other bodies, not far off.

A solid figure emerged and a shout went up: 'Ho, young woman! Stand right where you are!'

Rose pushed Harry away from her. 'Run!' she ordered him. 'Quick!'

'There he goes! Cut him off before he reaches Christ's Pieces!'

The thud of several pairs of boots giving chase confused him further. He managed to cut into an alley and discover a broken doorway to hold himself against, hoping for the sounds of pursuit to die away while he steadied his breathing. It was at this point that he decided to stuff his gown and college scarf behind a grille in the wall nearby – a hastily thought out attempt at establishing anonymity, should he be apprehended. It was clear to him that he was now a person on the run.

*

At about the same time as this disturbance was taking place, and some way off, Constable Cyril Morley gave a nod to his colleague Constable Jack Rimple when they passed close to each other, creating a foggy draft of air which threatened to bind them in some sort of artificial pact. Morley was about to start work while Rimple was on his way back to the Police Station at the end of his beat. 'Rather me than you this night, boy' observed Rimple, at the end of his shift, to the unfortunate Morley, who was about to embark upon Night Beat No. 8, the one they called the Barnwell Beat.

Ah, Barnwell… Ostensibly, this region – which, fifty years previously, housed a sixth of the population of Cambridge – does not exist. It has long since merged seamlessly with the town itself, this suburb of open cesspits, feral cats and dogs and baleful vapours of decay curling through an extended warren of shabby tenements, cramped passages and overcrowded dens. Nevertheless, the entity known informally then as Barnwell was certainly there on this unfortunate evening. It stood, muffled, in all its murky squalor, about as far removed from the University buildings as a busker is from a magistrate though they shared one boundary. All that can be said is that a hundred years before these events there was a village called Barnwell, and there were open fields separating it from its grander neighbour, Cambridge. Then it was consumed by the town. More recently, the Bishop of Ely had been heard to refer to it as 'a dark spot, close to the very focus of light,' a hideous place, a place of disorder, pollution – and lewdness. But Barnwell's economy at that time to an extent depended upon dubious goings on.

Constable Cyril Morley flicks a globule of snot from his nose, aiming it towards the pavement where it will join the other sickly green gobs hawked from many another congested pair of lungs. Barnwell Beat is not a popular one. He is Harry's age and already has a wife and baby at home nearby, Isaac, they called it. It was a "mistake," but Cyril had done the honourable thing and married the girl in question. Maybe there will be a chance to sneak in and warm himself for five minutes during the course of what promises to be a most dismal shift that will last until six the next morning. This drear fog might provide some cover for such a tempting deviation. It is strictly out of bounds, of course – as is a tempting dip into the Jolly Ragman, from which a wan draft of beery air escapes when the solitary constable passes by, as if to lure him in. There will be pickpockets out in force tonight, he knows, fine-wirers, they call them, fanning the unsuspecting with their deft fingers. He is on the lookout for them. As he will be later for a fellow constable trudging thereabouts, who he is obliged to meet at a "conference point" at around 4.00am. For sure, he will be there when the time comes. Failure to attend conference is penalised, even on a night of such uncompromising weather, and Cyril Morley is glad of his waterproof cape and his winter boots and trousers.

What he doesn't expect at all in this sorry region is to come across a shivering young gentleman. They eye each other with caution. 'Are you getting behind yourself, sir?' he enquires of the foolish undergraduate. 'It will be time for the curfew very soon. Come, where is your coat?'

'Shh,' motions Harry through stiff fingers.

'You will have fallen foul of the Proctor, then?' guesses Cyril, correctly.

'I must place myself at your mercy, Constable,' whispers Harry, arms crossed and hands now returned to his armpits as he tries to calculate odds on the man apprehending him. He decides upon the truth: 'I have no idea of where I am.'

'Where is it that you would go? Which of the colleges?'

But Harry will not risk telling, for fear of being reported.

He tells another truth instead. 'At this moment, I can go nowhere. There was a frightful hue and cry and I must lie low.'

The policeman surveys his quarry once more. All things being equal, he has nothing against the young gownsmen of the University who, by and large, tend to keep to the law. The rule is that if there is any breach of the peace short of a felony, then undergraduates should merely be returned to their college or lodgings for the matter to be taken up by the University. He has some sympathy with the young college men, bound as they are by many restrictions – apart from when they take advantage of his good nature by playing japes on him, especially by knocking off a fellow's helmet, an object much prized by some of the more boisterous amongst them. If a young man refused to state the name of his College when asked, it was only then that they could be taken to the Police Station. Did he feel like going through the whole rigmarole with the shivering specimen in front of him? Sizing Harry up, he instructed: 'Follow me.'

Harry had little choice but to be led hither and thither along a number of streets he was sure he had never encountered during all his time in Cambridge. He tripped over a mound of horse droppings kicked willy-nilly across the pavement. He bruised his shoulder against a swaying figure looming into visibility when he was almost upon them, a man who let rip an evil curse. Cyril Morley voiced his supposition that this one was 'tight as a drum' and raised his truncheon arm to indicate that the drunkard had better move off quickly unless he was looking for trouble. Harry, following blindly, was roused by the disembodied scream (or was it a hideous burst of strained laughter?) of a female somewhere in the vicinity, which had an air of danger about it. In a vertiginous state brought on by anxiety, too much drink and coldness, he formed the odd impression that people were deliberately pursuing each other hereabouts in some sort of macabre dance.

The policeman took his arm and led him to a coal repository where canvas sacks were neatly piled, smelling of tar. 'You take a couple of these and wrap them round you, I would,' advised Constable Cyril Morley. 'Here you are.' And this is what Harry did, providing himself with a pauper's cloak that would surely not deceive anyone about his real identity. 'Listen carefully, now, and I will direct you back towards St Andrews Street, and from there you should be close to where you want to get.'

Alone again, Harry reached for his inside jacket pocket where his fob watch resided – a gift from his father – keen to ascertain whether there was still any chance at all of beating the 10.00pm curfew. But only its chain remained, hanging loosely. He sought his cambric pocket handkerchief, sweetly embroidered with his initials by his devoted twin sister Kitty but it, too, was missing. He recalled the way several people had used the poor visibility to come into contact with him, ridding him of these items, no doubt.

In complete ignorance, and no longer in the company of the policeman, he wandered past the modest brothel kept by Mrs Shed of Fitzroy Street, and that of Mrs Gurney of Fields Court, the Doo sisters of New Street's establishment, the parlours of Mrs Benton of Carters Yard, Lizzy Cartwright's in Eden Street, and more … And occasionally he caught sight of an array of straw beds behind windows without curtains, dingy openings to back yards, women gathered by cheerless kitchen fires smoking their acrid pipes and hapless men playing "blind all fours".

'Come, gentleman, ain't you going to stand a gallon of ale? I got a drop of Betty's beer, ducky,' came a salacious snarl in his direction which made him increase his pace. A peel of baleful laughter pursued him.

The growl from a stray mutt with matted fur conveyed a promise that it would nip him, given half a chance.

In one house he thought he saw a goat by the window, gazing out at him. His nose rebelled at the smells issuing from ill-fitting windows and shrouded dens – the onions and carrots and beets being boiled, the herrings toasting on forks before miniature fires burning in shabby grates. His shoes squelched in this treeless region, not on dead leaves but on discarded vegetable peelings and the contents of chamber pots.

He reached into his pocket and touched his interview with the great man for some comfort and reassurance. But to his sorrow, all that was left was the last page of it. Whoever plundered him this time was not in for rich pickings, he thought to himself, with no satisfaction at all. But it led him to recall the one hopeful thing the editor had written in his estimation of him – that he had an eye for detail. He began to note the dark entry-ways more closely from then on, refuge of petty criminals and other scoundrels, the zig zagging passages where a thief could disappear without trace, the stench of dissolute living, the dung heaps, and the air of desolation all about.

The door of a shabby inn opened suddenly to release a man and a woman, both in the easily recognisable uniform of the Salvation Army. Harry was saddened by a mixture of revulsion, sadness and thin-lipped resolve on the woman's face as she turned her back on the collection of men inside sending forth their curses.

He hurried on.

At last he came to Fitzroy Place, heading – surely – towards Maid's Causeway at last, and thence to Jesus Lane where he would be in the vicinity of the University once more – oh, please let it be.

When –

'Pssst …'

A very small hand grasped his wrist, pulling him towards a dark door.

'Why, Bernadette, is that you?'

'Shhh … you come with me, sir. You look properly frozen.'

Four silent creatures even smaller than Bernadette were squashed into one chair in the small front room into which she led him. They stared in awe at the unexpected visitor clothed in coal sacks. 'I'll put a kettle on the fire,' said Bernadette's mother, needing no prompting. Harry's lips were blue by then and he had acquired a parched, wild look. Bernadette had evidently told her family all about the young man who was calling on Miss Travers, and this kindly family seemed to understand a dangerous situation when they saw one.

He was urged to squat by the glow of the coals and thaw himself out before travelling on. With a sense of profound gratefulness he allowed the warmth of this poor Irish family to seep into him. They asked nothing of him. He was provided with a bowl of soup, then a clean blanket was urged upon him as a replacement for his coal sacks. A little while later he was ready to be on his way once more. On the doorstep, he reached in a side pocket for a coin, but his last guinea had flown, along with the few sixpences and shillings he kept about him by way of small change. To his shame, he was left with nothing to give them.

It was approaching eleven o'clock when he eased himself over Downing's long, western boundary wall road, banging his head and grazing himself in the process. The fog was easing a little by then. He could just about make out the glow of a few lights behind thick curtains as he ferried his aching body across the Great Court towards his rooms. He caught the merry notes of a phonograph coming from somewhere. A window was flung open for the release of smoke, and out flew a collegiate gale of laughter from members of the Griffins who had presumably dined that night. One or two others, bearing books under their arms, were to be seen making their way to their rooms in this scene of frightful normality that he, feeling like an intruder, was preparing to surreptitiously re-join.

It was only as he approached the familiar staircase leading to his set of rooms that it occurred to him to wonder, with a cold sense of dread, what might have happened to Rose Whipple.

5 – GOING DOWN

'Christmas is coming, the goose is getting fat,
Time to put a penny in the old man's hat.
If you haven't got a penny, a ha'penny will do,
If you haven't got a ha'penny, a farthing will do,
If you haven't got a farthing, then God bless you.'

There was a nip in the air as sharp as a starling's beak, though a weak winter sun was trying to penetrate bundles of angry looking purple clouds speeding low overhead. The ill-clad beggar was shaking his hat towards the crowd shuffling slowly past him and a gaggle of stunted children took to bawling bits of Christmas carols in competition with him. Positioned next to a slow-moving queue of assorted humanity is, of course, an admirable pitch for those who hope to gain by it, thought Harry, as he dropped a few pennies into both camps. But equally important – this struck him forcibly as he strove to preserve his anonymity in the midst of the queue – such a thing as a queue is a perfect forum for the voice of the un-voiced, whose medium is gossip. His ears began to register some of its darts as they sped back and forth along it.

The Cambridge Assizes, towards which all were heading, were convened in an auction hall not much more than a week and a half after the night when Cambridge had been visited by one of its more memorable fogs. The court was to hear a single case. The barn of a building where the trial was to take place would not be large enough to admit all those in the queue stamping their feet against the chill, blowing out icy clouds of their none too sweet breath. That was why it had begun to form early. Current whispering seemed to lean towards the notion that it might turn out to be something of a trumpery case – that of the Crown versus Rose Whipple. This in itself was an extra incentive for anyone who could find fair means or foul to escape their normal duties that morning. They'd come out *en masse,* driven by the bad odour of it. Conveniently for some, the University's end of term had already begun, so there was at the same hour a somewhat lesser counter movement of people heading in the direction of the station, either by tram or on foot, bearing with them their bags for the Christmas vacation.

Harry had delayed his own anticipated return to Suffolk in order to anxiously follow these proceedings himself first hand, as a matter of honour, prior to setting himself the task of working out what must now be done.

The morning after his frightful night-time experience in the fog he had been summoned to Lucien Prideaux's study to take his place in another queue – this one outside the tutor's room – alongside a number of other Downing men. Each was summoned inside at roughly five minute intervals – sometimes shorter. Every time the heavy oak door opened for one undergraduate to exit, the line shuffled forward a few steps, in a state of mystification. The last person to enter prior to Harry spent less than two minutes with Prideaux before making an indignant and (considered Harry) a rather flamboyant exit, exclaiming in a loud voice: 'No, sir, it was certainly not I. I do my whoring in London.'

Then it was Harry's turn.

Prideaux gathered himself quickly after the last rude encounter. 'Kindly look at these garments, Mr Hobbs,' he instructed, without inviting Harry to sit, 'and tell me whether you can identify them.'

Harry carefully viewed his discarded gown and his college scarf laying scuffed and besmirched on Prideaux's desk.

'No, sir,' he affirmed. 'I cannot. As you can see, sir, I am in possession of my gown. My scarf, I believe, is in my rooms.' He had lost no time in borrowing a substitute gown from Francis Travers, knocking him up with some urgency after passing a sleepless few hours in dread of what may lie ahead.

'You see,' persisted Prideaux, 'this is unmistakably a *Downing* scarf, would you not agree?'

Harry nodded his assent. 'But I am not sure what it has to do with me, sir … ?'

'Do not trouble yourself with idle speculation, Hobbs. The fact is that last night at near nine thirty a *Downing* undergraduate was seen in the presence of a local woman who was later arrested for soliciting.'

Harry's eyebrows raised themselves slightly.

'Not I, sir.'

'Not you. Of course not you,' replied the don in a caustic tone. 'Or anyone else, it would seem. But listen to me carefully, Hobbs:

Be in no doubt that I shall be pursuing this distasteful matter. It is just the sort of thing that brings dishonour to the College. I shall not rest until the owner of these items is run to ground. Is that clear?'

Harry offered a shrug of incomprehension to the next man in the queue as he made his way from the vicinity as quickly as he dared. Trusting that Prideaux's sleuthing would not stretch to presuming upon his tailors, his next move was to purchase replacements after returning the gown he was wearing to Francis, who would need it himself for a similar quizzing in due course, no doubt, poor fellow. As soon as he returned to his rooms with the brand new items he doused them in his wash basin then crumpled them in an attempt to remove some of their obvious newness.

*

But wait! All around him at the Assizes, the people of Cambridge are slowly beginning to take their seats.

Harry strove to merge seamlessly into the throng, hunching his shoulders and shuffling along at their pace. He picked up at once an atmosphere of nervous tension establishing itself inside, expressed in pockets of chattering that rose up in a percussive hiss throughout the tall space. He made a furtive scan of the underlings of the audience settling themselves, principally to check for anyone who might recognise him. Ah, yes: there, surely, was Mrs Mawkins, the landlady at the lodging house in Warkworth Road. Harry instinctively bent his head. And wasn't that Cynthia Dawes sitting right next to her? What were they doing here? He also made a mental note of *The Mercury* reporter Walter Magson on the press bench, though he did not know him by name. A brief disturbance near the public entrance revealed one other figure Harry thought he recognised, whose fur wrap tossed extravagantly around her shoulders revealed a florid woman who alerted the attention of those close to her as she pushed her way forward. He recalled that it was almost a year ago that he had watched that very lady in combat with his tutor, both of them fairly galloping on horseback past where he stood on the pavement in town one morning, and he was not proud, now, of the fact that he had readily joined in the general sniggering. He also recalled her wanton abandonment of a certain hat, decorated with a white feather. What place had she here in this courtroom today?

Shame on you, the woman's appearance reminded him, that you

did not stay and defend poor unfortunate Rose Whipple, whose only crime on *not one but two* occasions was to be in your vicinity. What right, he asked himself, have I to be roaming free while this poor young woman is in the throes of wholly unjust charges, let alone an irreversible assault on her reputation? What on earth had possessed him to flee without a thought for her on that fateful fog-bound night? How disgracefully easy it had been to run away at her brave command, how equally easy to lie about his movements to Prideaux the following morning. No, worse than easy – instinctual. *I am a toad*, he concluded, while he eased himself into a seat. A poor specimen of toad at that: a toad who is a coward and a liar. It was true that his face had become tight and his complexion pale ever since that fateful interruption. His man had even enquired whether he was, in fact, ill. Well, he might be. Nothing, it seemed, was mendable, let alone this pitiable self. Was there any point in pursuing his time at Cambridge further? Surely his whole undergraduate life was an absurd pursuit for one destined to be a country man anyway? If he could not quite accommodate his new, unmanly self, any more than he could turn an honest face towards the authorities and all the other people he had let down by coming clean about his lying and misdemeanours, well then ... His remorse had begun on the day after Rose's arrest on that night of mayhem, after which he knew that nothing about his life could ever be viewed in the same light again.

*

Three days after the night of the fog, Harry had found himself wandering dank streets once more, unable to settle to anything and allowing a mean-spirited drizzle settle on his new gown without troubling about it. He set off in the opposite direction from the town centre, away from all traces of the university and the chaos of the roads. The last thing he wanted was to be sequestered by an acquaintance and obliged to put on a tiresome display of bonhomie.

In due course he happened upon the new Catholic Church, and to his surprise saw that its main door was ajar. Curious about why this should be on a weekday he found himself putting his shoulder to it. He walked into a dry nave resonant with a peculiarly velvety quietness. To his astonishment, he was by no means the only visitor – perhaps thirty others were silently, separately kneeling or sitting there: women with shopping bags on the seats next to them, ladies wearing black lace head coverings, men on their knees holding themselves with straight backs as they faced the altar. He felt a gentle tap on his shoulder.

'I have a feeling we have met before,' came a gentle voice. 'It was at the house of Mr William Travers the newspaperman was it not?' the voice continued. Casting him a furtive look, Harry brought to mind the unlikely intersection one day between the priest standing in front of him now, the great editor himself, William Travers, the little servant girl at Park Terrace, Aurelia Travers in a fizz about a cake – and himself.

As though anticipating Harry's eagerness to be off as quickly as he had stumbled upon this scene, the priest immediately thrust out his hand. Harry could barely force a greeting in return – knowing himself to be unworthy, *so* unworthy of any kindness, if this was what was being offered.

'You know, we Catholics sometimes feel a little apart from the town,' continued the priest. 'But as you can see, people find peace in our church.'

There was something about the idea of such simple grace that disarmed Harry at the same time as it made him wonder whether he was about to be unpicked. Here he was in a place that – although different in tone from the interior of his own parish church – did not strike him as being particularly un-English, or an enemy of political and social justice, science and the legitimate progress of the day, as some critics would have it. This priest's welcome was so clearly genuine that he experienced a great discomfort threatening to force itself out from deeply within him – in a girl it would have been tears, he feared. 'I am a toad,' he whispered. 'I have let people down. There is no place for me amongst decent people, I'm afraid.' Without waiting for a response, he strode towards the door.

Then he sped back to the hell that Downing had become, in hot confusion, believing he had humiliated himself beyond recovery.

*

Eager for the trial to commence, local pundits were forming themselves in groups on the benches provided, devoting themselves to a variety of pre-emptive judgements as they congratulated themselves on the foresight of arriving early enough to gain a good viewing position. The court was full of people a good half an hour before the case of The Crown v Rose Whipple was due to be heard.

Meanwhile, *Mercury* man Walter Magson was in a state of grave calm. He had already won his first battle of the day. This particular case coming up was considered by his editor to be an important enough hearing for the newspaper to designate a team of four to its coverage, and Walter Magson, whose shorthand speed had recently reached an Olympian 180 words a minute, had been awarded the opening shift during which the prosecution case would be outlined. With luck, he would be able to read his own words in the early edition of *The Mercury* later, and once again after he took over from the last of the four to complete reportage of the day. He had plans to "fudge" the story to some of the London papers as well, ambitious to earn a few extra bob through that endeavour. It would depend upon how long the judge decided to sit, of course, and on how sensational a story it turned out to be. Oh, wouldn't Mildred be pleased. And she'd play her own part on her telegraph machine, too, tapping his story abroad. What a team they were.

'No smoke without fire, surely,' muttered one sage sitting in the throng behind Mrs Judith Mawkins and her small entourage, who turned as one to glare back at him.

'It's about time people heard out loud about how *innocent* girls are being taken and charged with *imaginary* faults,' said Mrs Mawkins to her companions, articulating her words carefully. Cynthia Dawes sniffed her agreement.

'Hasn't this one been at the Spinning House before, though? You can't help but wonder …' added another provocateur. They duly turned the other way to stare him down as well.

'But I'm not sure we should be too confident on Rose's behalf,' put in Cynthia Dawes.

'Why ever not?' asked Mrs Mawkins, who had been greatly inconvenienced by her housemaid's sudden removal.

'Well,' explained Cynthia. 'Just look at what Rose is charged with here: unlawfully escaping from imprisonment in the Spinning House. It doesn't mention the original charge against her, does it?'

'Well, I don't know about that,' said the landlady. She was hopping mad that her maid had been taken – *again*. What was the town coming to? In such a degrading manner, too. She had every sympathy with Rose, along with around two thirds of the spectators in that court room, according to the tenor of their voices.

'Well, I'd say there's more to this than meets the eye,' Cynthia went on while they waited for the judge to arrive, and one or two people next to them leaned towards her to hear what more a clever woman had to say.

'I ask you, what right has the University?' posed Mrs Mawkins.

'Precisely. It's going to be about rights, and the legitimacy of the Spinning House, at least in part. I do wonder what sort of organisation is so frightfully fearful of the morals of the young men in its care that it views powerless young women of the town as such a threat.'

'As though we were all of dubious character.'

'By implication, yes. As though any young girl will as a matter of course regard the proximity of a multitude of young men as fair game.'

'As though a housemaid like Rose is a *predator*.'

'As though young females were *by nature* parasitic on the colleges.'

The mounting degrees of indignation shared by this small group caused some shoulder hunching in agreement nearby, but a few arms were folded in opposition to such ideas.

Harry's perch was near the front of the arena and he continued to keep his head down. Unbeknown to him, there was another figure already present who was equally eager not to be noticed. This was Lucien Prideaux, who did not take a seat but positioned himself high up at the back of the gallery, which would offer an easy means of escape if need be. He was well aware of the potential this case had for rousing the rabble. Small wonder the University had accumulated useful legal privileges of its own against the friction that was liable to break out as a result of it, as far as he was concerned. What Prideaux feared was an eruption of civil disobedience now, regardless of the way the verdict fell. At the same time, it didn't stop him congratulating himself on the correctness of his recent foreboding concerning order in the town.

If Harry and Prideaux each had their own private reasons for attending a town court, there were two others present who also seemed to be taking an interest in the plight of Rose Whipple. Harry picked them out on one of his surreptitious glances to survey the mood of the court room, since they stood out in their Salvation Army uniforms. With a shock of unexpected recognition, he identified them from the night of the fog when they had surely been the two figures departing from an inn he found himself passing, its venomous interior as acid as the insults that pursued the pair. What could be their business here, today, he wondered. He also questioned the presence of the odd academic in a position of authority sitting incognito amongst the crowd. Were such people here to see fair play? It seemed odd to him that a humble girl accused of a rather mundane misdemeanour should attract such attention. He also marked out a gambler from Newmarket by the brash yellow neck-tie he wore. This opportunist was surreptitiously offering a less than generous book to anyone who fancied a bet, favouring the University – 'because that lot always win, don't they?' Harry instinctively pulled the collar of his jacket closer to avoid being spotted by one other who was scanning the crowd just as he was. It would be more than unfortunate if this man spotted him, since it would undoubtedly raise – or even confirm – suspicion about his reasons for attending the Assizes on this occasion. This was William Travers, who had dropped by with the intention of watching for himself the progress of a case that was guaranteed to raise public interest.

At last, pitched loudly above much pre-emptive guesswork, came the clerk's cry:

'All rise!'

It was the first time Harry had seen Rose since the incident that put her into the Spinning House for the second time. He could barely take his eyes off her now as she was led in. He noted the neutral expression on her face – what, he asked himself, did this signify about her peace of mind, or lack of it? She appeared composed, but dazedly so. And yet this was, he realised, probably the first time in her life that she might be granted an opportunity to speak up for herself. He willed her to take the witness stand if it became possible. There was support in the room for her. Let her take heart from that. The rest must be left to Providence.

And so they all stood to attention, and instantly the restless susurrus yielded to a mood of studied anticipation.

To begin with, Cynthia Dawes's equivocation proved perspicacious: the first thing the Judge did was to announce that it was his duty before the trial commenced to first determine whether *de facto* the woman in the dock was in lawful custody for a criminal offence – or not. Had Rose Whipple actually broken the law of the land as constituted? Or was whatever she had done to cause offence to the Proctor merely the "law" of the Spinning House, which was surely not on the statute books of England, as every amateur in the public gallery well knew?

How would they deal with that, then?

Very easily.

A Royal Charter signed by James 1 and dated 1645 was immediately produced and laid out, a substantial, waxy item. It had been dusted down after a long period of inertia, retrieved from the ancient annals of the university intact. It did seem to ratify the Spinning House proceedings, because there it was, in no uncertain terms: the University had been granted the powers of a "Court of Record", which permitted a discretionary period of imprisonment if a case against one arrested by a proctor was found.

'So the University can toss them into the Spinning House, then, just like that?' whispered Mrs Mawkins. 'That's a pretty pass.'

'Hush,' replied Cynthia. 'Let us see where this is to be taken.'

A few groans were heard.

Counsel for the Defence leapt to his feet and ventured to ask his lordship if he could be heard on that very point – a point which he had been instructed to press very closely, he said. His lordship declined the request, pointing at the Charter. It was there in writing. He did not propose to slow matters by permitting equivocation.

The Prosecutor soon enough seized the momentum to proceed. 'The simple issue before you,' he pronounced, pointing towards the jury, 'is this: did the defendant escape from custody from a court *lawfully constituted* – I mean that held at the Spinning House – which passed its sentence *lawfully* on the defendant on the day following her arrest? That is all you are required to consider.' He reminded the jury that it was a given fact Rose Whipple had indeed escaped from the Spinning House. His open arms aimed towards the twelve good townsmen and true plainly recommended they consider the case against Rose Whipple already proven.

Defence Counsel arose, and it was now that Walter Magson's command of shorthand came into its own as he began to jot down the man's actual words as he warned: 'I must urge the most careful consideration of what you have just heard'. There was, in his opinion, grave danger in accepting the judgement of officers of the University using such monstrous power as they clearly had. 'I repeat,' he added for good measure, 'any respectable woman in Cambridge is liable to detention and subject to insults under the power which now exists. Granted, if the power is *discreetly* exercised mistakes might be avoided. But that is not the spirit of what has happened on this occasion. On the contrary, this is how the Spinning House "law" seems to operate: it is on record that on one previous occasion, this very woman in front of you, this Rose Whipple, was detained overnight – yes, she was,' he added, to quieten a perplexed murmuring. He repeated his point for effect when the Judge called for silence in court. 'And for what?' he resumed. 'Not for any interference with a member of the University. No, it was for – as I understand it – *waving*. A waving of her hand. Yes, for waving *towards* – though not necessarily *at* – a gownsman, who *happened* to cross her path whilst an *entirely unrelated* incident was taking place nearby. What a preposterous example of over-zealous interference, I suggest, on the part of the Proctor!' A ripple of laughter went round the public gallery, regarded sternly by the Judge. 'As for this *present* charge, do you consider the accused was in *lawful* criminal custody in the Spinning House?'

At this, the judge interrupted, calling him to order. 'I must instruct you,' said his Lordship, turning to the jury, 'that the question you are asked to answer is quite simply this, and no more: did she in fact *escape* from the Spinning House. For this is the charge we, as a court of Assizes, are asked to adjudicate. Nothing else.'

The Prosecuting Attorney, in opening the case, insisted that the facts were exceedingly simple, although of an extraordinary nature. The jury was now aware of certain powers affirmed by the Royal Charter in front of the court, granted centuries ago. It gave the University this power: that any proctor, upon finding any woman about on the streets of whom he had any reasonable ground of suspicion that she was a woman of ill-fame, or anything of that nature, had the right to take such a woman to the Spinning House where she would be brought before the Vice-Chancellor shortly afterwards, usually the following morning. That gentleman would duly visit the Spinning House and he had power, under the Act, to pass sentences of up to three weeks in duration. 'The latest sentence passed upon Whipple was indeed three weeks confinement,' he affirmed – to several cries of 'Shame!' from the floor.

But while her protestations of innocence in the street on the night of the fog had fallen on deaf ears, Rose Whipple was now, as it was her right to do so, pleading not guilty. The fact was that following that escape, she had not been apprehended by a proctor. Instead, at his request two passing local constables had held her in the town's own jail for fleeing her lawful imprisonment in the Spinning House. And so, since this was no University court but a court of the land, the accused had a right for it to be heard in full.

When it came to his turn, Defence Counsel called first for the Matron of the Spinning House to testify, who duly confirmed the fact of Rose's imprisonment on that fog bound night.

'And was the charge against Miss Whipple that she was talking to a gownsman in Trinity Lane?'

'Yes, sir.'

'Was the prisoner legally represented by Counsel of any kind at the Vice-Chancellor's Court?'

'No.'

'Is this Spinning House court of the Vice Chancellor a public Court of Justice?'

'No, sir.'

'I suppose there is some sort of form about the proceedings? Of course, they take evidence upon oath?'

'No, sir. They do not.'

'They do not? Well, then, were the proceedings taken down in writing?'

'No, unless you mean the name and charge. Those appear in the Record Book.'

Defence counsel paused, directing the arc of a knowing frown towards all present, followed by a shrug at the apparent absurdity of such a process.

'Then I suppose there is a clerk where this "court" is?' he continued.

'No, sir,' answered Matron, shifting her position.

'No? *No?*' His voice developed a squeak of incredulity, eliciting a snort of laughter from the gallery. 'And next, no doubt, you will tell me there was no jury?'

'No, there wasn't sir. There never is.'

'How long did the "trial" take? Can you tell me that?'

'Perhaps ten minutes – it might be that, more or less.'

'So. You are telling me that the unfortunate woman in front of us received a sentence of twenty-one days confinement after *just ten minutes* of interrogation?'

'I don't say that, sir,' ventured the poor woman, sensing where this line of questioning might be leading and knowing that anything further she said was not destined to represent her in a particularly attractive light. 'Not in that way, sir, the way you put it. I have no say in matters there.'

Several sceptical boos were heard. The judge warned he would clear the court if there were any more interruptions.

'Well, then, and what happened next?' persisted Defence Counsel.

'Well, sir,' attempted the matron. 'On her being committed to the Spinning House that night she was taken to No. 10 cell. As I recall, she complained of a headache early the next morning and was taken downstairs into the yard which runs in front of the cells and allowed to walk there to clear her head. About a quarter past nine the one who had been minding her went out to post a letter, leaving her alone in the yard. On returning after about ten minutes she found the prisoner gone. The curtains in the chaplain's rooms had been pulled down. They reckon she must have opened the chapel door and got into the chaplain's room and out of the window.'

Concluding his cross examination of Matron, Rose's Counsel appealed to the jury that only under two conditions could the prisoner be said to have "escaped from custody". One was if she had escaped from the custody of a constable of the town's Police Force, which plainly she had not, and another if she had escaped from a proper prison. No offence, he maintained, had been committed under common law.

('Does this mean she is to be found innocent, or that this is an improper charge?' whispered Mrs Mawkins at this point to Cynthia. 'Both,' replied Cynthia. 'But it is not a straightforward matter.' She put a finger to her lips.)

There was a faint intake of breath when Rose was asked to stand for questioning and a red spot appeared on each of her cheeks.

'You have pleaded not guilty, Miss Whipple. Are you a clever girl?' the Judge asked her before cross examination commenced.

'I have no way of knowing, sir,' answered Rose in a low but composed voice, uncomplicated by emotion.

A frill of titters running round the witness stand was subdued by the judge's gavel.

'Please describe your movements on the night in question, Miss Whipple,' began her Counsel, a little more encouragingly.

'I was walking to my home and place of work at Warkworth Terrace after visiting my family at about nine o'clock in the evening when I was taken up by the Proctor in Trinity Street. The Bulldog laid his hands upon me and said: "The Proctor wants you. What are you doing out at this time of night?" I replied that I was going home, but he pushed me into a doorway.'

A gasp of protest escaped from the crowd.

'And then?'

'The Bulldog told the Proctor I had been … street walking.' Rose tried to hide her face with her arm. No one present was in any doubt that Rose had sanitised the accusation by the words she chose to use, showing not only discretion but respect for the court. A sense of silent approval may have given her courage to continue: 'People here know that ladies of the highest respectability and belonging to the best families in Cambridge have been subjected to the annoyance of these proctors, let alone a servant like myself.' A crackle of spontaneous applause could not be suppressed.

'If I hear one single word more from that gallery, I will have it cleared,' growled the judge. 'It is most indecent. You are behaving in a criminal court as if it were a theatre. Officer, the next person who interrupts, report him at once to me. Now then, please continue.'

'And so,' said Defence Counsel, alert to an opportunity to re-attach the narrative to its relevant theme, 'we have heard from the Matron of the Spinning House what happened next. Let me now put it to you: is it true that you left the Spinning House of your own accord?'

'It is, sir, and I did. But I did not pull any curtains down. I untied them.' Hoots of spontaneous laughter were immediately strangled and turned into grimaces of approval. Not one onlooker wished to be evicted from the court at this stage of the proceedings. 'Anybody would be glad to get out of that place,' continued Rose, raising her voice, 'and I would do it over again rather than spend time in that Spinning House again. I was not with any University men at all, sir. Not that night nor any other one.'

At that, the judge called for an adjournment and Harry Hobbs watched with a heavy heart as Rose Whipple was taken down. What he did not register was the swift departure of the two Salvation Army people behind a door marked "Private". This was to have important implications for the fate of Rose Whipple. And, indeed, for himself.

*

During the afternoon of Rose's trial, an hour before the weak winter light began to fade, a hunched family could be observed emerging from their squat cottage just beyond the tenements of Barnwell. The eel man bore his equipment slung across his back and it was he who pushed a handcart loaded with goods and rough victuals tied up in linen cloths to see them through their impending journey. Following him, his wife and three small children each carried their baskets and bundles and there was no conversation between them as they made their way to the landing stage near Magdalene Bridge where the barges, emptied of their wares earlier in the day, would soon be setting off back towards Ely and King's Lynn through the rich, flat fields between Cambridge and the open fen. They were hopeful of a lift back to the "island" from which they had hailed, barely two years previously.

They had not seen their eldest daughter since she had visited them on the evening of the great fog, nor had they pursued her, once news of her arrest found its way to them. Both parents were in no doubt that Rose had fallen into bad ways. It made perfect sense, given their experience of others of her age who lived nearby and gave in to the lure of the easy money that seemed to be available in abundance in this town of two parts. Though brought low by the thought of one of their own following such an accursed route, neither of them had either the wit or the desire to think beyond the shameful spectre of a scandal visiting itself on the family. Nor did they possess the confidence to question why the brightest member of the family, herself the incumbent of a respectable post at a University approved lodging house, would consider such a thing. These were people who were accustomed to clinging to the barest sinews of existence, stoking the habitual self-enclosure of those used to always fearing the worst. So they had lived according to the whim of a dark fate governing the very few certainties they held close to them, arising from a way of life where thoughts of subsistence ruled the day and each day was a predictable unit of the limited time they imagined was their lot. Since gloom was the natural, watery element flowing through his body and soul in the same way that it saturated the watery fen with its weight, the eel man lost no time in declaring that they would now return from whence they came, before the shame of his daughter caught up with them. It – *she* – was henceforth deemed to have nothing to do with them. She must not be mentioned again. After that stark decision it wasn't very hard for him to effect a complete erasure of himself, his wife and children from the face of Cambridge within little more than a few days. And here they were now, with no return envisaged. The children, underdeveloped mites whose bloodshot eyes smarted from the cold and whose noses dripped haplessly onto their rough coats, trudged incuriously behind their father, the eel man. He knew he would leave no trace, either of the camouflage of his cleverly placed traps on the banks of the Cam where it slid past the backs of the great colleges or of his temporary sojourn on the outer rim of the town. He paid his dues in full to his landlord before setting out and took from his lodging nothing with which he had not arrived. It was not for him to linger while the price of eels would dip naturally during the Christmas vacation, though it would surely rise again in the Lent term according to the demand of the discerning epicures in the Colleges for this smooth delicacy, providing someone else with the opportunity he once possessed to supply them. Good luck to them, then.

By the time of the twilight, their hunched backs might be witnessed drifting up river on the flat deck of a barge, swaying to the steady clop of the big horse pulling it and subject to the occasional sensation of being invisibly stung by a tendril of cold air displaced by a swooping bat. A crescent moon shivered on the surface of the river and the evening star rose, appearing to dart backwards and forwards across the water in front of them.

*

At the end of the day, when a guilty verdict was returned by the jury – inevitably, since the case had always rested on something of a technicality – the Judge sought fit to sum up by saying: 'I can quite understand how the prisoner came to adopt a course which, at least, was not unnatural: she merely acted from her natural desire to be free. However, I am left with no choice but to order her return to the Spinning House where she must abide by the law that put her there, and conclude her sentence. Take her down, please.'

It was then that the small voice of Rose Whipple from the dock declared, over her shoulder: 'I thought England was a free country. But I find it isn't'. Then she was seen no more.

A collective groan of disappointment went up, followed by a small shriek from one who had found the whole thing too much, together with a chorus of: 'But she never did nothing!' Those twelve good men filed out quickly with bowed heads, evidently uncomfortable about their part in a result that had a feel of incompleteness about it, though it was no more than they were bound by law to give. So it was a fractious crowd who left the scene, potentially a mob in the making, and neither Harry nor, separately, Prideaux, could fail to sense their displeasure.

Meanwhile, instinct told Walter Magson to leap up after the departure of the judge and nip round the back of the court on a small diversion of his own in search of a quote from the foreman of the jury. He was not to be wholly disappointed. But that man would only stop long enough to inform him: 'We wished to protest that the Vice-Chancellor's court, as now constituted, needs revision, but it was not allowed,' before slinking off. This, Walter surmised, must have been the nub of the essential question that Defence Counsel had attempted to put to the judge before the proceedings got going in his attempt to get the case thrown out before it started, which the judge had refused to hear. Hearing this, Walter lost no time in a singular dash back to *The Mercury* to write up his final contribution that day for *The Mercury* – and also to transmit a version of it, post haste, up to London.

*

That evening, Lucien Prideaux, seeking to take refuge once more in his friend Travers's downstairs study in the house on Park Terrace, as he so often did when there was a situation brewing, was alarmed to find this mildest of men back home already – and in high dudgeon. 'It is humiliating,' announced Travers. 'It is as if we are being judged and found wanting in the matter of whether we are capable of running a police force like any other reputable town!'

*

In London that evening, in the smoky office where he had been awaiting it, and thanks to Mildred Dobbs's dexterity with the telegraph, the great editor received news of the Rose Whipple case from a copy boy and set about what he was famed for: turning a story into an issue through careful magnification, much generalisation and not a little high-handed rhetorical speculation. Echoing the indignation of the public was one of his particular journalistic gifts, enabling him to point the matter in a certain direction by questioning the frailty of justice and pursuing the matter of a court's vulnerability to its own tainted version of morality – pushing aside, for the moment, the matter of rampant immorality on the streets of Cambridge. He had spotted something about this case that offered much bigger pickings: a situation ripe for a new battle about power and authority. Of course, it was all about power, after all. This University, he began to think, could conceivably find its autonomy squeezed brutally if enough protests were made. 'Pressure of space prevents us from commenting at any length upon this case,' he jotted, when he had fuelled his own indignation by summarising the nuts and bolts of the proceedings. 'But the action of the University against this girl of 19 – an age when many of our daughters have hardly left school – has transformed this girl from an "unfortunate" to a "martyr".' He paused for a moment, warming to his theme. 'The gulf between the University and the town is today broader than ever it has been and nothing in the semblance of friendship can again exist under the present circumstances.' There. See how that would be received.

He paused once more, frowning and twiddling his pencil.

I shall call it "An Academic Star Chamber," he decided. What a case! Because of an outdated Charter, of course the judge's hands were tied from the outset, turning the jury into mere pawns in a disgraceful game. But people do not react well to being duped. Surely this roasting of a servant girl on the altar of "justice" might bring about change one day. As a self-proclaimed agent of change, his appetite was only whetted for further action. He was more than ready to light the touch paper to that.

*

Would that Rose herself could read such a peroration, thought Harry as he scanned the London press the following day, searching for signs of his own words that must surely form some of the tinder beneath the great editor's fire. At his own expense Harry had telephoned an impromptu report from the machine in the Porter's Lodge at Downing, calling himself "A Bystander" but adding his name in brackets in the hope that the great editor might one day be persuaded to recall his promise to look favourably on another attempt at journalism on his part. For despite the trauma of the last few days' distractions, there was a residue of determination within him to make something, however paltry, of the scant amount of self-respect he was left with. If effort was required, then he would make it. As would Walter Magson for his own reasons, though they were wholly unaware of each other's role in the business. At the bottom of the article in the London newspaper, Harry was gratified to spot that the great editor had seen fit to give out a word or two of anonymous credit, thanking "our local correspondent" for the information. Neither Harry nor Walter were ever any the wiser that there had, in fact, been two of them on the case.

*

The very next day, fresh letters were brought in on the hour for the attention of both the editor and the proprietor of *The Mercury*.

'I think we have a case here, Gilbert,' said William Travers at last. 'Do we run with it?' Overt intervention was not, until this point, the modus operandi of *The Mercury* – it had always considered itself a slow spin bowler rather than a bare knuckle boxer. Given the weight of the outrage and its persistence – and influenced by the fact that his friend in London had lost no time in taking a stand – William Travers now veered to the opinion that a rip tide might be building out there on the streets.

'Well, sir, to be the *vox populi* is what appears to be required by these communications, I'd say,' said his editor. Using the tip of his pencil he stirred the pile of letters they had just finished reading, nudging them back towards his employer.

Who hesitated, yet.

'You know, Gilbert, we have always striven to report – and I say *report*, not fulminate, not bluster – matters of interest to *all* our readers. Tell me, what proportion of these letters are on the side of the servant girl?'

'All but two.'

'Do we enter the fray, then, on behalf of all those who have been wrongly apprehended? Is this what you are suggesting? Do we embroil ourselves in agitation and mischief? I do not feel comfortable with too much sensation, you know. It feels irresponsible, to my way of thinking.'

Gilbert made an inward smile to himself. He had never thought the genial proprietor was a newspaperman as he would define it but – to give him credit – the governor was always astute enough to be guided by those who were. 'How about we simply print 'em, then, in the first instance,' he advised. 'Make a spread of 'em, and let people make up their own minds?'

And so they did.

*

'Oh, goodness gracious me!' shrieked Aurelia – and it should be noted that at that exact same moment a similar (though much riper) expostulation was being made in the kitchen below by Cook, drawing a startled Bernadette to her side to bend over the early edition and its report of the conclusion of Rose Whipple's trial. Half a dozen papers had been left for the family not ten minutes previously, just as they were every day, and it was the time of the morning when servants as well as gentle folk were used to pause to read the news in their own quarters with a cup of coffee and a freshly baked bun.

'Whatever is the matter, dear?' said Alice Travers. 'Has someone died?'

Hope Bassett hovered nearby. A frown of concentration crossed her face when she caught sight of the headline.

'Look! Look here!' cried Aurelia. 'They've devoted a whole two pages to letters addressed to the editor,' said Aurelia.

'I'm not sure this is quite the stuff for family reading,' said Alice when she began to absorb such raw emotions laid bare. 'What does father think?'

'I'm sure I don't know.' None of them had seen a great deal of William during the frenzy of the trial and the shock of its outcome.

'But I don't understand why they are making such a fuss. See, there's barely any letter from someone who thinks otherwise.'

Hope and Alice exchanged a look. 'Let us try to keep an open mind about girls who are led into bad ways,' said Alice. 'Their lives are so very different from ours, as we know from our visits to their neighbourhood. They are mostly poor and foolish, Aurelia.'

'And they have been causing proper young women much inconvenience lately,' added Aurelia. 'Foolish? Indeed, yes. We can be in no doubt now that this one was taken once before. Surely, this must be cause for suspicion?'

'Well, beware of making hasty judgements,' urged her mother. 'Remember, judgement upon the charge made against her has now been passed, in a court of law. But not for anything other than escape.'

'Wait a minute, mother. Listen to this.' Aurelia proceeded to read out loud a letter she had selected.

"Sir,

Let us indeed not lose haste to rally against the somewhat sentimental appeasement of the evil behaviour of local women. But could not the doings of such as these be dealt with better by our own constables? Mrs EH."

'Someone sounds as though they have worked themselves up into a foam!'

Hope, gliding nearer so she could see the page in question for herself, pointed to another of the letters, which read:

"I have no wish to encourage prostitution; but I want to feel that my wife, and lady members of my family, when walking out, are not in danger of being brought before our 'Varsity "Star Chamber". Surely, it is high time that the people of Cambridge rally for their independence! Why should we remain subjected to the caprice of the Vice Chancellor and his minions?"

'There you have it,' said Alice. 'I do believe it is not really about Rose Whipple at all any more. It's to do with whose authority should be paramount when it comes to the women of Cambridge – that of the proctors or that of our town's Police Force.' She frowned, before adding: 'It is the word "rally" that worries me a little.' She scrutinized these two letters again. 'It sounds like a cry for rebelliousness. I wonder, are those who approved this page prepared to take responsibility for the kind of restlessness such a comment might produce? Goodness knows, history tells us that people here are known to be volatile when there is disagreement between the town and the University.'

'Or anything that exposes flagrant injustice, perhaps?' added Hope.

'Probably. I dare say that's what it does amount to. We must be vigilant, Aurelia, especially during the next few days. It is a blessing that the Christmas vacation will no doubt put a stop to any immediate trouble.'

'Do you think it is likely to go away, though?' said Aurelia. 'Perhaps the situation has become like, oh, like a persistent outbreak of hives that must be scratched, even if common sense cautions otherwise.'

'Well. We shall have to see,' said Alice. 'The whole affair makes me uneasy. Let us not talk about it anymore.'

'What will happen to the girl?' pressed Aurelia.

'She was committed to return to the Spinning House,' said Alice, ringing for Bernadette to take away their used cups. 'Not for any moral lapse this time – if we choose to believe her – but for the lesser offence of escaping from custody. She will be released in a few days time, no doubt.'

As indeed she was.

*

During the remaining days of Rose's imprisonment in the Spinning House Harry suffered greatly, knowing her to be there without reason or true justice. Continuing to interrogate himself, he came to believe that he had crossed the boundary of his own understanding of morality. A sense of uncomfortable shame made him question whether he could remain in his familiar life when there were so many intractable loose ends. He could think of no solution to his worries. Should he run? He dared to confide in only one friend, Sidney Beaumont, the poor student of theology who lodged at Warkworth Terrace along with Arthur Moody and Cynthia Dawes. It would have been jollier to talk to Francis, no doubt but Harry's distress was too close for comfort to *The Mercury*, in whose pages the ghastly process of Rose's trial had just been laid bare. And, by association, to the house on Park Terrace, a location containing both Aurelia Travers and Hope Bassett, two of the women he believed he had compromised. He would miss those pleasant evenings at the Travers's, but to present himself there again would, he felt sure, be simply wrong. Consequently, desperate to hear the sound of his own voice after much solitary soul searching, Harry went in pursuit of someone and eventually found Sidney sitting on his trunk in the Porter's Lodge, hoping for a lift to the station from anyone going that way.

'Might I delay you for no more than five minutes, old chap?' asked Harry.

'Well, I am about to be off, as you can see. Otherwise …' The anguish on Harry's face left Sidney in no doubt of the necessity of agreeing to this last minute request, despite its inconvenience. 'Come on, then, let's take a turn round the court.'

Harry readily set off by his side and quickly summarised his part in the two incidents which had been the catalysts of Rose's downfall.

Sidney gave the story his grave attention. Part of it he knew about already – the part regarding the earlier debacle in the wake of a ribald scene on the street involving a local madam. But not this latest development on the night of the fog which had, according to Harry, precipitated the whole awful business of the public trial.

'Hold on a minute,' interrupted Sidney, raising a hand. 'It was *your* gown and scarf that Prideaux had in his possession, then?'

'It was, and I wish I could apologise for putting you and all those other fellows under suspicion,' said Harry. 'It can't have been comfortable.'

'I wouldn't concern yourself about that,' said Sidney. 'It is sure to go down in the folklore of our college and I will not breathe a word of it. So you will remain a shadowy figure hereafter, dear boy, don't worry. A ghost of history, if such a tale is told – forever unnamed!'

'This is no laughing matter,' Harry reminded him.

'Of course not. But can you not permit yourself – if not some mild levity at the more absurd aspects of the matter, then at least a less agitated assessment of your own part in it?'

This was not what Harry had hoped to hear. He wanted wrath, he wanted punishment, he wanted a scourge to be applied to his overheated conscience. He wanted ostracism, he wanted exile, even, for his shabby behaviour. Just as long as none of it was delivered by Prideaux and learned about subsequently by the people he loved.

'Listen,' Sidney persisted, touching his arm. 'I don't believe you have been guilty of anything much at all. On the first occasion, it was a case of mistaken identity. I mean, did you *deliberately* hail Rose out on the street? No, you did not. On the second, as you say, it was a fog that placed you in her path – the hand of nature itself. If you want to blame anyone, blame the mistaken zeal of the Proctor. Both times.'

'It's not quite as straightforward as that,' said Harry. 'Come on, you must surely admit that I am more of a toad than a man, Sidney, because each time, you know, I might have come forward and provided vindication for her.'

'Yes, but only by implicating yourself, with disproportionately fatal results, hmm? They would have no choice but to make a charge against you of behaving in a loose way yourself. Do you suppose any proctor would believe for one instant that an undergraduate did *not* have an ulterior motive for waving towards a girl on the street? You would never have been believed – how would you prove it? The onus would have been on you to do so. And what next? He would have reported you to our College. You would be sent down, without question. Your family would be exposed, by association. The stain of it could never be removed. And in any case they would still arrest the girl.'

Harry bowed his head.

'No – let me continue … And so you bump into a girl on the street on a foggy night. You have no clue whose body it is that touches yours – only that you can't see it, through no fault of your own. You can barely anticipate its closeness to your own, even as it shuffles towards you. Tell me, then, what must you feel guilty about in the second instance? Being out after dark without your gown is one thing, but they would have had you for soliciting a woman of the streets, once again. That is how these people proceed. You must have known that, Harry, when you took flight that night. And once again she would have been taken, regardless.'

'You should be a lawyer, Sidney. I wish I could let it go at that. But you know I can't. Not when *I* can get away with outwitting those people, but *she* never stood a chance.'

'So poor Rose is your responsibility? Is what you are suggesting? Or is it more about the discrepancy of your standing in the world compared with hers that really troubles you?' (As a poor student, Sidney knew a bit about the matter of "standing", and how the sensitivity of his fellows ensured it was rarely spoken about in his presence.)

'Perhaps,' said Harry, unable to progress his point any further. 'Look, I just wish for some sort of justice to be done, even at this late stage.'

'So maybe you will come out and appeal to our friend the newspaper proprietor to take up arms against a system riddled with injustice? I admire you if you are a true reformer. I never had you down for one, I must say.'

Harry shrugged.

'Well then, we navigate our way the best we can with the tools available to us,' suggested Sidney. 'That's what we do. It's all we can do.'

'And that's just it. With deepest respect, my friend, you and I know that just as I have a few more tools at my disposal than you, Sidney – no, let me say it – there is no doubt that I have many, many more than Rose Whipple will ever possess. It places her at such a disadvantage in these unfortunate matters, don't you see, and so vulnerable to injustice?' Harry began to feel that he was on the brink of something, that his words – the very utterance of them – were opening a kind of channel in his mind whose churning elements he must try to navigate towards a smoother, more reasonable flow.

By now, they had almost completed their walk and the Porter's Lodge containing Sidney's trunk stacked against an inside wall was in sight. Harry shuddered, and began to feel embarrassed about saying so much.

But Sidney was not quite finished.

'Go home,' he urged. 'Enjoy Christmas with your family. It will have blown over by the time we come back.'

They shook hands in a more sombre manner than usual. Harry did not relish going home at all and had not yet troubled himself to pack his bags. He felt that his ardent sense of obligation towards his father had suffered damage, through nobody's fault but his own, and an oppressive feeling began to encircle him again.

*

'Whipple? Pay attention. Folk are here to fetch you.'

Rose put down her work at the table she had shared in the Spinning House that morning with five other detainees during the final day of her imprisonment. Who could "they" be? Mrs Mawkins had already been to deliver her belongings to the Spinning House the day after the trial and, such as they were, they had been locked away by Matron, pending her release. She had no expectation of a family visit, guessing accurately the minds of those who had bred her and hardening her heart against the sadness this caused. So who was this? Surely not Bernadette, the little maid at the Travers's: no young woman would be so foolish as to present herself at this place. Miss Dawes and Miss Meadows, then? She'd spotted them from the dock and was touched by their presence, which had caught her by surprise. Could it be one of them? They needn't have troubled themselves, they certainly didn't have to come, and those ladies would not have been there out of prurient curiosity. Then whoever else was there? Fetching her for what?

It wasn't long before she found out. A grave-faced young woman accompanied by a short, ordinary looking man – both of them in Salvation Army uniform – advanced towards her, and she stood up to make a small curtsey, which was waved aside by both of them. 'There,' said Matron, watching this take place with her arms folded, standing under the draughty door arch of the dayroom. 'You are one of the fortunate ones, Whipple. You should be grateful.' Did she not already know that gratefulness was as natural as politeness to Rose? But grateful for what, this time, when she'd lost her job, her livelihood, her family and her reputation?

The Salvation Army people drew her to the side of the room where they could attempt a semi-private conversation in whispers. If Rose agreed, she would be taken to London with them, explained the lady, to a special house where she would be given board and lodging in return for light work, and where time would be made available for her "rehabilitation". Whilst none of this made a great deal of sense to Rose, neither did it necessarily raise doubts. In fact, when that word "taken" was spoken – so softly, so gently, by the young lady – she felt as though a blanket infused with curative properties was being thrown round her shoulders in her time of need. It made her feel as though the whole burden of these cruel, bewildering circumstances was rising, like yeast, to the surface of her consciousness, prior to a new incarnation where degrees of safety might await her. What a thought, though. It belonged more to the realm of dreams, surely.

They talked to her for about fifteen minutes, during which time she occasionally nodded to show she was following their words. Well, they could do what they liked with her. It made little difference. She had no future otherwise, as far as she could see. They seemed kindly. That was quite sufficient. There was nothing left for her in Cambridge. It had proved to be a most severe place, where mercy was lacking.

While they spoke, she recalled seeing Mrs Mawkins, for the first time unable to look at her squarely. It was when that lady had brought Rose's small case containing all of her worldly goods to the Spinning House. With great reluctance, the landlady had explained, she could not have her back at Warkworth Terrace despite Rose being the best of maids, because the University had told her it would remove her license if she harboured one who had not once, but twice, been shut up in that Spinning House prison. No, agreed Rose with the trace of a sigh, of course that would not be possible. 'I have slipped a little something extra into your bag, my dear. You do not deserve what they've done to you. I never for one moment believed any of it, you know.' For a fleeting moment Rose found herself in the peculiar position of offering a kind of comfort to her ex-employer, who had a few choice words regarding proctors and bulldogs and the University itself in a final show of awkward solidarity with the girl. 'Just look at your hands,' remarked Judith Mawkins at last, taking one of Rose's in her own and scrutinising the red blisters and cracked nails. 'If I could make them better …' But of course she could not. Even the best people have limits to their courage as well as their generosity. Rose bore no grudge towards any of them. Not even her persecutors. What would such aggravation profit her?

So the Salvation Army people took her away with them, the man carrying her case and the lady wrapping a simple shawl around her worn coat. 'Come along, then, Rose, we have a long journey ahead of us.'

At the appointed time, the door of the Spinning House opened to release Rose Whipple for the final time. She prepared to leave it, and her life in Cambridge, without a backward glance.

That station was a-buzz with activity when Rose and her two benefactors arrived for the London train. Porters were shouting at each other in their own private language as their trollies ferried the baggage of the last of the University people leaving for the Christmas vacation towards one or other of its two platforms. No-one gave the three figures a second glance. Rose pulled her hat down as far as it would go because it was cold, and if her eyes glittered that was because it was cold, too. Freezing. But she couldn't help thinking what a thing it was that she, of all people, had landed up here on the edge of the real world as it was known to her, facing an entirely unknown future for the second time in her short life.

On the train to London she found herself recalling her other train journey, her mission to deliver a letter to Mr Hobbs – from his sweetheart, Miss Aurelia, she supposed at the time. The excitement of using a train for the first time in her life – one which was going in the opposite direction to this one she was riding presently – it all seemed so very far away, and belonged to summer's simple pleasures. This image led her to a recollection of poor Mr Hobbs and the sight of his terrified eyes on the night of the fog when a whistle blew and she told him (*she* told *him*!) to be off. How topsy-turvy everything was. It was for the best, though, that gut reaction of hers on the night in question: she still believed this, despite all she had suffered as a result. There was no point in him being disgraced as well as her, because he had so much further to fall, to be sure. And he was a decent enough young man, to her knowledge, and she had not met many who were that.

So she had submitted, making little protest when they escorted her back to that dreadful Spinning House once more, where she attempted to re-iterate her innocence, just as she'd done the first time. But it was all too plain to her that she was nowhere near being a candidate for any sort of consideration. It was, after all, the second time that they had written her name in the Record Book.

Nevertheless, she was overcome by a fit of nervous sobbing when she was put down for the night in that place again, after being sworn at by another girl in the room for waking her up. Coarseness upon injustice upon humiliation … it all took its toll in a good weep on that horribly foggy night. But perhaps this was for the best, too, because instead of resisting the damp and cold as she had done in such a futile way the first time she was there, her exhausted limbs gradually gave way after such an outpouring, and she was able to sleep.

But I cannot stay here. This was her conviction on waking to the muffled, overlapping sound of a number of morning bells in the semi-darkness outside, heralding another day. *And I will not.*

*

On the last night he was to pass in Cambridge, Harry dreamed they were not only crowding in upon him again but this time preparing to pounce. One or two – including his tutor, Lucien Prideaux – were clamouring for answers about his failure to turn up to appointments during the last week of term. Fingers were being pointed regarding his unexplained non-appearance at a rather delightful sounding evening of musical entertainment which he had been invited to attend (and had accepted) with the Travers, *en famille*. An explanation was surely owed, too, after he failed to turn up to one last steamy evening in the Fountain with his close friends before they all went their own ways. And perhaps most of all, answers would be required when he faced his father. This hideous set of failures began to bear down upon him – *like Pelion on Ossa*, as the fearsome Prideaux would have said, no doubt. Bad decisions, mean evasions, feeble wavering: it was all starting to rebound on him with a vengeance. He could see no way out. It was all up.

And yet, however much he squirms he remains a young, healthy, potentially resourceful human being, capable of taking on despair and at least wrestling with it. *What about Rose?* Those three words impose themselves on his frenzy of regret with great clarity, only to be repeated, as if in one last clarion call to his conscience: Well, then, what *about* Rose? With everything finished –his self-respect, any sort of future in Cambridge – there was, of course, *nothing left to lose any more*, he told himself, startled by how obvious this was. Therefore, he determined, I shall make it my business to do something for *her*, at least, without delay. It wouldn't absolve him of the ramifications of his cowardice, of course – that would continue to shame him for some time yet – but he began to wonder whether Sidney Beaumont had been partially correct in suggesting that both he and the girl had been victims of an implacable system, voracious in its rule over them, which still could – and would, if it so chose – devour them like maggots.

What about Rose, then? Why, he must seek her out, see what reparation he could make, at the very least.

If he managed to ferret out her current whereabouts, there would be nothing left to prevent him making his own escape.

*

It did not take much sleuthing to track Rose down. Employing all the charm he could muster he teased it out of the landlady at Warkworth Terrace by assuring her that all he wanted was to make sure Rose had a little provision for her well-being. The place was empty of lodgers once more, yet sprays of holly were strewn across the mantelpiece in the front parlour reminding him of approaching Christmas, one he knew now for a certainty that he would miss at home.

'You look tight about the face, Mr Hobbs,' she observed, eyeing him. 'You must be the last University man to leave Cambridge.'

'I have been suffering from a cold,' he lied. But from that point on his honesty was sincere.

'I will not detain you longer than necessary,' he assured her. 'But I need to know what has happened to Rose, where she is gone.'

She eyed him with suspicion, though she'd always had a soft spot for this particular young man.

'Please help me to do something worthwhile for Rose,' he found himself pleading. 'I guarantee that she is innocent in every way. I only want to help.'

Bit late now, he could sense the landlady thinking, from the tilt of her head. But eventually she acquiesced, rummaging in the drawer of a sideboard in the hallway and coming up with a piece of paper bearing the Salvation Army insignia. 'You'd better copy this down, then.'

From that point onward he was in the grip of a strange sense of propulsion, as though he had stepped onto a moving conveyor belt whose destination was no longer entirely within his power to manage, leaving him less with a depleted will than a sense that he might be embarking on a re-configuration of his own destiny. Just how quixotic such a trajectory might turn out to be he refused to entertain because he knew that his mission ran the risk of not being completed if he allowed himself to dawdle in indecision and prolong those other black thoughts of late. Also, disgrace was now sniffing at his heels ever closer, and that was another incentive to take action.

Onward, then.

*

Harry deposited his trunk in a locker at Liverpool Street Station after a journey passed mentally composing appropriate words and useful phrases in preparation for several difficult letters he knew he must set about dispatching without delay. Maybe he would sit down in the Great Eastern Hotel that very night for the purpose. But first he had a destination to seek out. As it happened, it was not far away.

London must be a permanently smoky place he decided on this, his second visit to the city. The air had a hollow, rubbery feel to it, its heaviness oozing melancholy, and a sleety downpour was in progress.

He set out on foot for the address he had taken down from Mrs Mawkins. When he interrupted a street cleaner to ask the way he was told: 'Ah, you'll be meaning what they call Hope House, sir.' Indeed, a few minutes later there it stood: a gaunt, square building of three stories built solidly of soot blackened bricks with a placard announcing itself as the Hanbury Street Rescue Home.

He took the brightly polished brass door knocker in his hand and rapped three times. A rap is like a calling card, he mused while he waited, hoping his had sounded polite and tentative rather than arrogant or demanding, as some raps can.

Footsteps could be heard padding down a long internal corridor, and when the door opened he was confronted by a woman carrying in her right hand a small bonnet trailing white ribbons. She still smelled of the cold of the street and was busy unbuttoning her blue felt cape to reveal a brown linen uniform finished off with a scarlet collar and cuffs. Her floor length apron was so white, Harry noticed, that it gave the impression of illuminating the duskiness of the hallway. She smiled at him with a brisk confidence he was generally unused to in women (though, come to think of it, Cynthia Dawes had surely been an exception to that), shook his hand firmly and ushered him in. He supposed these were the ways of working women, a breed of whom he had no experience whatsoever apart from those who were employed in service of one type or another. From now on, he decided, I am in *terra incognita* and must pay careful attention.

She led him into a small room which had the appearance of an office, where a colourful curtain adorned a single high, small window on the world outside. This, he surmised, was surely a place where such women as the one in front of him could command some influence.

'So what can I do for you, sir?'

He introduced himself and came straight to the point. 'I am a friend of one who is living here, I believe. And I have come here on her behalf.'

Again, as had been the case with Mrs Mawkins, Harry was surveyed, if not with outright suspicion then with a gaze of doubtful scrutiny.

'For what purpose, may I ask?'

'I am not yet sure. But I mean to be of help to her. She has been treated abominably, you know. She is entirely innocent of that for which she was charged.'

The woman retrieved a last hat pin from her hair.

'Are you aware of what we do here?' she asked, side-stepping his request.

'I am not sure.'

'We have a mission,' she told him. 'That mission is to take in and protect young women who have been exploited by men. There are many of them, you know. A great many.' She searched his face for a reaction. 'Are you such a man?'

'What?' spluttered Harry, succumbing to the provocation. 'Absolutely not. I am a Cambridge undergraduate who, on account of bumping into a servant girl I knew from the house where a few of my colleagues lodge – in thick fog, I may say – was the unwitting reason for her arrest as … as a woman of the night. I want more than anything to put matters right.'

'And how would you propose to do that?'

Something about her demeanour, which he summed up as a blend of intelligence and brisk compassion of a practical sort, encouraged him to confide some of the thoughts that had raged in his mind lately in words for the first time.

'I wish I knew. I think I shall know if I can speak to her. At the very least, I have some money I can put at her disposal. It has been weighing on my mind.'

She smiled briefly. 'You must be talking about Rose Whipple, then. She was brought from Cambridge the other day.'

'Yes! That is right. Oh, she is as sweet and hard-working and honest as the day is long. You probably know that already.'

'I think we do, sir, though she has only been here for a short while. Well. I think that first of all I should like to show you round our house. We are often misunderstood, and it is important you know how Rose is being kept. It may help you form an opinion of what is best for her.'

He followed willingly.

As they walked, she explained that the Salvation Army was known for its "visitations" here in the East End of London, the way its people knocked randomly on the doors of the hovels hereabouts offering to tend to those brought low by the fevers and diseases which were rife, thanks to the poor conditions in which they lived.

These doughty visitors were equally willing to set about scrubbing floors themselves if need be, or doing a bit of tidying for tired women grown hopeless, through their mission to make the conditions of those less fortunate a little more palatable. Harry had a fleeting vision of Alice Travers and her baskets of provisions taken to the denizens of Barnwell in Cambridge, though he couldn't quite imagine her getting her hands dirty in this way. He began to warm to the Salvation Army lady. She didn't mince her words and he admired that. How delicate, yet hard as steel, was the armour of her faith, making it possible, he surmised, to undertake such work and the churlishness of the streets that she navigated. Such exceptional endurance, he thought, was what he had caught a glimpse of in Cambridge on the night when fog obscured all but an outline of two Salvation Army figures he spotted as they left an inn they had been visiting. He also remembered thinking at the time how galling it must be to be ridiculed and insulted for such generosity of spirit on the part of those who persisted in pitting themselves against the grain of low behaviour in places like that.

She opened a door on the first floor to reveal what seemed to be a huge dormitory, full of several neat rows of – coffins. A small gasp escaped him.

'Don't worry,' she said. 'This is where our women sleep. See those boxes? They each have a mattress filled with seaweed. It is a light and soft place of rest. And see the covering? It's a leather sheet with a strap to tie around the neck to prevent it falling off. *No-one* is cold here. That in itself is a blessing for many.'

'Ingenious!' cried Harry.

Another room was dedicated to light industry and he was permitted to stand by the door which she opened a crack so that he could see what was going on in there. 'Those who come in from the streets, they sew and they knit, and the trifles they make are sold to pay for their board and lodging.' A soft hum of discrete murmuring merged with the whirring and click-clack of various needles.

'They are allowed to talk?'

'Why should they not be? Do you think we should be in the business of punishing people? Quite the reverse. It's very simple, if I my say so: this is a place of safety for young women, most of whom have never experienced such a thing before. They receive love and support and help to earn their own living. Then they will be able to return to respectable society as a part of it.'

'A haven.'

'Perhaps. Hopefully. Some of them have never received so much as a kind word in their lives and don't know how to cope with it. It makes them appear rough, like corrupted bits of metal. Oh, they have learned how to be devious, many of them. They are not attractive to people of worth in the community – even less to some who just manage to keep their heads above water, who would have them further brutalised. But you see, Mr Hobbs, we are not interested in their sins. Only in the sinners themselves, and our work is helping them rid themselves of the evil in their lives.'

'So they are not locked up?'

'No. They are free to leave here at any time.'

As the door was pulled to he thought he caught a glimpse of Rose – those black, anxious eyes – but he wasn't sure.

The Salvation Army woman led him back to the front door. 'Come back tomorrow,' she told him. 'Then we shall see what might be done for Rose Whipple.'

Was he being tested? Would he be found worthy of talking to Rose, even for a minute, in order to discharge his most immediate duty and pass over to her some of the money he had accrued after selling his entire collection of books and all his other belongings, back in Cambridge? He hoped he would be able to conduct himself properly.

*

'Do you know how easy it is to buy a child in this city?'

It was the following day, and Harry found himself helping two of the Salvation Army "Slum Sisters," both possessors of red cheeks and brisk smiles, to load boxes of the "trifles" he had seen in the making the day before onto a cart. The woman who had talked to him the day before was now addressing him in front of the front door of Hope House, with her arms folded and her cloak drawn close. As it happened, Harry, along with a large, scandalised readership, was partially aware of the unthinkable vulnerability of ragamuffin children thanks to the machinations of the great editor himself, who had outrageously "bought" one such girl himself when she was still a child in order to prove how easy it was to do so, and then told all about it via his newspaper. This entirely new sort of journalism fascinated him, but its appeal, he realised, could turn

184

out to be in inverse proportion to the sympathy it was meant to engender, and he wondered whether such investigations merely served to titillate, while callously exploiting its hapless subjects. But –

'Rose isn't a child,' he responded.

'No, but she is young, and on her own, it seems.'

'She has me to fight for her.'

'Do you know what you are saying?'

'I am willing to take responsibility for her.'

'Oh, big words, Mr Hobbs.'

'And I mean them.'

She cast an eye over her shoulder. Rose was at that point passing from one room to another across the corridor.

'Rose!' he called out. 'It is me! Come and speak to me!'

'No need to be impetuous. Let us see first what the girl wants. It would do you good to remember that no man has done much for her so far, beyond letting her down.'

They re-entered the building and this time, when she allowed him to stand by the open doorway of the room where the girls were once again at work, she did not interrupt when Rose herself, about to return to her chair, turned to face him, with a hot flush on her cheeks when she saw who it was.

'Mr Hobbs, what the devil are you doing here?' she managed to blurt out before staring at the floor in extreme embarrassment.

'I have come for you, Rose' (no point in beating about the bush, explanations could be worked out later).

'Come for me? For what purpose?'

'I have left Cambridge,' announced the ex-undergraduate. 'I have a few matters still to attend to, but I am free to offer my services to you. I am only too aware that great wrong has been done to you and that I have played a part in it. Through no design of my own, but nevertheless …'

She raised her eyes and looked at him full in the face. And laughed out loud.

'Please, Rose, hear me out.' He turned to her keeper, who was smiling at this unexpected turn. He felt like a schoolboy, but persisted. 'May Rose and I go for a short walk?'

'Rose?'

Rose had no idea what to make of this, but she made a small nod so the Salvation Army woman told her to collect her coat and to make sure to be back in time for evening prayers.

*

They strolled side by side in thoughtful silence at first, both of them alive to unfamiliar sounds magnified by the oppressive closeness of buildings each side of cobbled streets and alleyways. The grinding squeal of a procession of carts bearing a troupe of street entertainers shouting at all who passed to mind out or they would be squashed obliged Harry to take Rose's arm and place it in his own, further guarding her passage with a walking stick he had brought along with him. A sudden flurry of bare-footed chalk-faced children flitted here and there like starlings, their hands reaching out for pennies but not always lingering in hope of a response. Fearful of an ear-boxing if instant returns were not forthcoming, these urban urchins would disappear as quickly as they had materialised, Harry was beginning to perceive. Was Barnwell – that awful part of Cambridge that had consumed him for a dark hour or two not so long ago – like this during daylight hours? No, thought Harry, this is chaos on a meaner scale altogether. Even the apparently permanent layer of hovering smog seemed more acrid than the one he and Rose had been caught out by in Cambridge. It would be true to say that each of them was partially struck dumb by the strangeness of their situation and the many sights assailing them in this city. So they walked a little stiffly, until they reached a groyne by the enormous river's new embankment and leaned against a wall, watching flotillas of small boats coming and going and inhaling the bitter smell of the sea on the incoming tide.

'Well, Rose,' began Harry, who had prepared the first part of his intended speech. 'First of all I would like to ask you to forgive me, if you can find it in your heart, for not stopping with you when the proctor pounced.'

'But it was I who told you to run, as I recall.'

'Please allow me to say what I need to say. I have suffered dreadfully lately for my cowardice, you know, and I want to put it right.'

'Truly, there is no need, Mr Hobbs. I wish you wouldn't think like that.'

'I am sorry. There. I have said it.'

'Very well. If it makes you feel better.'

186

'But it is you who should be made to feel better, Rose. I believe that it is my duty to help you.'

She looked askance at him.

'I'm sorry. That sounded patronising.'

'To be sure, you have no obligation to me.'

'I have put my studies behind me,' he continued.

'More fool you, then.'

He let that pass. 'What I am trying to say is that I came away with enough money from the sale of my belongings to be able to make a plan for what I might do next.'

'I am pleased to hear it. It is nothing to do with me.'

'Might you be persuaded to just hear me out, Rose? First of all' – he delved in the pocket of his great coat where he had stored a brown envelope – 'I want you to have this'.

Her cheeks turned an angry red as her eyes squarely pierced his own. To his own discomfort, he caught sight of her fear, mingled with what he put down to mild disgust.

She took the envelope, opened it, briefly surveyed the contents (he had raised a sum of five pounds for this purpose) and firmly held it out to him.

'What makes you think I would take money from a gentleman?'

'Oh, Rose, I am your friend.' At the same time, he belatedly recognised her point and felt bound to accept the return of his offering, chiding himself for clumsiness and insensitivity. It occurred to him that to be a man at all he only too easily risked being perceived a potential menace to women, whatever his motives. *Toad.*

'We had better set off back to Hope House,' said Rose by and by, taking his arm once again. By now a residue of peachy sunlight lying low on the horizon began to dapple the river in a florid display. They were alerted to the time by the start of an exodus of vehicles to outlying villages from the City nearby, accompanied by much racket and rumbling.

'Mind now,' she said to him at one point, absorbing his thoughtful mood as she nudged his knee so he would not tread in a mound of horse droppings left to steam. No more was said as they walked back to Hope House. Harry was invited in to take part in an evening service punctuated by rousing hymns that he was able to join in with the required gusto, knowing them of old. Rose thought it was sweet to watch him adding his enthusiasm to that of the residents and staff. Then he set off back to a gentler sort of hospitality altogether at the Great Eastern Hotel, with nothing resolved.

*

Meanwhile, back in Cambridge a few days after this, another chilly morning was getting underway. In the house on Park Terrace, Hope Bassett did not appear to flinch even though a conversation between Aurelia and her mother was beginning to take an ominous turn. She listened with one ear cocked towards them, a pen poised in her hand.

'My darling, think of it as an adventure,' offered Alice. 'I wish that I had had your opportunities.'

'What is this truly about, mother?' demanded Aurelia. 'Why do you want to send me away?'

'No, no, no … you are not being sent away,' insisted Alice.

But Aurelia is not stupid, though she suspects people sometimes may mistake her inexperience for ignorance. So she comes out with it: 'Is this about Harry Hobbs? You don't like him, do you? You think him rude for not joining us last week? There will be an explanation, I'm sure of it. Anyway, I'm not sure I care.'

Oh yes, there certainly was an explanation, Alice knew, aching for what she sensed was about to be Aurelia's first experience of full blown disappointment – and what a sore thing that would be. Soon, but not now, she would explain all to the daughter who stood in front of her. Lying in bed with William a few days previously during that short and often productive interlude before drifting off to sleep she had learned from him about Harry Hobbs's defection. William did not hesitate to relay to her Lucien Prideaux's suspicions regarding the undergraduate. 'It appears,' Prideaux had announced, 'that the boy has upped and jumped ship. His rooms are empty and his family know naught of his whereabouts.' From the little more that Prideaux had laid before him, William decided that Harry Hobbs was not just suffering from a temporary phase of philandering. Perhaps he was a dilettante, or a dangerously careless youth – but no, it went further than that, since his daughter was caught up in it – as he duly reported to Alice. 'So you see I'm afraid Harry Hobbs is a bolter,' he announced to Alice. This now became a matter of honour. Or, rather, dishonour. It was likely, Prideaux had suggested, that, according to his investigations, Harry Hobbs

188

was somehow implicated in the recent *cause celebre* of the housemaid who escaped from the Spinning House. That girl, thought Alice, would have been known to her son Francis as well, of course, whose own lodging had once been at her place of work in Warkworth Terrace, not a stone's throw away from where they lived. It began to make the scurrilous issues being reported in *The Mercury* seem awfully close to home.

Oh dear, oh dear.

Complicating matters, Alice considered, was a new tone the *The Mercury* was choosing to pursue regarding the sorry case of Rose Whipple at the recent Assizes. It was as if the newspaper had decided to work itself into a sort of boomerang curve concerning this issue, now that a question about the Spinning House's very validity was being questioned in some quarters and the original story seemed to be galloping off on a new course of its own.

Alice had followed not only the expostulating letters but also a number of fervid "commentaries" written by journalists working at *The Mercury* in their wake. The unusual passion of these writings served to expand and sometimes explain a few of the latest rumours travelling round the town. In fact, Cambridge was now a-buzz with speculation, to the distaste of die-hards like Lucien Prideaux and a number of his ilk at the University. It was as though an ill-starred surge of self-righteous energy was sweeping through the markets, the shops, the public thoroughfares and the drawing rooms, made pleasing especially to many townsfolk of all ranks who had long felt uncomfortable with the authority the University possessed over parts of their lives. *Mark my words*, was the kernel of the muttering Alice was picking up. *The University will have to answer for it, one way or another.*

But for now: 'He's gone, my love,' said Alice to Aurelia with an air of finality, bringing herself back to the matter in hand. 'You must accept it, and we must only look forward.' As far as she was concerned, to produce some form of replacement for Harry Hobbs in the manner of a healing diversion was vital – the sooner the better. For her daughter to become the butt of any stray gossip here in Cambridge was not something her mother could tolerate. It could all be averted, softened, risen above, as long as …

'You see, you will meet new friends,' persisted Alice. 'You will learn new accomplishments, you will see new places – and it's only for a year and a half.'

'Have you enrolled me already?' Aurelia's perplexed, bruised spirit was not inherently a rebellious one, nor one given to cynicism. But even as she asked this a minor part of her was grudgingly opening a door in her imagination. After all, would it be *that* awful to join an establishment for the cultural enhancement of young ladies like herself in Florence?

It was at this point that Hope turned to face them both head on, although they were too preoccupied with each other to notice her interest in what had just been declared.

'You will miss me,' proposed Aurelia.

'Of course I shall,' said her mother, sensing that the first stage of the battle was within reach. 'And so will your father. But I shall have Hope while you are away, won't I?' Hope stared at her in disbelief. Had she forgotten about Hope's own departure to take up the University place she had been awarded in London and very recently accepted, dependent only on the acquiescence of her father?

'Hope will defer her university experience, won't you, my dear,' said Alice. This was not put in the form of a question.

*

A crushing wave of thwarted anticipation attacked Harry after he sat himself down at an escritoire in the lounge of the Great Eastern Hotel, brought on by longing – he was able to identify it at once. It had become a regular visitor. He picked out the very chair where he had sat mesmerised by Hope Bassett, but this was not the reason for him being struck by sudden anguish. No. It was the revelation that he was too far along on a course that was all but irreversible, and he knew that it meant abandoning all reasonable possibility of ever seeing in front of him that exquisite young woman who was capable of engaging his thoughts to the exclusion of all others. But now he was confronted by the most pressing need for letters to be written and dispatched. And he would do it. By God, he would. Without delay, he would contact those dear, dear people who, after all, deserved to know first-hand about his defection. Then he would be able to finally cut loose and concentrate on what must be done next.

First: his father. He pictured a moment of disbelief on that kind man's opening of his letter, but he had to trust that it would be quickly absorbed into the melancholy tomb of that most esteemed parent's permanent management of loss, the handling of which he was an old hand. Harry knew well that while he himself was positioned not far away from the excitable bobbin of progress, his father was absorbed by a grief in small part ameliorated by time, but by no means dictated by it. For John Hobbs, life and death were, in the end, the enclosing of a coming and going of passing details, dictated by the changing seasons and the small moments of interim satisfaction they offered. Such as the sight of lazy steam coming from a heap of compost in December, a frozen cobweb lacing an ironwork fence in January, the early morning sun sending a bright spear down a deer's backbone as it stood in a meadow in June. These things, Harry hoped, would surely stitch their way across the absence of a son, eventually. How he hoped for this outcome.

He wrote with deeply felt tenderness to his father.

This was followed by a much shorter note to Prideaux, stopping short of admitting his ownership of the lost scarf and gown but apologising for his unseemly exit from the University.

Aurelia Travers, he considered, would not be well served by any approach from one who had disgraced himself in his relations with her.

His most important letter he saved for last, and it took him a long time to complete.

Eventually, he read over what he had scripted in this final letter, probing it for flaws – less of composition than of how he could best express his honesty, with heartfelt affection. All he hoped for, he explained, was to somehow talk truly to her once more, without making much call on her time, if that was what she would wish. Putting things right with Hope Bassett: it was the last demand he would make of himself that night. That said, he did feel a little nourished by the writing of it. He replaced the lid on the inkwell and put his pen away after wiping it, just as he always did. The involuntary sigh he exhaled while making for the lift to his hotel room was therefore not one of regret for what once might have been, but one which aimed to disperse the final remnant of this, the greatest disappointment of all. He imagined the letter speeding towards Cambridge like a small piece of severed thread at the mercy of the world. He planned to remain until Christmas at the Great Eastern Hotel. If she wished she could correspond with him and then perhaps, later, he could follow her progress at university, which he dearly hoped she would be embarking upon. It would be a genuine delight for him to hear that *her* course, at least, was set fair, he told her.

The next thing he must busy himself with was to put his new plan to Rose Whipple. But that would have to wait until the morrow.

*

Back at *The Mercury* all were becoming attuned to the fact that a sensation, as they defined it, generally resembled nothing so much as a balloon quickly inflated then rudely released. Such sensational stories were like the instability of mercury itself, lending themselves to re-invention and embellishment. *The Mercury* believed itself to be a winged messenger, after all, a purveyor of news, whatever form it might take.

After its conclusion, the Rose Whipple case at the Assizes might have lost its bite after a few press runs, with any clippings recording it dated and left to turn yellow in library boxes. After all, this was the destination of all those other stories of audacious crimes with a hint of the salacious about them which had tickled the public in times gone by. But the Rose Whipple case was not to be disposed of as quickly as that. 'It is like a boil which has been partially lanced,' observed William Travers to his editor one day. 'It festers.'

He had at that moment in his possession a University document of such high-handedness that it was tempting to publish it as it stood, although it was a private document and therefore he knew he would not. It contained such a blatant snub to the civility of the town that Travers felt a deep frustration as he studied this document. He felt increasingly certain that behind this document was a University assuming the guise of an implacable, semi-conscious monster in its disdain for his town, his Cambridge. *'It is a matter of experience,'* opined this circular, which he noticed Lucien Prideaux had signed, along with signatories from all of the Colleges, *'and it has been pressed upon Proctors by residents in the town of Cambridge that, when they have for special reasons abstained for a time from exercising their powers to the full, there has been a marked increase in the number and persistency of women of bad character in the streets'.*

What were such words if they weren't a direct disdain of Cambridge's ability to keep its own peace?

'Weasel words,' agreed the editor. 'But they have the law on their side, as things stand. How hard would it be to get the law changed?'

'Do you know, Gilbert, I think we must try,' said Travers, pointing towards a letter received that morning from "a respectable married woman" and addressed to *the Mercury*. It called for a "mass indignation meeting". It concluded: *'I do not in any way view with pleasure the present sad state of our streets, as things stand, but if these fallen ones are to be dealt with, let them be brought into open court, where they may at least have some opportunity of defending themselves, and where the public shall be satisfied that they have at least common justice meted out to them'.*

'Put in in,' commanded Travers. 'I shall write a comment myself tomorrow. Please leave me space.'

On his short walk back home to Park Terrace that afternoon a further realisation dawned on him: that "as things stand" was, in all probability, a stifled criticism of his own complacency of late, joined to that of all institutions of influence in the town, not just its police force. It was on this basis that he began to mentally compose the promised commentary which he perfected during the evening, sitting alone, his frustration curdling into anger.

This is what his broadside declared when it appeared, un-edited, under a sub-heading "The Spinning House Scandal":

> *'This newspaper is proud to respond to indignation in the town about University powers. A fund has been established to be used to secure the repeal of the Act which has given University proctors the right to shamefully insult our womenfolk.'*

It was with this statement that *The Mercury* first demonstrated its desire to enter into a new intimacy with its readers. As a proxy for their own views, it made it its duty to take up righteous arms against their mighty cohabitee by pledging to keep the story rolling until the heart of the matter was resolved to the town's satisfaction, however arduous that battle might be turn out to be. The proprietor concluded with a vow that only then would the very dignity and pride of the town be restored, if *The Mercury* had anything to do with it.

*

Salvage. That was all John Hobbs hoped for while he absorbed the contents of Harry's letter – some sort of salvage he might be able to reclaim out of the debacle of his son's shameful absconding. A day or so later, the trap which had been ready to collect Harry and take him home for Christmas instead bore John Hobbs to the small station in Suffolk not far from the rambling home he shared with his four daughters. Kitty insisted on accompanying him. It returned to the estate empty, while father and daughter, with some misgiving and much apprehension, boarded the train to London. The pleading with Harry that took place at the Great Eastern Hotel later that day on both their parts was not something to be subsequently dwelt upon by either of them. It had been harrowing. All arguments they put to Harry to cease his rash course of action had already been rehearsed by Harry himself, many times. He deemed them all wanting. He heard out his father and sister in acute discomfort, burned by the pain he was causing them, but he held his ground. His plan for Rose had, after much argument, been accepted by her. Now, it was a matter of keeping his mind trained on this alone, for only in this way would it stand a chance of being accomplished. It was hard for him to keep from weeping when Kitty herself became tearful, but at the end of an excruciating hour in their company he offered his hand to his father, who took it, then turned to his sister and hugged her close.

With heavy hearts and nothing accomplished, Kitty and her father did not linger. On the way home they decided to break their journey home by stopping in Cambridge, where John Hobbs felt a need to make things right with the Travers family, hoping this might be possible.

So the following day, William Travers and his old friend closed the study door behind them in the house on Park Terrace, while Kitty was left in the company of Aurelia.

'My dear, I am not going to apologise for the circumstances of my brother's unexpected departure from Cambridge,' began Kitty. 'I can't, you see. He is upset about it as we are.'

Aurelia waited for more.

'You see, he believes he is doing the right thing. It is a bad business he finds himself mixed up in. But he is not a bad person.'

'Do you suppose I care?' said Aurelia. 'I am going to Italy, you know.' She proceeded to describe what she hoped to be doing there and Kitty nodded as she spoke, encouraging her to provide details which she was happy to do, although she suspected this all might be a show of bravado on poor Aurelia's part.

'Wouldn't you like to come too, Kitty? It would be such fun to have you there,' said Aurelia, who was not entirely fearless about what hazards and interruptions to the familiar state of things such a change might entail.

'I don't think so, not now. Father is certainly not in the right mood to pay for another of his children to be educated at great expense. I would be too afraid of disappointing him.'

'Just like Harry did?'

Kitty regretted the careless opening she had created for such a comment and shook her head. 'I am quite, quite sure that Harry regrets any errors he has committed.'

'Wherever he is.'

'Well, well, well, let's not dwell upon it. It cannot be altered and you must surely be excited about your trip. Tell me about the clothes you are planning to take with you and what you will be doing when you are there.'

'Oh, silly things … frivolous things … interesting things, no doubt,' replied Aurelia vaguely, unwilling to expand further.

After they had all but finished their tea, Kitty's eye was arrested by the passing shadow of Hope Bassett and the sound of her footsteps on the stairs.

'Would you excuse me for ten minutes, my dear?' asked Kitty. 'I should like to pay my respects to Miss Bassett, briefly.'

Aurelia shrugged, and Kitty lost no time in following Hope up to her room on the third floor.

*

'Come in,' came the voice from within the instant Kitty knocked, almost though she had been expected.

'Hope! How lovely to see you again,' said Kitty, a warm soul, though they were barely acquainted.

Hope pointed Kitty towards the single easy chair in the room, then sat down with a straight back on the edge of her bed.

Her eyes caught Kitty's and Kitty was relieved to perceive that there seemed to be no bitterness in her. So she came straight out with it, since she was aware there would not be much time for this conversation, mindful that it might seem odd if she stopped too long with Hope.

'Hope,' she began. 'I must be quick. I have talked to Harry. He is in London at present.'

She paused to let this news take effect.

'So he really did abandon his studies altogether,' said Hope. 'I heard them talking about it in the house. How fortunate for him that he had such a choice.'

'I think he felt he was left with *no* choice. You must know that he was swept along by events not entirely of his own making?'

'I am in no position to form a judgement about that. Nor is it my business.'

'Do *you* consider him a fugitive, entirely unworthy of consideration?'

'Why are you talking to me about your brother?' she parried.

'Oh, I have long been his confidante.'

Hope frowned.

'I must say this very quickly now,' Kitty persisted. 'I am talking to you for a purpose, on his behalf. I did not manage to have many minutes with him alone, but this was what was on his mind. He tells me that he has written to you, but he is unsure whether you have received his letter?'

Hope looked at her as though she was simple. 'Who, in this household, would pass to me a letter from Harry Hobbs, especially if it indicated the name and address of the sender?'

'Which I have no doubt it did. Because he would have been seeking a reply from you. He urged upon me how much he would value remaining in contact with you. That is all.'

This appeared to cause some suspicion in the figure sitting on the bed. What did Kitty know? Nothing that could incriminate Hope, it quickly transpired. Harry had been discrete, then, about their night at The Great Eastern Hotel.

'I really don't know what to say.'

'Say this,' urged the intrepid sister in a whisper, with a glance towards the door. 'Say that you will acknowledge that he clearly, *dearly* wants to contact you, and say that you will allow me to be the conduit. That way, I can supply you with his correspondence and you can use me to forward anything you might like to write to him. He is all alone, you know.'

'What? Is there no Rose Whipple with him?' asked Hope. 'The talk here is that she eloped with him. As you can imagine, he is not a popular person in this household for other reasons as well.'

'Rose? Oh, Hope! *No.*'

Hearing Aurelia's voice at the foot of the stairs calling out for her,

Kitty jumped up, kissed Hope on the cheek, squeezed her arm and left.

*

Then one more year in Cambridge turned on its axis, after which another springtime tripped playfully into summer, summer heralded autumn with its waning light, and autumn was consumed by winter once again before yet another spring rang with the sound of madrigals…

Oh, the ambivalence of this mighty and esteemed University towards our town, thought William Travers from time to time. Might it be that a turning point could be reached concerning certain aspects of power sharing before the old century had spent itself? What must be done? The Council of the Senate of the University and Cambridge Borough Council were much preoccupied with hammering out a solution. Back and forth travelled the barbs, the speculative darts, the appeals to reason, the squabbling, the eruptions signalling an affront had been received, the bitterness, the stubborn prevarication. There was a keen undercurrent pulling both ways as each side jostled for supremacy on matters relating to the scourge of the Spinning House and all it stood for. Concerted manoeuvring set in for many months during an initial period of uncertainty. But early on during these machinations, *The Mercury* was able to neatly summarise the sticking point of their quibbles: *'Many townspeople believe there would never be a better opportunity to sweep away, root and branch, a disgusting relic of 16th century tyranny; but not a few members of the University consider that if the right of the Proctors to arrest prostitutes was impaired, the streets of Cambridge would nightly be scenes of flagrant immorality.'*

The main story, in the absence of an accord, began to dissipate somewhat and form other tributaries. What would happen, for example, posed *The Mercury* one day – with women students in greater numbers than ever, despite having no hope of gaining a degree to seal their achievements – what might actually be the result if the dreadful *status quo* regarding University powers of arrest were to be maintained? It was a shocking proposition, argued *The Mercury*, predicting catastrophic slip-ups resulting in even more flawless females being wrongly challenged by the Proctor.

In time, readers of *The Mercury* may have grown a little weary with picking their way through the faithfully reported milestones in this long drawn out process. (But the record must be kept, insisted *The Mercury*.)

At last, eighteen months after the Rose Whipple case, some clarity began to emerge in the form of a cautious compromise after much ricocheting back and forth between the two parties. The proposal was that suspicious women might still be arrested by proctors, but that they would then need to be charged before the Borough Magistrates, if it was considered that they had erred. So it was conceded that the town's police should at last be invested with the same powers as those currently possessed by the proctors in this regard.

'Ho, ho, ho,' gloated Mrs Blanche Marchmont, perusing her copy of *The Mercury* whilst tucking into a succulent saddle of mutton since she, along with many who had vested interests in the matter (especially in the Barnwell region) felt it their duty to follow the unfolding negotiations rather more closely than some others. 'This surely means there will be no need for a Spinning House any more, if it succeeds.'

As eventually it did. Owing much to the tenacity of *The Mercury*, a new Law replacing the ancient Charter was passed by Parliament, phrased in such a way that neither side was seen to entirely lose face.

*

Over time, it seems that most ostensibly irreconcilable issues and all leaping opinions tend to melt into either better or worse versions of themselves, their traces diluted or buried in history's repository of forgotten causes. This was the conclusion of William Travers as he quietly congratulated himself for his role in the resolution of the matter in years to come. Maybe the inclination of time is to cleanse, on the whole, or at least to make available that possibility. This must have been when once dank river Cam – mired in a town's ordure, its flow blighted by the foulness of being an open sewer – was on its way to being clarified. One day, he surmises with confidence, people will surely remark how delightful their river is on its whimsical ramble through Cambridge, clarity shot through with sunbeams in due season.

And another thing, he sometimes has cause to reflect. Almost imperceptibly, a state of wellness in the town is starting to overlay a certain unhealthy fascination with "lewd women", those "suspected of evil" or "incontinence", along with the "light in character" which have absorbed the readers of *The Mercury* ever since the overheated period leading up to the Rose Whipple case. As a result, girls who hitherto offered their own bespoke services in the alleys and back streets may now begin to think it wise to be a little less forthright in their endeavours, and a little more cautious about the prospect of being named in *The Mercury* should they be brought before the public Magistrates' Court where Walter Magson and his fellow reporters will surely be waiting to expose them to public gaze in such a way that the Spinning House, with its private court, could not. If the brothels of Barnwell continue to prosper for a while, perhaps they will be obliged to do so with more discretion as their business levels off. In time, most of those dismal places will shut down altogether, and as for the village once called Barnwell and known as a devilish place – well, that is simply one of the poorer parts of Cambridge, where poverty continues to be a spur to a residue who succumb to clandestine activities, as it always will. Alice Travers still maintains that those who do succumb are those who need care most of all. Supported by the loyal endeavours of Hope Bassett, and following a successful public appeal, she will go on to establish a refuge in the Barnwell area for women who always believed themselves beyond redemption, and through her not a few of them will be helped to a more hopeful, dignified life during which they might be accorded value in the eyes of those who encounter them.

Constable Morley – he who continues his responsibility for either the day or the night patrol of the ramshackle Barnwell beat No 8 – is proud to exercise *in an official capacity* his discretion regarding whether an arrest is the best action to take or not, which he does with admirable discernment, being all too familiar with the lives of many of the individuals who live thereabouts.

And what if *The Mercury* did permit itself to gloat a little about the way it had acted as a mediator in this choppy period of significant change, presenting itself as an agent who set out to reflect the culture of both a town as it matured in executive responsibility, and a University anxious to maintain its rights based on medieval hierarchy and patronage but equally determined, it maintained, to get on with its neighbour? Where once it held conflict at arm's length, in the end *The Mercury*, thanks to the misfortunes of Rose Whipple, correctly identified that reform was not only desirable but plainly unavoidable, on the whole. At the same time, the groundswell of popular voices clamouring to hear their opinions expressed in print left *The Mercury* in no doubt about the importance of public opinion generated by "the people" – while also attempting to identify who, subliminally, "the people" *really* were. And this was how it discovered its true soul.

The great editor visited Cambridge soon afterwards to congratulate his friend on seeing the light.

SIX YEARS LATER

Dear Harry,

I do hope you receive this letter because I see your fortune is now in the ascendant in New York. Can it only be six years or thereabouts since we walked along Hunstanton beach together?

Thank you for posting me a copy of the newspaper you have joined, containing a rather thrusting piece written by yourself, if I may say so. I have attached it to my notice board here at The Mercury where I honour its style! But you must not imagine I am cloistered within some cubby hole in our head office in Cambridge. No, I write from Norfolk, where Father has established a new title in the Mercury brand, as well as one in Lincolnshire and another in Essex. He has put me in charge of the Norfolk office. We are expanding.

I have come to believe that the case which was the reason for your departure was foremost in these developments, since The Mercury, I'm delighted to report, is now poised for the new century and is making itself heard in an altogether – I was about to say "louder" but perhaps "keener" is a better word to use – manner. No more can it ever be accused of peddling "mere perfumeries and pigeon-wings" as one of your American editors has accused British journalism of doing. I therefore send you a "souvenir" of how it looks today. Note the bold type, the strong headings, and the occasional illustrations which make it easier on the eye. I mustn't go on about it, but you will appreciate Father's desire neither to shout from the pulpit nor shamelessly pander to people's lower appetites as some newspapers do nowadays. Tawdry iconoclasm is not our way, either. So we have remained true to his original premise while endeavouring to place our finger on that mysterious pulse of the local psyche defined by the essential locality of where we find ourselves. This is our authority. This is our voice, after the Spinning House affair. I maintain it is a proud one.

We were a little challenged to keep up interest in the pages of The Mercury by the time it took for the authorities of our town and its University to come to an agreement over the Spinning House goings on. So much hot air, I remember thinking in the end, when I joined a small crowd to watch that unwholesome place tumble to dust, and I must admit that I added my hands to the round of applause which accompanied its demolition. The foundations of a new building are already in place and will quickly consume any lingering trace of its shameful presence, not even granting it the dignity of a temporary sense of its own absence in memoriam. Any stray wisps from its collapse that may seek a foothold to cling to will find none of its material remains to haunt. It is all part of the record now, and as we know, records themselves grow dusty with time. But I think that the name of Rose Whipple – though nothing is known of her since her final release from the Spinning House – will be written into the annals of the University as well as the cuttings library of The Mercury, should any future explorer wish to dig deeper. It is her name alone that will survive out of that sorry business.

But it is all water under the bridge now.

Let me end by giving you news of a more personal kind which I know you will welcome. Of Cynthia Dawes I can only tell you that she appears to be the main support of infirm parents and has a small post in a library nearby. Our friend Sidney Beaumont is to be ordained soon, according to plan. Our tutor continues to work on the book he has been writing for the last twenty years or so. Arthur Moody is a different case. He has chosen illnesses of the mind as his medical speciality and is a follower of a German doctor whose experiments are gaining some notoriety in London, I believe. The word is that he will go far.

You will appreciate that I do not feel inclined to talk to you about my sister.

But I believe you did the right thing, my friend, when you left to start afresh elsewhere. I salute you for it.

F. Travers.

My dear Rose,

This is the third time you have sent me these dollar bills which you say you owe me, which I have denied as many times as I return them to you. All I did was furnish the price of a boat ticket. Do you not understand that nothing gives me more pleasure than to hear you are settled now, a good many miles west of here? Just as I was delighted to wish you well when you no sooner disembarked than you decided to join a Quaker group setting out for the interior of this great country, you will recall. This time, however, you will be relieved to hear that I have persuaded myself to accept your dollars. I must thank you for them. I do this only so that we can regard each other truly as batting on the same pitch from now on, if I may put it this way. Yes, at last, I grant that I do understand your uncomfortable feelings of indebtedness to me which, though they have always been entirely unfounded, cannot be a pleasant state to maintain. Therefore – yes, I accept that you rightly chide me not to cause you to feel beholden to me any longer, and I in turn beg you to forgive me that it has taken me so long to concede to your wishes.

I have one shard of news from England for you and I hope it will not cause upset if I mention the old "S.H." because – it is no more! With rude haste, once the University relinquished its right to imprison local women, it was razed to the ground, I hear. So there it is, Rose: history is pockmarked with foxholes for the purpose of drawing down and burying unpleasant memories, it seems. The whole business has become something rather strange to me now, my dear, as I hope it is for you.

With sincerest good wishes to you and your family
I remain
Ever yours

H.H.

My dearest Beatrice,
It is high summer and we have moved almost straight

away to a new house, tho' it is what they call here an "apartment" – of which we occupy the second and third floors. Please note the change of address. Our home is called a "brownstone" after (I suppose) the colour of the bricks used for its construction. It is a grand place – four storeys high with a steep outdoors staircase rising to the second floor (one of our floors). This they call a "stoop" and during our long, hot evenings neighbourhood children play on these steps – this is a city which resounds with children's laughter as well as their games and mischief, I can tell you. It is a young place. They are of all sorts, just like their parents, coming from every country in the old world. How I wish I could describe to you the cacophony of accents and strange words straining to be heard in bits of Hebrew, Italian, German, Spanish ... from what I can make out. The resulting variety of "English" has a strong Irish flavour, but it seems to be the dominant voice here.

Well, my dear. Let me tell you that I have just taken up my fourth cordial of the evening and I see that fans are out and brows being mopped in the heat outside, tho' it is near ten o'clock at night.

I shall not dwell on trivia, however, because I know you are all yearning to know how we are getting on after our first six months here.

First, I will record our safe arrival and Harry's joyful welcome. The dear boy put us up at his own expense in a hotel for fully a week while he made sure all was ready. He himself remained in his lowly lodging, a place frequented by dubious characters by all accounts which he was most pleased to vacate as soon as the time came. This place was all he could afford when he arrived here. It was above a "saloon" where alcohol was sold and where gambling took place openly, I gather. But he is doing awfully well, you will be relieved to hear, dear sister. Each morning he sets out by "street car" (this is a horse-drawn carriage which slides along on rails in the road at a frightful pace, between hordes of people, animals, and the new motor vehicles going in every direction!) for his office at the New York Times, a most reputable newspaper. He arrives back home wide-eyed with the challenges presented by his working life, eager to tell us all about it and eager also for his supper in the middle of the evening – and you can be sure that the meal is always ready for our table. He has little time for writing letters himself as he has been promoted to be an investigator of sorts, I believe, and this work, the manner of which he so admired in a great editor in London who helped secure his livelihood here, is proving to be something he is very good at, I am glad to report (yes, I am become a reporter here myself, via this letter to you, ha, ha!). He has invested in a typewriter which resides in his office alongside the machines owned by his colleagues and can already tap out his stories as rapidly as gunfire using his two index fingers!

"The Sun" and "The World" vie in competition with "The New York Times", let me tell you – a newspaper of principle which professes to be politically independent. To give you a flavour of it so that you can picture Harry there the better, here is its slogan: "All the news that's fit to print". (How admirably to the point, don't you agree? No, it does not define "fit"). Heady scandal and sauciness it leaves to the other papers, along with the advertising of immoral books, fortune tellers, female pills and the like. We laughed when one evening Harry read out to us the paper's original aim fifty years ago – a much more long-winded and bumbling affair in my opinion. (How times are a-changing.) Here it is, I will copy it out for you: "We shall be Conservative, in all cases where we think Conservatism is essential to the public good; – and we shall be Radical in everything which may seem to us to require radical treatment and radical reform. We do not believe that everything in Society is either exactly right or exactly wrong; what is good we desire to preserve and improve; – what is evil, to exterminate or reform." Perhaps this is what "fit to print" means, then! The newspaper's editor has taken Harry under his wing, teasing what he refers to as Harry's "Cambridge voice" while admiring it. This man has invited us to supper and we are at the moment considering what we can purchase that will be suitable to wear for this occasion. We are partisan about wanting to represent Harry to the best of our ability, you can be sure.

You may wonder how we spend our days. Shopping for food is carried out every day at markets laid out on streets which conveniently face either north to south or east to west, in straight lines. This is most helpful when finding one's way about. There is a great deal of construction going on everywhere at a most furious pace – ladders and cranes, carts bearing rubble away, wooden scaffolding snaking up to dizzying heights and much noise and hullabaloo. A large, square park is being constructed not far from our dwelling, and the shanties and tenements and vegetable gardens of this formerly wild place are disappearing at a great rate.

Harry, who is still reeling, I think, from the exaltedness of having us by his side – he can scarcely believe such a blessing – takes great pleasure in escorting us on various excursions on his day off. He is eager for us to feel properly at home here in our new country. Last Sunday we visited a funfair many times bigger than anything I have ever seen before. It is called "Coney Island" and the striking thing about it and about this audacious city is that people of high and low standing are mingling quite easily in places like this. I know, my dear, that each time we attend church on Sundays, Harry gives profound thanks that the girl at Park Terrace (Bernadette, I think he said she was called) undertook to bear his correspondence to Hope upstairs after I passed it on to her. What a mercy that turned out to be, and each of them treasures their bundle of letters and the rekindling of an esteem that was denied them by circumstances at the time. Hope insists that for a long time it was the only thing which compensated her for her inability to take up the university place in London offered her, due to the demands of Mrs Travers. Now, she is finding time to pen her own stories and one has been published already. I, as appointed housekeeper, keenly await additional duties when Something Important for Mr and Mrs Hobbs arrives soon after Christmas.

What will you make of all this, dear one? I have droned

on, I'm afraid, and I am reminded of this by Hope, who comes in to this room urging me to take to my bed, bearing a candle and a sisterly smile. It is important to me that you should be assured that all is well with us, for I know you worry.

How I long to see you again one day. I wonder whether you might be tempted to visit on one of these steamers which bring crowds of people from Europe every week? I do day-dream about this, I confess. In the meantime, I send you warmest love from all three of us, and trust you will you convey that same love to my sisters and to our dearest father as well.

Your most affectionate sister,

Kitty Hobbs.

The End

Acknowledgements

Many thanks to my dear family and friends for keeping the faith. Also, grateful thanks to Dr Jenny Ulph, Archivist at Downing College, along with the staff at the Central Library, Cambridge, whose patience, knowledge and enthusiasm during a number of visits I very much appreciated. Special thanks, too, to Dr Mike Petty, Cambridge historian, whose extensive research is so generously shared in his Cambridge Collection at the Central Library where I learned about the true cases of Daisy Hopkins, who sued the University, and Jane Elsdon, who escaped from The Spinning House. The following books in particular provided the flavour of Cambridge at the end of the 19th century, and and the rapidly changing landscape of popular reporting:

●Noel Annan, 2000, *The Dons: Mentors, Eccentrics and Geniuses*, HarperCollins

●JW Clark, 1908, *Cambridge*, Seeley & Co Ltd, London

●DA Winstanley, 1947, *Later Victorian Cambridge*, CUP

●W Sydney Robinson, 2012, *Muckraker*, The Robson Press

●Town & Gown Rivalry:

http://www.iankitching.me.uk/history/cam/town-gown.html

●Joel H Wiener, *The Americanization of the British Press*, 1830-1914, Studies in Newspaper and Periodical History, 1994 Annual, London: Greenwood Press

●Margot Holbrook, *The Spinning House*, Cambridgeshire Local History Society Review No 8

●Maurice and Sheila Hornsey, 2009, *Glimpses of Life in Cambridge*, (C.44.47)

●Arthur Randle, 1969, *Fenland Memories*, Routledge & Kegan Paul Ltd

●Elisabeth Leedham-Green, 1996, *A Concise history of the University of Cambridge*, CUP

●Laurel Brake, 1989, 'The Old Journalism and the New: Forms of Cultural Production in London in the 1880s', in Papers for the Millions, ed Joel H Wiener, Study of Mass Media and Communications No 13, Greenwood Press.

About the Author
Jane Taylor

Jane Taylor, is the author of The Spinning House Affair, and Over Here, also published by ThunderPoint. She is a journalist and has taught news writing and the history of journalism at a number of universities in and around west London, Surrey and Hertfordshire.

Gaining a doctorate in Creative and Critical Writing from the University of East Anglia allowed her to explore themes of loss, memory and the blurring of genre boundaries, all of which she intends to pursue further as she develops her own fiction.

Her ideas are fuelled by travel, a fascination with history, walking, and a broad experience of people gained variously through volunteering at a homeless hostel, chaplaincy and co-hosting retreats. Plus a stint managing a trendy wine bar in London.

She was runner-up in the Long Barn Books competition (author Susan Hill's publishing company) for first time writers in 2006 and has published a short story in *Pretext*, the literary magazine.

Over Here
Jane Taylor
ISBN: 978-0-9929768-3-5 (eBook)
ISBN: 978-0-9929768-2-8 (Paperback)

It's coming up to twenty-four hours since the boy stepped down from the big passenger liner – it must be, he reckons foggily – because morning has come around once more with the awful irrevocability of time destined to lead nowhere in this worrying new situation. His temporary minder on board – last spotted heading for the bar some while before the lumbering process of docking got underway – seems to have vanished for good. Where does that leave him now? All on his own in a new country: that's where it leaves him. He is just nine years old.

An eloquently written novel tracing the social transformations of a century where possibilities were opened up by two world wars that saw millions of men move around the world to fight, and mass migration to the new worlds of Canada and Australia by tens of thousands of people looking for a better life.

Through the eyes of three generations of women, the tragic story of the nine year old boy on Liverpool docks is brought to life in saddeningly evocative prose.

'…a sweeping haunting first novel that spans four generations and two continents…' – Cristina Odone/Catholic Herald

A Good Death
Helen Davis
ISBN: 978-0-9575689-7-6 (eBook)
ISBN: 978-0-9575689-6-9 (Paperback)

'*A good death is better than a bad conscience,*' said Sophie.

1983 – Georgie, Theo, Sophie and Helena, four disparate young Cambridge undergraduates, set out to scale Ausangate, one of the highest and most sacred peaks in the Andes.

Seduced into employing the handsome and enigmatic Wamani as a guide, the four women are initiated into the mystically dangerous side of Peru, Wamani and themselves as they travel from Cuzco to the mountain, a journey that will shape their lives forever.

2013 – though the women are still close, the secrets and betrayals of Ausangate chafe at the friendship.

A girls' weekend at a lonely Fenland farmhouse descends into conflict with the insensitive inclusion of an overbearing young academic toyboy brought along by Theo. Sparked by his unexpected presence, pent up petty jealousies, recriminations and bitterness finally explode the truth of Ausangate, setting the women on a new and dangerous path.

Sharply observant and darkly comic, Helen Davis's début novel is an elegant tale of murder, seduction, vengeance, and the value of a good friendship.

'The prose is crisp, adept, and emotionally evocative' – Lesbrary.com

The False Men
Mhairead MacLeod
ISBN: 978-1-910946-27-5 (eBook)
ISBN: 978-1-910946-25-1 (Paperback)

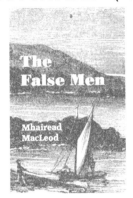

North Uist, Outer Hebrides, 1848

Jess MacKay has led a privileged life as the daughter of a local landowner, sheltered from the harsher aspects of life. Courted by the eligible Patrick Cooper, the Laird's new commissioner, Jess's future is mapped out, until Lachlan Macdonald arrives on North Uist, amid rumours of forced evictions on islands just to the south.

As the uncompromising brutality of the Clearances reaches the islands, and Jess sees her friends ripped from their homes, she must decide where her heart, and her loyalties, truly lie.

Set against the evocative backdrop of the Hebrides and inspired by a true story, *The False Men* is a compelling tale of love in a turbulent past that resonates with the upheavals of the modern world.

'…an engaging tale of powerlessness, love and disillusionment in the context of the type of injustice that, sadly, continues to this day' – Anne Goodwin

The Oystercatcher Girl
Gabrielle Barnby
ISBN: 978-1-910946-17-6 (eBook)
ISBN: 978-1-910946-15-2 (Paperback)

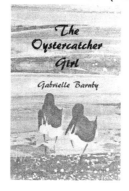

In the medieval splendour of St Magnus Cathedral, three women gather to mourn the untimely passing of Robbie: Robbie's widow, Tessa; Tessa's old childhood friend, Christine, and Christine's unstable and unreliable sister, Lindsay.

But all is not as it seems: what is the relationship between the three women, and Robbie? What secrets do they hide? And who has really betrayed who?

Set amidst the spectacular scenery of the Orkney Islands, Gabrielle Barnby's skilfully plotted first novel is a beautifully understated story of deception and forgiveness, love and redemption.

With poetic and precise language Barnby draws you in to the lives, loves and losses of the characters till you feel a part of the story.

'The Oystercatcher Girl is a wonderfully evocative and deftly woven story' – Sara Bailey

Mere
Carol Fenlon
ISBN: 978-1-910946-37-4 (Kindle)
ISBN: 978-1-910946-36-7 (Paperback)

"There's something about this place. It's going to destroy us if we don't get away."

Reclaimed from the bed of an ancient mere, drained by their forbears 150 years ago, New Cut Farm is home to the Askin family. Life is hard, but the land and its dark history is theirs, and up till now that has always been enough.

But Con Worrall can't make it pay. Pressured by his new wife following his mother's death, Con reluctantly sells up.

For Lynn Waters, New Cut Farm is the life she has always dreamed of, though her husband Dan has misgivings about the isolated farmhouse.

As Con's life disintegrates and Dan's unease increases, the past that is always there takes over and Lynn discovers the terrible hold that the land exerts over people - and the lengths to which they will go to keep it.

'Mere reflects on the impact the ghosts of history have on all of us, and how that shapes and sometimes destroys lives.'

The Birds That Never Flew

Margot McCuaig

Shortlisted for the
Dundee International Book Prize 2012
Longlisted for the Polari First Book Prize 2014
ISBN: 978-0-9929768-5-9 (eBook)
ISBN: 978-0-9929768-4-2 (Paperback)

'Have you got a light hen? I'm totally gaspin.'

Battered and bruised, Elizabeth has taken her daughter and left her abusive husband Patrick. Again. In the bleak and impersonal Glasgow housing office Elizabeth meets the provocatively intriguing drug addict Sadie, who is desperate to get her own life back on track.

The two women forge a fierce and interdependent relationship as they try to rebuild their shattered lives, but despite their bold, and sometimes illegal attempts it seems impossible to escape from the abuse they have always known, and tragedy strikes.

More than a decade later Elizabeth has started to implement her perfect revenge – until a surreal Glaswegian Virgin Mary steps in with imperfect timing and a less than divine attitude to stick a spoke in the wheel of retribution.

Tragic, darkly funny and irreverent, *The Birds That Never Flew* ushers in a new and vibrant voice in Scottish literature.

'…dark, beautiful and moving, I wholeheartedly recommend' scanoir.co.uk

Printed in Great Britain
by Amazon

66514316R00129